FALLOUT
A Post-Apocalyptic Novel

Harmony Kent

ISBN: 9781070495217 (Paperback)

ASIN: B07S6PJ3L2 (Ebook)

Any references to historical events, real people, or real
places are used fictitiously. Names, characters, and places
are products of the author's imagination.

Front cover image by Harmony Kent.
Book design by Harmony Kent.

Printed by Amazon POD, in the United Kingdom.

First printing edition 2019.

Publisher:
Harmony Kent Author Services:
https://harmonykent.co.uk
harmonykent@gmx.com

For my husband. Without whom, this book would have been finished much sooner! Thanks for making real life better than fiction.

'Fear is the engine that drives the human animal. Humanity sees the world as a place of uncountable threats, and so the world becomes what humanity imagines it to be. They not only live in fear but use fear to control one another.'

Dean Koontz

'Totalitarianism [...] extends the civil power beyond due limits; it determines and fixes [...] every field of activity, and thus compresses all legitimate manifestation of life—personal, local, and professional—into a mechanical unity of collectivity.'

Alexander Solzhenitsyn

CHAPTER ONE

1

Event +56 Days (E56)

At noon on a swelteringly hot day, thirsty, hungry, and exhausted, Priya saw a dirty young man on the deserted corner of what passed for main street. She walked toward him, intending to ask for help. Not something she would have done, typically. But then, these were a long way from normal circumstances.

Nervous, she stopped a few feet away from the guy. The hard stare with which he'd watched her progress morphed into a slow smile.

'Um, hi,' she said.

He glanced around the area, suspicious, and then continued to watch her.

'I'm lost.'

The guy shifted away from the wall he'd stood slouched against and moved toward her. 'Where're ya headed?'

Priya swallowed around a lump in her throat and crossed her arms. Now she felt silly. 'I don't know.'

He shoved his hands in his pockets. 'Not from around here, are you?'

She shook her head. 'Zone five. I thought ...'

The guy scrubbed at the days-old stubble on his begrimed chin. 'The city got too dangerous.'

Priya nodded then plucked up courage. 'Can you help?'

For a couple of seconds, he stood and watched her. His eyes glinted in the sun while his brain calculated. Then he shrugged. 'Sure. We have a house ... an old farm. I can take you there.'

Her hunger and desperate need for rest and safety overrode her jittery nerves and doubts. She moved so that she stood by his side. 'I'm Priya.'

He held out his hand, which she shook, trying to hide her grimace at how sweaty and gritty his palm felt. 'Jimmy. Pleased to make yer acquaintance. We don't see too many pretty ladies around here. Not no more.'

Silent, Priya chewed her bottom lip and nodded. What did that mean? Had the virus taken out mostly women around here, or had something else happened to them? More doubts crowded in, but the heat and the thirst and the loneliness of the past weeks, scavenging for food and water, had turned her brain spongey. She reassured herself that he'd said 'we' and not 'I'.

Safety in numbers and all that, right?

Lost in her thoughts, she failed to notice that he didn't say much while they walked. Not until he broke the long silence at a dilapidated gate.

'Here it is.'

She hesitated. Alarm bells ringing. 'You don't talk a lot.'

Jimmy grinned and shrugged. 'I guess I haven't made up my mind about you just yet.'

Her eyes widened. 'What? Whether you can trust me?' Priya laughed. 'And there's me wondering if *I* can trust *you*.'

Jimmy chuckled with her and stepped onto the dirt driveway. Over his shoulder, he said, 'You coming?'

Priya shoved her hands into her jumpsuit pockets and followed. The building looked run-down, but loud laughter drifted from inside. It sounded like a sizeable group. Relief relaxed her shoulders. She'd made it. Jimmy showed her into a large kitchen with a range cooker lining one wall.

The occupants fell silent and stared at her while she stood cowering behind Jimmy. He'd said nothing about his group being all men. Terrified, she took a step back, toward the exit. An unknown somebody closed the door behind her with a dull thud of finality.

Jimmy spoke to a big guy seated at the head of the scuffed and worn kitchen table, 'Hey, Hank, I got some fresh meat for ya.'

Hank licked his lips and rose to his feet. The suffocating silence held. Then arms wrapped around Priya, pinning her limbs. He strolled across the room until he stood in front of her, and then he reached out a lazy hand and squeezed one of her breasts. She tried to squirm away, but the man behind her held her still.

'No, please. Don't do this.' Her words came out breathless and squeaky.

A large, meaty hand slapped her across the face. Her head whipped to the side. Pain ignited through her cheek and jaw. 'Now, now, little Priya. You don't speak unless I tell you.'

Shock froze her. Then she stammered, 'H-how do you k-know my name?' Jimmy hadn't given over that information.

Hank grinned and straightened his spine, which gave him another inch or two of height. 'I'm one o' the ones who got the telepathy. Don't need none o' these telling me stuff.' He nodded to indicate the rough-looking group of guys, and then he grabbed both of her breasts and squeezed hard, making her whimper.

'No.'

Her weak protest earned her another slap.

Hank leered at her, still squeezing. 'Just like I don't need you to tell me you ain't never had no man before.' His words elicited a ripple of low laughter. The menace in the room hiked up to full volume. Priya knew, now, what was coming. Knew that when he'd done with her, he'd make a gift of her to his sycophantic followers. Why the hell hadn't she listened to her instincts?

Until now, she hadn't met an infected who'd developed psychic powers. And she had doubted the rumours. She cursed her ignorance and bad luck. Whatever plan she might come up with to get out of here, he'd know it.

Hank punched her full on the face, and her nose flattened and smashed in a blaze of pain and a river of blood.

Priya saw stars. Her vision went black around the edges, and her consciousness narrowed to a pin-prick.

The guy who'd pinned her arms to her sides pushed her to the cold stone floor. More men rushed in and grabbed her arms and legs. Dazed and helpless, she shivered when rough hands ripped her clothes from her. Then she heard the ugly clang of metal on metal and forced her eyes open all the way. Hank stood unfastening his belt. Priya tried to scream, but only a hoarse, whistle-like whisper came out.

With his face like thunder, Hank punched her on her broken nose.

2

E58

The gloom cleared bit by bit from Kaleb's momentary day blindness. A substantial black rat gnawed busily on something in the corner. Kaleb looked harder. A pile of filthy rags held the rodent's attention. Disgusted, the army special yelled and kicked the ugly brute. With a squeal—more of outrage than pain or fear—the rat scurried away.

Kaleb squatted by the rags to get a better look. Not rags. A dead body. A female. Dirty blonde hair snaked out from beneath a filthy tarp. Without thought, he followed all his years of training and reached out long fingers to check for a carotid pulse.

There.

Thin and thready.

Weak.

But there.

Alive, then.

He rolled her over.

Blood and bruising and swelling obscured her features. The old and dank neosilve throw that had covered her fell away and exposed her nakedness. More blood and swollen bruises marked her torso, her thighs, even her feet. A glance at her hands showed defence wounds, snapped and bloodied nails, broken fingers, a dislocated thumb.

Kaleb swallowed the bile that had risen to his throat. He didn't need to ask who could do such a thing—rape and beat a woman and leave her for dead—not in this day and age. The virus …

He shot to his feet. Right, the virus. His mission was to find the lost vial, which supposedly held the only known cure, not to get side-tracked rescuing damsels in distress. Annoyed, he wiped his bloodied palms on his black army jumpsuit and took a step toward the door. On the floor, the woman gave a soft groan. Then he noticed a single tear tracking down one disfigured cheek.

A sudden vision invaded his mind—his pet puppy, Oscar, getting torn apart by a raptor. The creature had come out of nowhere and gutted the tiny Labrador within seconds. Then it had loped off, laughing much like the Hyenas that had populated Earth. It hadn't even hunted for food. Just for pleasure. Why Exxon had brought *every* creature up to the terraformed planetary system when they settled it, he had no clue. What possible purpose could they *all* serve? The humans had enough on their plates dealing with the native predators such as the raptors and the tubers—the former made you think of dinosaurs while the latter resembled Earth ferrets, only much more aggressive and dangerous.

Emotions grew around the visual memory like mould. Unwanted and poisonous. He had been but a boy. Young and weak and ignorant. He hadn't known the way of the world. Not back then. And still, the old feelings held him prisoner so that he could not simply walk away from the woman bleeding out on the dirt floor.

Pity and remorse squashed his logic into a dark corner. He had to help her. The responsibilities of his mission—what they meant for mankind—warred with his desire, his need, to help the young victim.

Duty pulled his left leg toward the exit. Pity drew his right toward the woman. If he didn't make up his mind soon, he'd end up doing the splits. With a sigh of frustrated annoyance, he squatted by the beaten body again. Only then did he notice what the rat had been chewing on. Her left little finger was missing, gnawed down to the lowest knuckle joint in a mess of bloodied flesh and gristle.

A grin lit his features. Bitter, but a grin all the same. If he played this right, he could have the fries and the burger. It didn't have to be one or the other. What if he fixed her up and then enlisted her help? He wouldn't have to compromise the mission at all. He could get her scavenging for him while keeping her on a strict need-to-know footing.

Dreams of glory set his heart racing. His grin turned into a full-on smile. It transformed his features into those of the young and carefree farm boy he used to be. If he found the lost vial, he would also find redemption in the eyes of his superiors.

His rapid rise up the ranks had ensured that they would send him on the initial recovery mission for the downed helipod. After all, he'd earned their trust. Had proven his loyalty. But then he'd failed to find any traces of the antidote. Due to the extreme durability of the neoplast, which encased the vital liquid, it seemed highly unlikely that the crash had damaged the vial, let alone obliterated it so completely it left no trace.

Not only had Kaleb failed to secure the antidote, but he'd also been unable to locate and identify the body of the lead scientist who'd been charged with transporting the vial in the height of the initial crisis. No matter that all the bodies had burned to an unidentifiable crisp. Worse still, he couldn't even confirm whether this crash site was *the* crash site or just some other misfortune fallen.

Happy now that he'd found a workable solution, Kaleb wrapped the victim in the discarded neosilve throw and then completed his search through the cellar of the derelict farm building.

Other than a few packets of dried provisions, his scavenge turned up nothing useful.

Next, he fashioned a travois, using a couple of metal poles he found in a corner and more neosilve tarp, together with the everseal that he carried with the rest of his essential supplies.

+++

It took him an hour to get her back to his temporary base ... an old farmhouse well away from civilisation. Far enough out that the roving gangs left him alone. There, he settled her in the back downstairs room, which would once have functioned as a sitting room, and did what he could for her injuries. He would need to report the existence of another gang to the major so that the patrols could eradicate it. President Terrence had imposed a curfew and banned any groups from forming. Kaleb gritted his teeth. Perhaps fewer people would end up like this young woman if they could come together for protection.

By the time she began to stir, the light had

mostly leached out of the day, and Kaleb had made the necessary changes to keep her in the dark about who he was and what he was about. He got a clean cloth, soaked it in water, and squeezed a few drops onto her dry and cracked tongue, all the while telling himself that what she didn't know couldn't hurt her.

For now, he had no idea of her political affiliations, and he couldn't risk exposure. Couldn't risk her working against him or telling the wrong people about the vial. A lot of folks called President Terrence 'President Terror', or worse still, 'Dictator Terror'. Kaleb disagreed. He lived for the man. Would kill for the man. Would die for the man.

3

E72

Nightmares born of recent weeks smothered Priya, and she struggled to reach the surface.

The holographic sign she'd lived with her

whole life winked out of existence.

'Exxon 1. Zone 5'

There one second—gone the next.

(Blink.) Some guy wearing the green of a farmer squeezed drops of water onto her tongue. Cold. Delicious. (Blink.)

The power went out. Never in the planet's settled history had that happened. For days, the newsnet had told of an unknown pandemic. But why would that make the power fail? Priya looked out of the window. The whole city seemed to have gone down. People wandered out of buildings and onto the street, and soon, angry crowds had gathered.

(Blink.) Darkness. From another room, muffled conversation. Shivering. Thirsty. Pain. (Blink.)

The riots lasted for days. Not knowing what

else to do, she stayed hidden in her tower block deep in the city.

Then her food ran out.

When her neighbour turned, it changed everything.

(Blink.) The harsh light of morning. A little more alert. Pain. So much hurt. She was alone. (Blink.)

Terrified, Priya crouched behind the apartment door and listened to his raving. An hour later, someone shot him. The silence that followed sounded much worse than had his screams and rants. Her neighbour's chip had failed. Had made him into an animal. What did it mean that hers had stopped working sometime in the night while she slept? Had she gotten infected too? Or was it because she couldn't recharge her unit?

So many questions. But the only thing she knew was that she had to get out of the city. Find somewhere safe. Zone 9 was rural. Less populated. So she headed there.

(Blink.) The green-clad farmer came back. Priya cowered beneath the blanket, too weak and drowsy to mount a defence. The man squeezed more water into her mouth. (Blink.)

Priya made it all the way to the outskirts before the rest of her implants failed and she lost all navigational ability. For days, she wandered around in circles, well and truly lost. Perhaps a local could direct her to a good place?

(Blink.)

She woke up. A man in a green jumpsuit sat watching her. When she roused, he came and knelt by her side. Priya panicked. A scream roared up and out of her throat. 'No, no, nononono.' She tried to fight him off. Tears poured down her cheeks. Not again. Why couldn't she have died?

CHAPTER TWO

1

Event Horizon (The Point of No Return)
E-Zero

Nobody knew her. And she intended to keep it that way. It's easy to fool others. All you have to do is believe it yourself, and you make it real. People want to be manipulated. It keeps life simple for them. You watch and learn what their desires are, what their morals are, and what you can give them in return for what you want from them.

For the time being, it worked for Sasha to sleep with Ellie's husband. And she enjoyed keeping the true nature of the lab project a secret, even from the boss. It was too funny: the lead scientist not having the first clue.

Sasha set up the accident perfectly.

She arrived late for work, flustered, and holding a reusable cup of coffee, which—in her rush —she dropped. Then, affecting horrified dismay, she mopped up clumsily. And the next thing you know, the test tube lay shattered on the hard tile floor of the lab with amber liquid pooled all around it.

Eloise Martins cried out and dashed to Sasha's side. What would the boss do?—Given that she had no idea of the real nature of Specimen 7. After staring for a full three seconds at the substance seeping across the floor, Ellie jerked to attention and clicked her fingers.

'Everyone, out. Now. Quick.'

The lab emptied faster than the box of chocolates Sasha had given the nurses in thanks for looking after her parents. As soon as they'd opened it and put it on the nurse's station, hands snatched and mouths gobbled until nothing remained but colourful screwed up wrappers.

The utilitarian room looked like that emptied
box now. Half finished projects littered the counters, while pens along with sheaves of paper
filled with scribbled notes lay scattered on the
floor.

'I'm so sorry,' Sasha murmured with a horrified hand pressed to her mouth. 'What will we
do?' She raised imploring eyes to her boss.

Ellie grabbed two sets of gloves and masks
and handed one to Sasha. Then she donned hers.
With utmost care, she knelt and suction-tubed the
glass and liquid. Then she fixed a worried gaze
on Sasha, 'We have more of number seven, yes?'

The young protege nodded. 'In the cold
room.'

Ellie pursed her lips. 'Okay, here's the way
it's going to go.' She put her hands on her hips.
'I'll go and let the others back in. I'll tell them it
was just a control tube that you dropped.'

Despite Eloise's virtuous approach to life and
morality, Sasha hadn't doubted for a second that
the woman would come to her aid. Especially
when she didn't know what the test tube had
actually contained. As far as she was aware, it

was a trial nano-drug to cure ageing. No harm done.

Sasha nodded encouragement.

Ellie said, 'Good. Nothing more to worry about.'

If only she knew.

Nobody suspected that Sasha had done it deliberately. Ellie had no idea what had just happened. Or of the disaster that would unfold over the coming days and weeks. New Year's Eve had offered the perfect timing for Sasha to put her plan into action. The richest planet in the Exxon system would revel and party, meaning all but the barest essentials would cease to function for the next three days. Most of the populace would head for the capital, all the way across the continent in zone 1. People would awaken with what they believed nothing more than well-earned hangovers. It would take at least a week for the first chips to fail. Two weeks for people's personalities to undergo drastic changes. And shortly after that, bedlam. A world in chaos.

2

E35

The weeks passed quickly, and Sasha made her plans. One evening, when everyone else had clocked off for the day, Ellie stood in the doorway of the empty lab, arms crossed.

'Sasha? Can I have a word?'

'What is it?'

'I think you know.'

She'd never heard her boss speak so sternly or look so grim. Had she worked it out? Sasha shrugged. 'I swear—'

Ellie held up a hand, forestalling further protestations of innocence. 'You should have told me. I would have treated the spill so differently. But now. ... It's far too late.' Her face looked haunted. 'We did this.'

Then she shook her head. 'No. You did this. You and my husband and the bloody president.'

Sasha grinned—no point in hiding her real feelings anymore. 'He told you. John.'

Eloise refused to dignify the statement with a response, which just added to Sasha's enjoyment. She had one more card up her sleeve. One that neither Mr Martins nor President Terrence had any knowledge of.

In mimicry of her boss, Sasha crossed her arms and leant against one of the counters. 'I've been working on an antidote.'

She paused to give her words their due weight.

Ellie's eyes widened. Then she blinked. 'We have to move it. Now. The riots. People suspect the virus came from us. From here. They're coming to burn us down.'

Sasha jumped. And the silly cow had waited this long to warn her?

Ellie demanded, 'Give me the vial.'

Not trusting herself to speak just then, lest she alert the other woman to her schemes, Sasha went and did as asked. Mute, she handed the tiny neoplast container to her boss. Through clenched teeth, she said, 'I was just about to come and find you. The president wants this at his secure base immediately.'

Ellie's next words saved Sasha from having to fashion an excuse to send her boss instead of accompanying the antidote herself. 'I'll take it. You've done more than enough already.'

Sasha hung her head, all meekness and chagrin. According to John, the president wanted the vial for himself. He had no intention of replicating it and giving it to the masses. As with any virus, some people would have natural immunity, but most wouldn't. Terrence had just come up with a great way of destroying his enemies while ensuring his supporters had reason to feel even more grateful to him.

Only Sasha knew of the existence of a second vial. Only she knew that the helipod would never make it across the nine zones to the military stronghold in zone 1. She had suspected that John Martins would spill the beans when he believed his wife could do nothing about it, and so she had devised a back-up plan.

3

E35

Grim-faced and sweating despite the evening chill, Ellie climbed into the helipod, clutching the precious vial in a clenched fist. She wouldn't let go of it until she could pass it to Professor Giles Stephenson, Terrence's head scientist at the presidential lab.

What had begun as hurt at the betrayal from both her husband and her young protégé hardened into seething anger. Ellie clenched her jaw against its urgings to destroy them all. The most important thing was to get this antidote to safety. Take it to the one scientist on the planet who could replicate it quickly and get it distributed to the population of Exxon 1. Then she could decide what to do about the man and the girl.

No, not just this first planet. With horror, Ellie hung her head and wiped away an errant tear. By now, the virus would have spread to the other five planets in the Exxon system. And it was all her fault. She had covered up the spill. That she'd had no idea of the real nature of specimen 7 gave no excuse.

Is that the president's intention? To infect the whole system? Does he aim to take control of them all?

A loud bang and the sudden juddering of the helipod stopped those thoughts before they could get going properly. Then the small craft plummeted, leaving Ellie's stomach way up above. With her free hand, she grabbed one of the hanging straps and braced her feet against the vibrating floor.

Smoke oozed into the cabin. Within seconds, Ellie couldn't see, and her eyes smarted and watered. Then she broke into a coughing fit. The four-man helipod continued to plunge toward the ground at an alarming rate. Damn the president for banning any and all portable access into zone 1. That would have offered the quickest and safest way for her to get the antidote where it desperately needed to be.

The craft went into a spin. Then the front end

angled sharply downward. Chaos ensued. Any object not strapped down flew around the small cabin, making lethal weapons of even the smallest items. A metal box hit Ellie on the left temple. In pain and reeling, she screamed. She had time to reach a hand up to the wound and see it come away bloody. Then she passed out.

4

E35

Two hours later, Sasha received a frantic call from Mr Martins. The helipod had crashed enroute. No survivors. All the vitals had gone dark on the monitoring chips. The president had sent in army specials to try and retrieve the vial before the looters could get to it. But first, they had to determine the precise location of the downed helipod.

With the riots spreading throughout the city, she doubted they'd find it anytime soon. Somebody had taken out the power hub, leaving the whole of Exxon 1 without an energy supply. The pod's tracking would have gone offline almost immediately after takeoff. And the absence of power rendered all the transport pods useless, except for those restricted for army use only. She had no access to those.

As Sasha ended the call, she grinned and tossed her secret vial up in the air and then caught it in her palm, which she clenched shut around it. From the window of the hotel penthouse, she watched the lab complex burn. Already, the blaze had consumed a whole commercial block.

The flames reflected in her eyes and warmed her soul. With Ellie out of the way, Sasha's secret remained safe. Only she, the president, and his second-in-command—Mr Martins—knew what had really happened in the lab all those weeks ago. And nobody but she knew about the second vial, or that she'd immunised herself. Time to get over to the presidential base, where she could offer to make herself useful.

CHAPTER THREE

1

E79

From the lumpy old mattress on the front-room floor, Priya strained to hear his side of the conversation—futile, though, as the thick walls prevented anything but muffled rumblings from reaching her.

Frustrated and a little afraid of him, even though he'd nursed her from the brink of death, she chewed on her thumb. An unconscious thing she did whenever she felt nervous or worried. Her once long and neatly manicured nail had foreshortened to a ragged thing that barely reached the top of her nail bed.

Abruptly, the talking stopped, and Kaleb strode through the door separating the back kitchen from this room. Priya watched him.

Although he wore the green jumpsuit of a farmer, he didn't move like a farmer. Didn't speak like one either. However, he did seem to know about things. Like plants—what was poisonous and what was okay to eat. How to do things you'd expect a guy who'd grown up in zone 9 to have developed skills in. How to read the weather and time of day just by studying the sky.

Priya, having lived in zone 5 her whole life, had no clue about anything. From her earliest memory, tech had been there to do for her. Never had she needed to learn how to cook, develop a sense of direction, read people, or any number of other things that now meant the difference between surviving or perishing.

She missed her implants and all the valuable information they'd fed her constantly on every aspect of life, including if anyone within a few meters of her posed a threat.

Now, all of that had been stripped away from

Harmony Kent

her. And she'd discovered in the most brutal of ways just how much she would have to learn if she were to make it in this new world.

Right now, all she knew was that the man who'd helped her was no farmer. Or, at least, he hadn't been for a lot of years. Which version of Kaleb had come back in here? The kind and caring boyish guy, or the impatient and indifferent man? She didn't care at all for his wild swings between the one and the other.

2

E79

Annoyed at the dressing-down the major had just given him, Kaleb dropped the mic to the worn tabletop and stomped into the front room. He hadn't had any way to defend himself because he hadn't told his superiors about the girl. They only knew that he'd stayed in one location for way too long and questioned his motives and commitment.

Priya sat on the makeshift bed, watching him

30

with a face full of wary suspicion. That just added fuel to his bad mood. What way was that to repay him for all he'd done? Determined to get this over with as quickly as possible, he set his jaw and dropped onto the only other piece of furniture in there, a hard metal chair at the foot of the bed.

'You have to get up,' he told her. 'Get moving. You've lain around too long.'

When she gasped, he hardened his heart against the physical pain such action would bring her. She hadn't yet recovered enough. But they had to relocate. The part of him that had urged him to help her now wanted to tell her the truth. To explain his seeming cruelty. The more rational side would have none of that. No way could he jeopardise his career—his life, in all honesty— for some little woman. No, she would either go with him or go alone.

Kaleb stood and moved to stand by her side, then he grabbed her wrists and pulled her to her feet. Priya yelled and tried to yank herself away from him. Disgusted in so many ways, he turned and strode to the doorway leading to the central hallway.

'We leave within the hour. I'll go and pack.'

His foul temper gave him extra momentum, and he'd finished the packing forty minutes later. When he returned to what he'd come to think of as the sick room, he found the woman standing at the back window, arms hugging her upper torso and staring outside.

The yellow jumpsuit he'd dug up for her hung baggy and big on her petite frame, and the colour of a waste worker did nothing for her pale and mottled complexion.

'What colour did you used to wear?'

His unexpected question made her startle. It took her a second or two to recover and process, but then she said, 'Blue.'

He nodded. Office worker. It figured, with her coming from zone 5. She would be of no use out there. In general, the city folk from zones 1 through 6 had no clue about fending for themselves or how to get by.

She eyed the enormous black duffel bag on his back. 'Where'd you find that?'

Her voice held an edge to it that made him

cautious. He shrugged. 'Same place as I got everything else.'

A thin smile stretched her lips but didn't reach her eyes. 'Right. Your scavenging.' Disbelief oozed from her every pore.

Kaleb ignored both what she did and didn't say. 'You ready?'

She unwrapped one arm to push her thumb between her lips. Her words distorted around it, 'Where to?'

He lost his temper. 'For God's sake, Priya.'

She flinched.

Kaleb softened his voice, 'We have to keep moving, or the gangs will find us. If you want to survive out here, you can't settle down. We've stayed here too long already.' He ran a hand through his hair. 'I have an idea, but we'll need to scout the place out first. It's a week since I saw it.'

Mute and wan, she nodded.

3

E79

The silo came into view. Kaleb held up a hand, his back straight and stiff. Priya stopped walking. Stilled. Waited. She felt like a disinterested bystander, or as if she were merely watching this unfold on the telecast, reducing it to nothing more than a fantasy of an apocalypse that couldn't hurt her.

Ever since she had burst into consciousness and panicked, thinking that Kaleb was yet another man attacking her, not quite leaving her nightmare flashbacks behind in the dark, this dead detachment had descended.

Though she knew it for what it was, she couldn't seem to do anything about it. Priya had become an automaton. A machine with just the one program: Escape. While the fake farmer had treated her with kindness—and had undoubtedly saved her from death—she couldn't (wouldn't) trust him. And his mood swings from that pleasant warmth to the cold and uncaring stranger scared her badly.

As the days had morphed into weeks, Priya became more convinced than ever that Kaleb had been in the military when all this went down. Suspected he might still be. So why all the secrecy? What did he have to hide? And what did he really go in search of when he went on his scavenges? A little while ago, he had spoken to her about her accompanying him when she grew strong enough. Had said she should show him, in particular, anything she found out of the ordinary.

If he had to keep his true purpose so tightly under wraps, then to her mind, it wasn't worth getting into, and surely not something she wished to become involved with. All she wanted was for the world to go back to how it had been before: safe, ordered, controlled, everyone knowing their places, and with tech running every aspect of life.

Some people had bucked against the totalitarian regime of Exxon 1 with its non-elected government, but Priya had always found it comforting. It meant not having to make difficult decisions. It meant no chance of someone attacking you out of the blue. It meant a peaceful and quiet existence.

Who had broken it, and why? If she ever found them, she wasn't sure what she would do. In breaking the system, her world, they had broken her. And even if she did ever find that imagined utopia of safety, she could never again believe the illusion or false promises. After all, she had just seen it all turn on a hairpin.

A gruff male voice broke into her thoughts. A man with a machine gun hailed them from across the dusty yard. Moon dust covered the whole of the planet; only in the cities did they manage to keep it at bay. Except for when the storms came, and then you breathed, ate, and spat dust for days afterward. It gritted between your teeth, and your eyes stung and smarted.

Priya tensed and moved so that she stood directly behind Kaleb, who raised his hand in salute. 'Whoa there, friend. Don't shoot us. We mean no harm.'

So, he'd gone for the affable farmer type. Silent, she stood and watched and listened.

The stranger lowered his weapon, but still

held his fingers at the ready near the trigger. Kaleb took a couple of steps forward, exposing her to view. A woman stepped from around the side of the silo. When she clocked Priya, her eyes widened, and she cast all caution aside and strode up to her.

'What happened to you?' She stared at Priya's still-healing wounds.

Priya shrugged, remaining on high alert. 'Men taking what they want.'

The woman cast a sharp glance at Kaleb. Priya hurried to absolve him, 'No. Not him. He found me. Nursed me back to health.'

The guy with the gun now lowered it fully and relaxed. Then he came over and joined the trio. The woman held out a hand, which Priya shook.

'Jenny.' She hooked a thumb at her companion. 'This is Jeremiah. He's the impromptu leader of our little gang.'

Kaleb answered for them, 'I'm Kaleb, and this is Priya.'

While they exchanged greetings, Priya zoned out. The mention of a gang had set off alarm bells. But, then, everything seemed to set off those warning clangs these days. She found it easier to let Kaleb do the talking. Far better for her to watch and listen and learn.

The fact they had found other people here complicated things for her, and—she suspected—for Kaleb. Priya planned to leave that night, and more people meant increased difficulty in getting away unobserved. Kaleb had something to hide, and company meant he couldn't hold his radioed conversations in private. He would have to keep his high-tech kit packed up and unseen, or it would raise unwanted questions for him.

The upshot was that Kaleb agreed they would spend the night with the group, and then go on their way in the morning. Priya pretended agreement and acquiescence. She would bide her time. Watch and Wait. A small smile hid at the corners of her lips. WAW (which sounded, in her mind's eye, uncannily like War) had become her new motto.

Inside the silo, she discovered that the so-called gang was more a group of families and the odd single refugee who had found one another and come together for mutual support and protection. They'd best watch out for the patrols, though. The president's edict stated that any formation of groups, sects, or societies was strictly outlawed. A couple of young kids shadowed their mothers, while two teenage girls sat off to one side and giggled with one another. Why couldn't Priya have stumbled across a group like this, instead of falling prey to the likes of Jimmy and Hank and the rest?

The woman, Jenny, had latched on to Kaleb. If she didn't know any better, Priya would say she was flirting with him. Kaleb didn't seem to mind, and neither did Jeremiah. So, the two weren't a couple, it seemed.

Then the pale lilac of Jenny's worn and dirty jumpsuit impressed itself upon Priya's brain. Lilac. The colour for escorts … a kind word for a well-paid prostitute. Her old profession didn't shock Priya, but more that the woman hadn't found a less obtrusive colour to wear in these unstable and dangerous times.

The gathered adults welcomed Kaleb and fussed over Priya and her injuries. All too soon, they became immersed in conversation, each of them having to fend off a myriad of questions. As soon as she could, Priya found a quiet corner until someone announced that dinner was ready.

The corn chowder tasted surprisingly good, considering it had been made by hand with few ingredients. For the first time since the assault, Priya's appetite returned with gusto, and she wolfed down her portion. It turned out they had plenty to go around, and most of them—including Kaleb and Priya—had second helpings.

Throughout the meal, Jenny sat by Kaleb's side. Priya did her best to keep herself to herself. She would get out of here tonight while everyone else slept. With any luck, they would post only the one guard.

The evening passed slowly, and Priya spent it people watching, trying to learn their tells … anything to indicate what they might think or feel or intend. The collapse of society and the implant failures meant that Priya had to work this stuff out for herself from now on.

Eventually, in dribs and drabs, folks drifted away from the circle around the fire. When she felt it would look innocuous enough, Priya did likewise and found a quiet corner by some dry bales in which to curl up and feign slumber.

Not having any way to tell the time, she lay and waited until no sounds of conversation or movement reached her. Inch by inch, she shifted position so that she now knelt behind the tallest stack of bales near the rear doors.

Alert, cautious, and wary, she eased one foot in front of the other, whispering across the solid floor, and then edged the door open, holding her breath in case it squealed. Mercifully, it didn't make a peep, and nobody stirred.

Priya let out her breath on a silent sigh and crept out into the night. Gasps and subtle movement from off to her left made her go still and rigid, hiding in the red-tinted shadows of the building. From childhood, she had hated the red glow Exxon 1's two moons cast down upon them.

Her eyes adjusted. Two of the deeper shadows revealed themselves to be bodies. One stood upright, head back and green jumpsuit unzipped to reveal a hairy chest glistening with sweat; the other knelt in front of the stander, with her dark head of long hair bobbing in front of his groin.

Fascination held Priya rooted to the spot. The guy was Kaleb. The woman, Jenny. As she watched, Kaleb grabbed Jenny's head and pushed his hips forward. Then he made a guttural sound and staggered. Jenny gripped his buttocks, steadying him. Then she eased backward and gazed up at him, smiling.

The whole thing disgusted Priya. And with the system down, he wouldn't be paying Jenny with credits. Just what had he offered her in return? Then it dawned on her that the pair would be certain to return to the silo via this door. She had to get out of the way, or they would surely spot her.

Just then, a guy with a gun walked around from the far side of the structure, obviously on patrol. He shared a laugh with the pair as Kaleb hurriedly zipped himself up. Jenny tidied her hair, joining in the banter unashamedly. The noise gave Priya the distraction she needed to slip back inside and return to her space behind the bales.

Perhaps tomorrow would bring a better opportunity for her to sneak away. In the dark, a small voice in her head nagged at her that with Kaleb, she had safety and a measure of protection. Insisted that she had no skills with which to fend for herself out in the changed and cruel world. Maybe if he'd been a female, she might have chanced it. She shook her head at herself. No. Whatever her saviour's gender, Priya needed to spend some time alone so that she could process and heal. She suspected her mental scars would take a lot longer than her various cuts and bruises to mend.

CHAPTER FOUR

1

E40

John Martins rolled off her, panting and sweaty. Sasha lit mineral cigarettes for them both and handed one to the recent widower of her old boss. Sprawled on his back, legs splayed open and one arm above his head, he took a long drag and blew the smoke out on a long exhale.

Sasha sucked on hers more daintily and fiddled with his chest hair, planning her opening words. It had taken a lot of lying, conniving, and using her body to get across the zones and inside the presidential complex in zone 1. She couldn't blow this now, not when she'd come so close.

She extinguished the stub and flicked it into the disposal unit, which had floated to the bed as soon as they lit up. John finished with his, and the unit swallowed that too, then it drifted back into its corner. When she felt ready, she rolled onto her side, continuing to run her fingers through John's chest hair and over his nipples.

'It's so good to see you again,' she said.

'Mmm.' He grinned down at her. 'That was a reunion worth remembering.'

Sasha giggled and let her hand slide down to his groin, where she squeezed his balls. 'I hope there's more where that came from.'

He took her hand and returned it to his chest. 'I didn't expect you to show up. Not after every-thing.'

His mood had turned unexpectedly serious. Sasha worked hard to match it. After the barest of pauses, she said, 'I had to come.'

John peered down at her, where she lay with her head on his shoulder. 'Oh?'

Before replying, she sucked on the nearest nipple and then let him be. 'I have a lot to offer.'

His chuckle didn't hold its earlier amusement, but—rather—sounded dry and cynical. 'I can get sex anywhere.'

That hurt, but Sasha pressed on, 'Not just in the bedroom, silly. In the lab too.'

Beneath her, his body tensed. 'Just tell me what you want. I don't like playing games.'

Her smile came forced this time, and she stilled her fiddling fingers. 'I want to offer my services in the lab. You know I'm better than some ignorant little protégé. I come highly qualified.'

The silence held for way too long. Had she pushed too far too soon? At last, he said, 'That's not my decision.'

She shook her head. 'No. I know. But you can get me in to see the president.'

Without mirth, he laughed—a single short bark. 'You don't ask for much, do you?'

'Please.' She hated to plead, but so much hung on this.

If he wanted more sex, she could live with that. She'd gotten used to selling her body since a young age. And soon, if she prevailed, she would become the one in charge. She would have the choice of who she slept with.

John spoke slowly, 'If I do this, you'll owe me.'

Sasha nodded. 'Yes. Anything.'

In a sudden movement, John rolled them so that he had her pinned beneath him, his erection finding new life already. His fierce green eyes blazed at her. 'And I don't just mean in the bedroom. You'll owe me big time. I'll own you. Do you understand?'

She swallowed, suddenly cautious. But she couldn't back out now. 'Yes.' To emphasise her compliance, she nodded.

He smiled and then pressed his lips down on hers, hard, punishing her with his mouth and teeth. The sex was hard and fast and short, which suited her just fine. Soon after, John's snores rumbled throughout the room.

Sasha crept from the bed, careful not to disturb the slumbering man. Just as much as needing his agreement to help her get into the president's good graces, she also wanted to have a thorough snoop around John's apartment. Who knew what useful stuff she might find?

2

E42

The next two days dragged by, especially as Sasha had failed miserably in her quest to find anything useful in Martins' apartment suite. He must have a hidey-hole elsewhere. Did he suspect her? Or was he merely cautious in general?

At last, John escorted her in to see Terrence. The president dismissed him right away and beckoned Sasha into his large, plush office within the extensive presidential suite. The tall two-wide doors swished shut with a dreadful thud. All of a sudden timid, she moved forward—one tiny step at a time.

Head bowed, she said, 'Sir, thank you for seeing me.'

A low rumble indicated his amusement. 'You come highly recommended.'

How to take that? What had John said about her? Just what had the two men shared? How close were they? For the first time in a while, doubts assailed her. Still, she'd come this far. No option now but to continue on.

Her greatest solace lay in that they didn't know her, not truly. They had no knowledge of her past, of what she had endured, of what she had done. She had taken pains to ensure that people only saw the successful young woman, orphaned at a young age, who had educated herself and risen high. Just as importantly, she did her best to make sure that nobody suspected her future plans and goals or her current schemes.

Why did she put herself through this? Because it kept her safe. Security lay in power. And she intended to get as much of it as she could. With that in mind, she adopted her most winning smile and batted her eyelashes, looking up at Terrence demurely.

'So do you.'

Amusement lit his eyes while he waited for her to go on.

She eased around the desk to where he perched on one corner. Not quite daring to touch him just yet, she let her hand trail over the smooth mahogany—a rare material in this day and age. It must have cost a fortune to grow the trees, especially.

'I hear you're the most powerful man on the planet.' She let her tongue sneak out and lick her lower lip.

He guffawed and slapped his leg. 'And what, little lady, do you need this big, powerful man to do for you?'

Now, Sasha did let her hand drift to his knee. 'I worked on the virus. I created the antidote. I can help. Put me to work with Professor Stephenson. I'm certain the two of us can recreate what was lost.'

She stopped and watched him expectantly. He proved a hard man to read, which put her on edge. His demeanour gave her an inkling of how he'd earned his nickname of 'Terror'.

Though she tried her best to decipher his expression, his features remained inscrutable. He held her vivid blue gaze with his cold grey one. 'And you made just the one sample?'

Her heart almost stopped. She swallowed around the lump in her throat and nodded. 'Mrs

Martins wouldn't wait. She wanted to get the antidote to you as early as possible. I begged her to at least let me make one replica as soon as I realised it should work on the virus, but she wouldn't have it.'

Sasha kept her head lowered throughout her charade, ensuring that she had to look up at Terrence in a faux deferential manner. She waited for him to chew over her words. Either he would believe her or he wouldn't. And she felt confident she could deal with his response one way or the other. These days, she had a lot more going for her than just her slim, petite body which men found beautiful and irresistible. And though she used her physical attributes to her advantage often, she did not have to rely on that solely.

The president lay his large, heavy hand over hers, which still rested on his knee. 'You can remember what you did? How we can kill the nanobots?'

Best not to come across as too confident. 'I think so, sir.'

Terrence grabbed her hand, lifted it from his thigh, and yanked her in close, trapping her between his knees and bringing them nose-to-nose. Sasha gasped with the shock of the manoeuvre and then forced herself to relax. He brought his palms to her buttocks and cupped them, stroking with his thumbs. Sasha let him.

'Is that all you're putting on the table?' he asked.

She weighed up the situation. Assessed whether he would put her in the lab without her offering herself. Had he not pulled her in and started fondling her, she might have been able to spin this differently. Now, however, his vanity had come into play, as well as his libido.

Sasha wriggled in closer so that her abdomen rubbed against his groin. 'You can put me on the table too if you like.'

The most powerful man on the planet made that low rumble again, indicating a laugh, and squeezed her backside, hard. He didn't kiss her. Didn't offer any affection or intimacy whatsoever.

To display the power he held over her, he shot to his feet and bent her over the table. With rough hands, he ripped open her zip, shoved her trousers down to her ankles, and with his boot heel, pushed the crumpled garment off over one foot. Next, he tore her panties from her. Then he pushed his knees between her legs and entered her.

She was too dry. Not ready. It hurt. And he was a big man. He pummelled her. Sasha bit her lower lip and held in her whimpers, keeping her end goal in mind. One day, she would make this man pay for degrading her in such a way. At least with John Martins, he made love with her. Left her with some semblance of dignity. Not Terrence.

This was sex and nothing more. The man fucked her hard and fast with no connection or feelings in there. When he'd finished, he tucked himself in and left her to put herself back to rights.

Sasha waited for him to acknowledge her, but he kept his back turned. His words came like a slap in the face, 'Get out.'

The man liked control. Power. Which she could understand. Could relate to. Could work with. Slowly. For now, she would give him the win.

For now.

Without protest, she walked on quiet feet to the vast doors. There, with a hand on one handle, she couldn't resist saying, 'Just this once, Mr President.' And then she left.

In the ante-room, John Martins sat and looked at her, his eyes asking the question. Sasha shrugged and murmured, 'I think so, but you'll have to ask him.'

While she covered the distance back to her temporary room, she hung her head, deep in thought. Terrence had manifested as an animal she hadn't quite expected, despite the many rumours. Had she convinced him? Was her mission successful? Not since her childhood had she floundered this badly. Ought she to have turned him down flat? Should she have shown more backbone with him? She couldn't see the way forward, and that was unacceptable.

Untenable.

Furious with herself, she bit down on her tongue, which drew blood. The pain removed the sting of the tears that had snuck into the corners of her eyes. Sasha lifted her head, straightened her shoulders, and strode back to her room.

3

E42

Seconds after the young protégé left the presidential office, Terrence came to the door and waved for John to join him. Martins rose and stepped lightly into the vast room. The president stood at the drinks cabinet pouring two scotches. He handed one to Martins.

The two men settled in a couple of armchairs, which faced a hologram fireplace. John sipped in silence, waiting for his companion to open the conversation. After a long three minutes, however, he couldn't hold himself back any longer. 'So, what did you think of her?'

Over the rim of his glass, Terrence studied Martins. 'You were right about her being a bombshell, but you didn't tell me how manipulative she is.'

To gain thinking time, John took another sip

of his whisky. He allowed a slow smile to spread across his lips. 'You can handle her, no problem. I take it she delivered?'

'I didn't give her an awful lot of choice.' Terrence laughed.

Martins pushed out a complimentary chuckle. 'You always were the ladies' man, Denis.'

They fell silent while they enjoyed more of the warming spirit. John hoped that the man hadn't hurt Sasha too badly. Still, she was a big girl, and she'd gotten herself into this. After another moment, John said, 'Will you have her? In the lab?'

The president shrugged, looking bored. 'For now. Until she's no longer useful to us.'

John nodded. Things seemed to have gone the way he'd expected. Though he did worry about the president's cavalier attitude toward the girl. She knew stuff. Knew a lot. Could inflict irreparable damage with the information she held. And then there was her past. His head jerked up, and he gave Denis a sharp look. 'You know about her history, yes?'

Terrence rubbed his thumb around the rim of

his scotch tumbler, studying John right back. 'That she was abused emotionally and psychologically as a child?'

'Yes.'

'That she engineered the accident that killed her parents?'

John nodded.

To his surprise, the president went on. 'That she killed the kindly aunt who took in the wretched little orphan?'

Mixed amusement and malice lit the man's eyes. John started. He hadn't known that last. Too late, he realised he'd given away his ignorance to Terrence.

Denis said, 'Know your enemy.'

John nodded, thinking furiously.

The president said, 'Know them inside out.'

At a near whisper, John admitted, 'I thought I did.'

The night he'd received the call about the helipod crash that had killed Ellie rose to the front of his mind. He'd had his doubts, but now …

Had Sasha set that up? Had she killed his

wife? He shook his head. To deceive his spouse, who also happened to be the lead scientist on the nano project, was one thing. But to have her assassinated? No. Too far. Too much. He glanced at his old friend seated across from him, empty glass in hand.

The look on the man's face told John all he needed to know. He accused, 'You knew. You knew that too. Ellie.'

Terrence gave his head the tiniest of shakes. 'I know it all.'

Slowly, it dawned upon John that more hung in the air. He watched the president and waited. Eventually, the man said, 'Were you aware that Ms Novikov manufactured a second, secret, vial?'

John dropped his glass, which bounced twice on the plush carpet and spilled the last mouthful of whisky. The fumes rose up, harsh on his nostrils. Terrence's words felt equally as harsh on his ears. He opened his mouth to ask how, but Denis answered, preempting it.

'She didn't know about the surveillance. The girl was clever enough to disable the main security system while she worked out of hours, but she had no clue otherwise.'

Stunned, John sat there. What other ways had Sasha used him? Abused his trust? The irony that he had used her too didn't pass him by, but still, how could she? The little bitch. He would show her.

After a couple of minutes, he calmed enough to speak again. 'Then why have you agreed to have her around?'

Terrence showed his teeth. Straight and white and polished. Menacing. The sort of teeth that would rip out your throat without blinking.

'We can use her. You and I.'

John scoffed, 'We can get sex anywhere.'

Denis grinned. 'Yes, but it's more fun letting her think she has the upper hand, don't you think?'

John nodded. He could use her in other ways too.

The president said, 'So, you keep her occupied on a night, just like you have been. In the daylight hours, we'll keep her busy on useless work in the lab. Giles will keep her in line, and

I'll have her whenever it suits.' He gave John a piercing stare. 'Are we agreed?'

Mute, shocked, but not daring to disagree, John once again nodded. 'Agreed.'

CHAPTER FIVE

1

E80

Well, now, this changed the balance. Priya stared, openmouthed. What to make of it? Perhaps Kaleb *was* a simple farmer after all. Surely he wouldn't have Jenny around, otherwise. It surprised her enough that he'd allowed Priya to stay with him this long, injured or not.

Jenny stood with a scuffed and dirty black backpack slung jauntily over one shoulder, contrasting sharply against the relatively clean lilac jumpsuit. A few members from the rest of the group stood huddled together a couple of feet away. Evidently, they'd come to wave her off. Priya just bet that the escort had made herself popular.

The woman's presence both threatened her and made her feel safer around Kaleb. At least, now, he could satisfy his appetites without involving Priya. What annoyed her more than anything, though, was the complete lack of discussion on the subject. Neither one had approached Priya to ask how she might feel.

With little fanfare, they set out from the silo, leaving the dust and friendliness behind. What drove Kaleb so hard? Why, if he were a farmer, couldn't he stay in one place? Why would he refuse to remain in the safety of the group? But, of course, the biggest why settled on his weekly radio conversations. To whom did he speak? And for what?

Largely, Priya ignored the pair while they walked and scouted, seeking out a safe place. Belatedly, after about three hours, she realised that she'd seen nothing of Jimmy on street corners, nor of any other folks, come to think of it. Intrigued, and not quite as highly keyed-up as she had been all morning, she called out to Kaleb.

'How come there's no one around?'

His shoulders stiffened, and he came to a standstill. Priya caught up to him and Jenny and stood with them, waiting for his answer. Already, she had her suspicions. Not all his absences had been about scavenging, she felt sure.

Quietly, he told her, 'You won't see him. You won't find any of them.'

Priya stared at him. 'You took care of it?'

He set his jaw. 'It would have been stupid not to.'

Priya nodded. She'd told him about the size of the gang. He wouldn't want to risk running into any of them unexpectedly. But, then, farmers didn't go around *taking care of it.*

Silent, Kaleb set off walking. Jenny hung back with Priya, and the two women brought up the rear. Although they didn't exchange any conversation, Priya appreciated the gesture and the company.

After another half an hour, they finally found a place that looked suitable, at least from the outside. The trio approached cautiously, intending to scout it. The old house appeared abandoned and run down. Priya's whole body hurt, and she hoped fervently that this property would pan out. She needed to rest.

When Kaleb had the two women wait just outside the boundary while he went ahead to check the place out, Priya didn't know how to feel. On the one hand, it was incredibly male-chauvinistic. On the other, she appreciated the way he protected Jenny and her. And, although he hadn't gone in holding any sort of weapon, she suspected that he would have a gun or something to hand once he'd left their sight.

Five minutes later, he returned, offering a tight smile. 'All clear.'

Priya mumbled, 'Thanks.'

Jenny stepped up to Kaleb and kissed him on the mouth. 'You're so brave.'

Priya turned away and rolled her eyes. Sometimes, Jenny made her feel like puking. Kaleb, however, seemed to lap it up. Priya stomped off ahead, leaving the love-puppies to follow. If she'd thought that going in first would give her the choice of sleeping room, she would have been mistaken.

As soon as Kaleb and Jenny entered, he started organising them and giving orders. For himself, he took the back downstairs room, which looked like it used to be a kitchen. He put the two women on the upper floor in one of the front rooms.

'Why do we have to share?' Priya scowled from one to the other. 'There's plenty of room.'

Most annoyingly, Jenny and Kaleb shared a knowing glance. Then, slowly, as if explaining to a small child, Kaleb said, 'Security. You're safer staying together. Right now, comfort should be the last thing on your list.'

Subdued, and a little ashamed, Priya clamped her mouth shut on a sigh and trudged up the stairs. Jenny followed on light feet and closed the door softly behind them.

'I'm sorry you're stuck with me,' Jenny said. 'Look, I know you don't like me. It won't be for long.'

The words startled Priya, who hadn't realised that she'd shown overt animosity to the other woman. She shook her head. 'No. That's not true.

I don't even know you well enough to dislike you.' God, that came out all wrong. She tried again, 'It's not you. It's me. I'm the one who's sorry. … Ever since the attack …'

'It's all wrong.'

'Yeah.'

Jenny smiled and nodded, and then she busied herself with setting out her thin bedroll beneath the window. Which suited Priya fine, as she preferred the back wall of the room, well away from any draft. She also felt much safer away from any points of ingress, regardless of the fact that Kaleb would stay up on watch throughout the night. He always did. How did he manage on just three hours sleep, day after day?

All settled, the three met in the downstairs front room—containing two long sofas that didn't appear too grubby—and grabbed a quick meal of tube food, which Kaleb had found on one of his scavenges. Dry and tasteless, it needed washing down with plenty of water, but it did satisfy her appetite even if it didn't fill her belly.

When they'd finished, Kaleb put the empty packets in his backpack to dispose of later. 'The less trail we leave, the better,' he said at their questioning glances. Then he turned and addressed Jenny, 'I plan on going scavenging now, before dark. Two sets of eyes are better than one.'

Jenny smiled and nodded. 'Count me in.'

Jealousy and worry infected Priya at the same time. Why hadn't he asked her? Completely forgetting her earlier determination to get away, she now found that she wanted inclusion and the feeling of protection which that brought. 'Three sets are better than two,' she said in a low voice.

Kaleb and Jenny stared at her for a second or so. Then Kaleb said, 'Sure thing.'

+++

That appeared to have settled the matter, and the three of them soon stood ready for heading out. Much to her surprise, Kaleb didn't split them up and allocate them each an area. Instead, he insisted that they should all stick together. Priya's cheeks flamed. Was that because of what had happened to her? Or would he have been so circumspect anyway?

Regardless, at least he hadn't made her stay behind. They reached the middle of town, and Priya went to high alert once more. Ahead lay the street corner where Jimmy had laid his trap. Or where she had behaved stupidly. Right then, it stood abandoned, and she breathed out a sigh of relief, even though she knew Kaleb had taken care of the gang.

Kaleb consulted a gridded map and took them left, toward a small commercial area. A cold wind gusted infrequently and kicked up dust. Priya zipped up her jumpsuit collar so that it covered her mouth and nose. By her side, Jenny did the same. Kaleb ignored the first two buildings, which looked like abandoned stores, and headed for a third, further down the road. She guessed he'd searched those previously.

Apparently, he'd found her on the opposite side of town, which made her think that he searched systematically from some central point. From where, though? And why?

The low building they entered struck her as utilitarian and unattractive. It appeared to have served as some sort of government centre. Wanting to test Kaleb's local knowledge far more than needing to know the purpose of the property, Priya said, 'What is this place?'

Without looking at her or breaking stride, he said, 'Feed and grain centre.'

Only then did she realise the futility of her question. Right now, she had no way of verifying his information. Had she always been this useless? Most likely. The technology had simply masked her inability. Perhaps tech and implants weren't such a good thing after all. Just how deskilled had humanity become? Only people like Kaleb, living off the land, had any idea anymore.

He led them to a room behind the main reception area, and there he stopped. 'I haven't looked through here yet. Let's see what we can find.'

Jenny moved off to a back room.

Priya wanted to know, 'What are we looking for?'

Kaleb shrugged. 'Food. Clothing. Medicine. Essentials, really. And if you come across anything out of the ordinary, show it to me.'

Priya pressed, 'Why?'

He rolled his eyes at her. 'Because, it might prove useful.' Then he walked away.

Still moody and dissatisfied, and hating herself for her mulishness, Priya trudged through the reception toward a side area. The smell struck her first, and she gagged at the stink. People had lived here for a time, and—it seemed—they'd used this room as a privy.

In the act of turning away in disgust, having decided that this space would turn up nothing but shit, Priya paused mid-step. Something that didn't belong had just flashed up in her torch beam. A bright orange container. Tiny. Intrigued, she wrinkled her nose and walked further into the revolting space.

The thing seemed to be some sort of vial, like the kind you might see at the med centre. Gingerly, still sore and stiff, she eased into a squat and reached out for the object. It looked intact, and when she shook it, liquid sloshed inside. Scratches, and one large gouge, marked its sides, but otherwise, it remained sealed.

What was it doing in here? Had someone

dropped it inadvertently? Or had they thrown it away, thinking it useless? Kaleb's words came back to her. This thing could be useful. It might even be the thing he was searching for. She gripped it in her fist, ready to drop it into her pocket.

A voice from behind froze her hand.

'What have you got there?'

Kaleb.

He'd seen.

Priya shrugged and turned to face him, keeping her fist wrapped around the vial. 'Nothing much. Just some bit of plastic.'

He advanced a step. 'Let me see.'

She ignored his outstretched hand but relented a little. 'Could be medicine. I'll show you when we get home.'

His jawline hardened, and he stood silent for a full minute, which felt more like an hour to her taut nerves. Then, he nodded—just the once— and strode back into the reception area. Confused, and her feelings torn, she followed after him. Where had her new stubbornness come from? What could she possibly benefit from withholding what she'd found?

Jenny stood by the front doors, holding a box. Kaleb called a halt to the search for the day, citing limited daylight, but Priya suspected he wanted to get back so that he could get a look at her find.

2

E80

Kaleb paced, fuming. She had the vial. He was sure of it. Number 23709103. He'd examined it not minutes ago, but still, she wouldn't let go, instead making him zoom in on the serial code without touching. The thing could save his career. Save the world. Why did she insist on keeping hold of it? In the back kitchen, he gripped the mic, hating the major's angry voice. His last words echoed inside Kaleb's skull, 'Just take it from her.'

The major was correct, of course. So, why hadn't he? Why couldn't he? It came back to the reason he'd helped her in the first place.

Emotion. Useless. Pointless. But there all the same.

'I'll take it tonight, while the two women sleep,' he gritted out.

'Civilians should never have been your concern, soldier.'

Kaleb bit his teeth together. 'Sir.'

After that conversation, he kept to himself, only joining the women for dinner—more tube food, along with some bottled water they'd found at the Feed and Grain Centre.

At this time of the year, night killed day early, and darkness soon cloaked Exxon 1. Kaleb bided his time until silence enveloped the house, then he crept up the stairs. For about thirty seconds, he stood and listened but heard no sounds. No signs of activity. Just about to pull away, he paused. A loud snore rattled against the door.

With a smile, Kaleb gripped the doorknob and turned, easing the door open a fraction. When no reaction came, he pushed it open all the way.

Cold, sharp steel pressed against his throat.

'What the fuck do you think you're doing?'

Priya.

Shit.

Slowly, he raised his hands in the air and opened his mouth to reassure her. A loud bang sounded from downstairs. Kaleb dropped to the floor, pulling Priya down with him. Window glass shattered. A dull thud followed. Cold air blew into the bedroom. He looked up.

The window above Jenny had gone—blown out by a pulse-bullet. Blood-red moonlight oozed through the holes that peppered the thin wall beneath. Priya threw herself across the room and to Jenny. Then she wrapped her arms around the woman and howled out her agony.

Full of dread, knowing already, Kaleb crawled over to the bedding and reached out a hand to check Jenny. Priya moved out of his way.

No pulse.

Sticky wetness coated his fingers.

Footsteps sounded from the bottom of the stairs.

Kaleb rose to a crouch and dashed across to the partially open door, with Priya crawling behind. After checking the landing, he took her hand and pulled her to her feet, then he steered her back to the empty window frame. A cautious glance outward showed him what he'd suspected. The intruders had entered the building. Whoever had shot out the glass must feel reassured by the lack of response from this room.

He took a chance and eased through the open frame, which held not even one jag of glass. Priya slithered through after him. The pair hung by their fingers, and then dropped in tandem to the dust below. Feet first, the drop was only a few feet. While it jarred his ankles, it did no damage. Priya got straight to her feet with only a single grunt. So far, so good.

Her bravery gave him a warm feeling inside. Her body had yet to recover from the brutal assault she'd experienced just weeks back. Not to mention her mind.

They ran to the woods and hid, watching and waiting. After about ten minutes, three men exited the house, all empty-handed except for the last guy, who carried the radio pack. Damn it.

Five minutes more passed, and their breathing settled to normal. Priya whispered, 'Jenny?'

'Dead.'

Priya stifled a sob.

'We have to run,' Kaleb said. 'Wait here. I'll go and pack what I can. If I'm not back in five, head out on your own. You have to get that vial you found over to zone 1.'

Priya tried to protest, but Kaleb gripped her forearm. 'You have to. It means the difference between life and death for millions.'

She acquiesced. Kaleb left her and approached the—hopefully—empty building. A quick recce proved his suspicions correct; nobody remained inside but the dead woman. Her death was a shame. He'd liked having her around.

Guilt stabbed him then. It wasn't Priya's fault that she laboured under such a dense cloud. The intruders had left the backpacks alone, so Kaleb grabbed all three. Not that they held much. He felt the loss of the radio much more keenly.

Back in the bedroom, he stared at the copious blood smearing the window ledge through which he and Priya had made their escape. Panic seized him, and he dashed from the room, down the stairs, and to the woods.

Priya tried to pull away when he grabbed her and aimed the bright torch beam her way. 'What are you doing?'

'Keep still. I need to see.'

Kaleb yanked down the zip on her bloodied jumpsuit.

Priya slapped him.

He pulled back. 'Sorry. I thought it was your blood.'

She glanced down at herself and gasped, hands going to her mouth. Then she scrabbled and clawed at her clothing. 'Get it off. Get it off. Get it—'

Kaleb shook her, not wanting to hurt her to bring her out of her shock. Thankfully, she calmed. Pale and too thin, she wore an appalled expression on her grim face. Then she whispered one word, '*Please.*'

Hurriedly, he riffled through his bag and pulled out a spare jumpsuit—a black one, but it would have to do. Kaleb turned his back to Priya while she changed garments. When she'd finished, he said, 'We have to move. Now.'

Her voice wobbled when she asked, 'Where?'

The time had come to give her the truth. He'd hated lying and prevaricating with her. The longer the farmer spent in her company, the less the soldier had a say. His stomach dropped when he realised that his feelings had grown much deeper than simple pity—the likes of which he'd felt for his ravaged puppy. He cared for the woman. Admired her grit and determination. Her strength.

'Each zone holds an army portal. So, even without power, they should operate. We have to get to zone 9's pod.'

Silent now, and with her jaw locked, Priya nodded, holding in the interrogation he'd expected. The two held hands as they picked their way through the woods. The scream of a distant raptor tore through the eery crimson darkness. Kaleb had dowsed the torch beam to lessen the chances of being seen by the wrong people.

By the time they made it to the road, scratches from thorny undergrowth and low-hanging branches covered both of them from head to ankle. Even the neosilve of the jumpsuits—like silk in feel, only much more durable and robust —hadn't provided adequate protection.

Priya staggered and stumbled at his side, obviously exhausted and on her last legs. The two moons shone balefully down on them, both highlighting and obscuring everything in their sultry red glow.

They left the relative protection of the trees and walked at a brisk pace along the deserted roadway. Priya found her voice.

'So, you're no farmer?'

'When I was a boy.'

'I thought as much. How long have you been in the military?'

Kaleb suspected that her questions were as much about distracting herself so she could keep going as about gleaning information. He shrugged and retook her hand. She didn't pull away.

'They took me when I was nine. I did too well on the zone exams for them to overlook me.'

Priya stayed quiet, mulling it over. Then she reached into her pocket and retrieved the neoplast vial. He breathed a sigh of relief. So many times now, it could have gotten destroyed or lost again, especially when she'd changed jumpsuits. A soft curse left his lips. He'd actually forgotten about the bloody thing in the aftermath of his panic about all the blood covering her.

'What *is* this?' She asked the question quietly but clutched the orange plastic as though her life depended upon it. Perhaps it did. Kaleb intuited that she needed a purpose after everything that had happened.

'I believe that's the lost antidote.'

She sucked in air. 'It's true, then?'

He nodded. 'A helipod went down while transporting it from ten to one.'

She pushed out her hand toward him. 'You should take it.'

Kaleb surprised himself when he shook his head. This was everything he'd wanted. What he needed. Why not take the vial and run? He didn't need Priya.

Oh but yes you do, a quiet voice mocked within.

His left hand spasmed. Jerked forward. Then

back to his side. His mouth dropped open, and he dragged in deep breaths.

'Keep it,' he said through tight lips, and then he shoved both hands deep into his pockets to avoid the temptation to grab.

Priya looked stunned, frozen in place with her palm still outstretched. After a few seconds, Kaleb told her, 'Put that thing away before you drop it.'

With a shaky laugh, she complied.

They completed the rest of the journey in companionable silence. To avoid deep thoughts about what had changed over the last few weeks, Kaleb recited the activation code for the portal over and over. They seemed to reach the secure space in no time at all … although, he didn't feel liked he'd been having fun so much, despite the time flying.

Still holding Priya's hand—gripping it, really —he rounded the corner.

A black-clad guy with a pulse-gun held at the ready stood in front of the portal. He saw them and straightened. Then he called over to them.

'Well, well, Special Moore. Long time, no

see.'

3

E80

With his finger over the trigger, and the gun raised and ready to fire, the soldier strode toward them, stopping three feet out of arm's reach. He pointed with the barrel toward Priya and then retook his aim at Kaleb. Malice glinted in his eyes. 'Who's the pretty little lady?'

She hated him on sight. By her side, Kaleb stiffened, gripped her hand, and then let go of her.

Still reeling from his confession earlier, she made herself breathe deep and slow while she watched this play out.

Kaleb spoke in a lazy drawl, 'She's nobody.'

Despite her resolve to stay calm, Priya gasped and stepped back, as if slapped. The soldier's eyes widened in surprise. Kaleb spoke again, 'It's been a long mission. I needed some distraction.'

His colleague chuckled and lowered the gun a fraction. Then his expression grew shrewd. 'You have the vial.'

A statement. Not a question. How did he know? Had Kaleb radioed in the find? Why would the army have sent in a second soldier to intercept Kaleb? Did they not trust him? That last thought rocked her on her feet. She chewed on her bottom lip. What had he done that was so bad even the military viewed him with suspicion? Cold and afraid, she waited for his response. Waited to see if he would drop her in it or not.

'That's none of your business, Marino. Why are you here?'

The soldier raised his weapon to the ready once more. Inexplicably, Kaleb relaxed further rather than tensing like Priya had. The trooper demanded, 'Give me the vial.'

Kaleb smiled, still at ease, and took a step toward the coffee-skinned man he'd called Marino. 'We'll go together. No need for the gun. We're all friends here.'

Marino said, 'Orders.' However, his actions belied his words when he lowered the weapon so that it pointed at the floor.

Kaleb took another step forward, then another. 'I know, mate. I'm not fighting you on this.'

Marino's shoulders came forward a little, and his spine lost its rigidity. Priya puffed out a soft breath of relief. This might work out yet. Then, in one fluid, sudden, and unexpected move, going from at-ease to a pouncing raptor in less than a second, Kaleb sprang. He grabbed the gun from the soldier, swung it ass-backward, and slammed the butt into Marino's jaw. The man crumpled to the ground in an unconscious heap.

'What are you doing?' Priya yelled. Soldiers shouldn't be attacking one another. 'You … he … Who *are* you?' She backed away, hands up in front of her, palms out, and cursed herself for not getting away from him before now.

Kaleb pulled wrist ties from his pocket and knelt by the fallen soldier's side, then he strapped them together, cinching them tight. As the man roused, Kaleb dragged him to his feet and pro-pelled him toward the portal. Over his shoulder, he told Priya, 'He means to steal the vial. The major said nothing about another special meeting me.'

Scared and horrified, Priya stood amongst the litter and debris in the red-tinted darkness. Marino struggled against Kaleb's iron grip but to no avail. He shouted to Priya, 'He's a traitor to his country. You shouldn't trust him.'

She had to hold in an ironic grin—the soldier had no idea of the relevance of his words. For definite, she didn't trust him. As Kaleb shoved the man toward the portal, the soldier called to her again, 'Get that vial to the president. No matter what.'

Kaleb gave him one last push, and he stumbled into the portal, where he stood trembling and wide-eyed. Priya couldn't decide whether his face paled out of fury or fear. Not that it mattered one way or the other. Either one made him dangerous and unpredictable.

The hairs on the back of her neck rose and stood on end, and she had to swallow a sudden rush of saliva. Her stomach knotted, and she had to fight down nausea. If Kaleb intended the vial to reach the capital, then why was he not working with Marino? What did he plan? But then he was putting the soldier in the portal to send him back to base, or at least, she assumed back to base.

She patted the pocket holding the vial and backed away, a tiny step at a time. Already, she knew Kaleb as a liar. He'd pretended to be a farmer when he was, in fact, a soldier. And now he'd turned on a supposed colleague, in spite of professing a wish to get the vial to the lab in zone 1. What else had he lied about?

Numb, she watched as Kaleb keyed in the code on the keypad. Instead of it emitting the usual hum and burst of white light from the portal, it remained silent.

It had malfunctioned.

Then it blew up.

Exploded in a huge fireball.

The concussive force knocked Priya off her feet. Dust and grit covered her and stung her eyes. Something wet and slimy stuck to her cheeks and nose. She raised a hand to wipe it off. Sickened, she realised that bits of Marino coated her. No longer able to contain the nausea, she rolled to her side and vomited violently.

What the hell?

Still retching and heaving, she jerked when Kaleb rested a hand on her shoulder. 'You okay?' he asked.

Priya wriggled away from him and then pulled herself into a sitting position with her knees drawn up to her chest, breath heaving. With the back of a hand, she wiped sick and saliva from her chin and lips. 'Did you know?'

Kaleb held up his hands and rocked back on his heels, nearly overbalancing from his precarious crouch. 'I swear, that wasn't me.' He shook his head and ran a hand through his dust-filled wavy hair. 'God. That could have been us in there.'

Shock drew his lips into a thin line and turned his complexion to chalk. Priya believed him. At least about the portal.

'What the fuck, Kaleb?' Venom laced her interrogative. Adrenaline pumped through her body, leaving her amped and ready to fight. It made a change from the constant running she'd done since the outbreak.

His poker face dropped into place, obscuring

any reactions. With his lips set in a grim and determined line, he said, 'We have to get to the next portal.'

When she remained silent, choosing to stare at him instead, he added, 'It's in zone 8.'

A bitter laugh rode on the back of a harsh sigh. 'We? What *we*?'

In frustration, he flung up his hands and then let them slap back down to his thighs. 'Going alone is suicide.'

Priya looked down at the dirt between her feet. An old Zing wrapper blew over her left foot in the stiffening breeze. She glanced at the sky. A haze now covered the two moons. Dust storm. They had to find cover.

They.

She shrugged. 'We stick together until we reach the capital.'

Opposite her, Kaleb nodded but had the sense to say nothing further.

Despite everything, Priya felt better. The need to protect the vial and get it to the right people had given her a purpose. A point to her life. Something upon which she could focus.

Anything had to make an improvement on her aimless flight from danger. And in this new world, the threats abounded no matter what she did.

Yes, better to stick with Kaleb for the time being, but from here on in, she would go it alone. She would only use him for added protection. An ancient saying from the days of Old Earth rose to the front of her mind, *Know many, trust a few, but always paddle your own canoe.*

What the hell was a bloody canoe when it was at home? Some sort of boat, she recalled. Regardless, the sentiment held true even all these centuries on. She might not know how to keep herself afloat these days, but she had always been a fast learner.

CHAPTER SIX

1

E50

At last, Sasha pushed open the heavy door to the lab. The reinforced metal felt cool to her touch. Comforting. She'd come home at last. Just to toy with her, the president had made her stew for a whole week in the thick soup of boredom before allowing her to begin work.

The sudden brightness of the lights stunned her for a moment, and she stood there blinking until her eyes recovered. Immediately, two things struck her: the tall ebony-skinned scientist—Giles Stephenson—was a woman. Secondly, she was beautiful.

Upon closer examination, the square jaw and angular cheekbones gave her a slightly masculine appearance, but neither detracted from her allure. Sasha realised that the scientist had turned and stood studying her right back and that she'd been caught staring for some time. Her cheeks coloured crimson, and she gave a genteel cough to try and cover her embarrassment.

'Um, hi. I'm Sasha. Sasha Novikov.'

'Yes. The president told me you'd be gracing my presence. Welcome, Ms Novikov.' Stephenson held out a long, slim hand.

Sasha accepted the proffered handshake. 'I can't tell you how happy I am to be here, at last, Professor Stephenson.'

The gorgeous woman shook her head, but a slow smile curved her lush lips. 'Giles, please.'

Sasha opened her mouth to offer her first-name terms too, forgetting in her fluster that she'd just done that, but at the last moment, decided to give her pet name that few knew. 'Shura.' She paused, then said, 'To my friends.'

The scientist's smile warmed and widened,

lighting up her every feature. Sasha almost swooned at the effects. Never in her life had any person ever affected her as strongly as this. She would have to watch herself. That warning, however, drowned in the overwhelming sexual arousal that snared her in its fevered grip.

Desperate to regain any sort of control over herself, she said, 'I need the bathroom. Could you show me?'

Giles's eyes widened for a fraction of a second, then she pointed the way. 'Just through there. First door on your left.'

It was all Sasha could do not to make a run for it. Somehow, she managed a sedate walk. When she reached the restrooms, she went straight to the sinks and waved her hand in front of the button for cold water. She let it run for a few seconds, then she plunged her cupped palms beneath it and splashed her red-hot cheeks.

What was this? What was going on? For Sasha, sex had only ever been about power and abuse. A tool of manipulation. Neither her childhood nor her experiences of adulthood had taught her any differently. Until now.

Five minutes later, she dragged herself back into the lab, no longer the comforting place she had grown used to. Giles changed all that. In dire need of distraction, she asked the rude question, 'Why a man's name?'

The scientist merely laughed—probably used to it by now. She leant against a gleaming counter and crossed her arms, but her humour prevailed. 'I was a man.'

Sasha heard a hint of a challenge in the words. This wasn't the first person undergoing a sex change that she'd encountered, and it didn't faze her. It would take a hell of a lot to throw her these days. Only the ghosts in her closet had the power to do that. And those demons, she fought minute by minute. The trick was not to let the outside world see.

Giles handed Sasha a lab coat, which seemed pointless given the white lab jumpsuit she wore. Made out of stainless and antibacterial neosilve, it contained climate-control features that cooled in heat and warmed in cold, as well as being waterproof. Mouth clamped shut and opinions held in check, she took the coat and donned it, eagerly waiting to hear what her position would be.

Giles watched her dress and then led her into a back room. It smelled musty and unused, the air stale. Plastic boxes filled the claustrophobic space, stacked from floor to ceiling. Sasha's stomach dropped.

No way. Now I know why the coat.

'You're to sort through this mess of old files and reports.'

Sasha stood akimbo, disappointment and fury leaving her speechless.

Giles said, 'We believe they contain clues to the virus and its antidote.' She stared Sasha down. 'It's important work.'

So much for getting ahead. Terrence couldn't have given her a more lowly position or one of lesser importance. The bastard. She gritted her teeth and nodded. At last, she managed to paste a smile on her tense face.

Giles moved right up to her and put a hand on her upper arm in a surprisingly intimate gesture. Into Sasha's ear, she whispered, 'This won't be for long, little Shura.' Then she slipped from the room.

Stunned, Sasha stood alone, trying to sort through what had just happened. Had Giles just tried to communicate something to her? And what did the president think he was playing at? That man had seriously underestimated her.

If nothing else, work would help her think. And at least she had a foot in the door. Access to the lab. She used the energy of the anger to rip into the stacked boxes and get started on the mind-numbing task.

Perhaps Sasha could use her attraction to Giles to her own advantage. *Right, if you can control yourself. You're smitten.* She shook her head, trying to dislodge that annoying on-board critic. Giles seemed to be drawn to her too, especially if that last interaction gave her anything to go by. *You're playing with fire.*

Such back-and-forth arguments and hopes sped the next couple of hours along. Then Giles pushed through the creaky doorway holding two steaming mugs and wearing a bright smile. 'Tea break,' she said.

Sasha grinned and took the proffered cup,

which smelled of coffee. 'I hate tea.'

'Just as well. I've banned it from the lab.'

Ah, kindred spirits when it came to hot beverages, then. Sasha held out an olive branch, 'I'll drink anything, so long as it's hot and wet enough to wash away all this dust and muck.'

Giles gave her a sympathetic smile. After a cautious sip of her scalding brew, she crooked a finger and beckoned Sasha. Mug in hand and highly curious, she followed the scientist on silent feet. The professor led her into a back corridor from a hidden panel in the storage space, and from there, down six flights of stairs, to a sealed room, deep underground. She closed the door behind them, plunging them into darkness.

Sasha froze and waited. Warm breath tickled her ear, then a hand eased the hot mug from her grasp. Every nerve in her body came alive, and the anticipation made her tremble. Giles must feel the same way as her.

Without a word, Giles nibbled on Sasha's ear, then she undid the lab coat and slipped a hand beneath it, searching for the jumpsuit zip, which she eased down. Her questing palm found pert breasts and erect nipples eager for her touch.

Sasha returned the passion, and they soon stood naked in the darkness, bit-by-bit learning one another by feel. Giles brought her to orgasm quickly and expertly with just her fingers, then Sasha murmured, 'My turn.'

She had expected to meet girl parts down below, but instead, man bits greeted her greedy groping. She gasped and stepped back. Giles chuckled in her ear. 'Another few weeks.'

Those three words told Sasha a lot. Even with all the technology still available within the presidential compound, Giles would need a week off work at a minimum to recover. Without thinking, she blurted her question, probably giving away an equal amount of information in that unguarded moment herself.

'Will the lab close?'

Giles chuckled, low and deep, in her ear. 'My little helper can keep things running.'

With that, the talking stopped again for a while. Ready to bring her boss to climax, Sasha dropped to her knees, but Giles lifted her easily to her feet. 'I want to take you up against the wall if that's okay? Wrap yourself around my hips and sit there.'

The words had Sasha wet and all afire once more. The actions that matched the words did that and more.

Afterward, the bedroom talk began, with both women sitting with their backs against the wall, chatting quietly. Giles had assured Sasha that this room was clean—no bugs, cameras, or any other surveillance.

Then the scientist ordered, 'Lights.'

The room lit to a fierce illumination as all the fluorescents fired together. Sasha put a palm over her eyes for a couple of seconds. When she dropped her hand, she saw that Giles sat watching her.

Then the contents of the room impressed themselves upon her senses. This was a fully fitted lab, with the kind of ultra-modern tech she could only have dreamed about.

Giles said, 'This is where your real work will get done. In secret. Each day, you'll spend a couple of hours in the box room—just enough time to make it look as if you've been searching the files—and then you'll come down here.'

'This stays between us, I take it?'

The scientist nodded and took Sasha's hand. 'Our little secret, Shura.'

2

E71

The restaurant favoured dim lighting and soft music to give a romantic ambience. In the background, glasses clinked and cutlery tinkled. Sasha and Giles sat drinking wine together. Expensive wine. The two women had gotten to know one another quite well, and frankness—it seemed—was the order of the day.

'I hear you're quite the ruthless manipulator.'

Sasha rocked back in her chair, splashing white wine over her trembling fingers. That had come out of the blue. Until that blunt statement, blurting out her love for Giles had filled her mind.

After a few seconds, she rallied, 'Some would say that those who judge merely hold up a mirror in front of themselves.'

Though Giles nodded, she didn't offer a smile or any encouragement. Instead, she sat waiting, her gaze fixed just over her companion's left shoulder. Sasha said, 'Is it so wrong for a woman to have goals? To want to protect herself?'

She aimed her gaze somewhere in the centre of the table, simulating submission, and twirled her half-full glass. After a suitable pause, she met Giles's eyes and batted her lashes. With a shrug of helplessness, she murmured, 'Jealous, inferior men. Let them say what they will.'

In a calculated move, she grasped the other woman's hand and looked up at her, imploring yet deferential. In that split second, Sasha saw that she'd lost Giles's attention. Her eyes had grown distant. And then she blinked and focused. Sasha realised that her approach hadn't worked. She tried a different tack, 'One day, I'll teach Terrence a lesson he won't forget.'

Giles stroked Sasha's fingers and then wrapped both hands around them. She leant over the table. Sasha had struck a chord. She sat and waited for the other woman to say what she suspected already.

'As a man, I was safe. He didn't even see me. Then it all changed.'

Sasha whispered, 'Tell me.'

Giles glanced over Sasha's shoulder, and then she tensed. Sasha followed her gaze. At another table, a bloke sat watching them. When he saw them staring, he blushed and lowered his head. Giles said, 'He's been eyeing us since we sat down.'

Sasha giggled. 'He fancies you.'

Giles' eyes widened. 'What? You mean …?'

Sasha winked and nodded. 'You're more woman than man now. Get used to the attention.' She reversed their hands and squeezed Giles' fingers. The two women shared a giggle.

Then Giles grew serious. 'He doesn't stand a chance.'

Sasha took a leap, 'I've fallen in love with you.'

Without warning, Giles shot to her feet and pulled Sasha up with her. 'Let's go. Now.'

Anticipating a long night of hot sex, Sasha went with her. She trailed Giles through the restaurant. When they walked past the man, she caught sight of his lapel pin. Which meant he was the president's man. She stopped and accused him, 'Seen enough? Heard enough? Want any more?'

All innocence, he held up his hands and laughed. Giles dragged her away, gripping her lower arm tight enough to leave bruises. Outside, Sasha pulled to a stop and demanded, 'What the hell?'

Giles held her shoulders, a little more gently this time. 'We don't want him telling our secrets. What you said about teaching the president a lesson. What I said.'

Sasha's terror pushed her onto automatic pilot, and she became all business. 'He's in a public place. We have to lure him away.'

Giles nodded. 'You confronted him, so it'll have to be me. I'll go in and seduce him. Get him back to my apartment.' She rooted in her purse. 'Here's a spare key. Go to the bathroom cabinet. You'll find a syringe.'

With a brief nod, Sasha bent and removed her fancy heels, then she set off at a run, her mind calculating her next steps the whole way. At the apartment, she found not only the syringe but a micro-drone as well. This, she used to track Giles and make sure that their plan didn't go awry. Heart fluttering with barely suppressed panic, she sat on the end of the bed and switched on the camera and microphone.

Giles and the man exited the restaurant. Sexual banter passed between them. The bloke caught Giles off-guard and shoved her roughly against a wall. Typically, nobody stood in sight. Sasha tensed, ready to flee to her friend's aid.

'It surprised me, you coming back.'

Giles rallied, 'I felt sorry for you. I don't know what got into her.' She gripped his buttocks and rubbed her hip against him, careful to hide her man-package. Then, gently, she eased him away from her. 'Not here. My place.'

Eager, the guy agreed and followed her, giving her bottom the odd pinch. As they neared the flat, Sasha put away the drone and found a place to hide.

Giggles and more innuendo preceded them through the door. Just as the pair stepped inside, the man asked, 'Where's your cute little friend?'

Sasha eased out of the dark alcove. She put the syringe to his neck. 'Right here, you little prick.'

A second later, he dropped to the floor with a solid thud. Sasha glanced at Giles, who wore a smile of cold malice on her face. 'What did you have in the needle?'

'He won't bother us anymore.'

A thought struck Sasha, 'What if he had that on a live feed?'

Giles grabbed her by the elbows and stared at her hard. 'What you said, in the restaurant. Did you mean it?'

A lot had been said that night. What did Giles want her to recall? Now that the heat of the moment had passed, she regretted blurting out her feelings the way she had. In her experience, it would be used against her at some point. But once you said a thing, you couldn't take it back, not ever.

Terrified and excited, she nodded. 'Yes. I love you.'

Giles smiled. 'And about getting your own

back?'

Sasha cringed inwardly but managed to keep it hidden from her companion. The redirection hurt. A lot. She nodded.

Then Giles made it a little better. 'Good. I love you too, little Shura.' She bent and kissed Sasha on the lips, letting it linger. Then she held the back of her head and looked deep into her eyes. 'We can be a team, you and I. We can do good things together.'

Eager to please, Sasha nodded. She hated herself for making herself vulnerable like this. For breaking the vows she'd made to herself all those years ago. But Giles was different, wasn't she?

Giles pulled her from her thoughts and to the bed, where she made love to her. The sex was the gentlest she'd ever had, the most sensuous and intimate. If Sasha hadn't been smitten already, that would have sealed her fate.

Afterward, they lay and exchanged pillow talk. Sasha felt desperate for a mineral cigarette, but Giles didn't smoke. Gradually, so that Sasha only noticed in the far back of her mind, Giles led the conversation back to the regime and the lab. Almost asleep, Sasha drifted along with it.

All of which meant that when Giles made her horrific suggestion, Sasha agreed when she otherwise would have had second—if not third—thoughts.

'We need another virus. You'll help me.'

3

E80

Jenny's chip data flatlined. Martins pulled up the screen and read the bad news in the absence of feed. Shit. Just when the army special had proven most useful and well positioned, she'd died. The screen blanked to black, showing nothing: her chip had just gone offline completely.

Trying not to panic, he pulled up the feed for the other army specials still alive. Of the twenty sent out on the original recovery mission, only sixteen lived. The missing four had either succumbed to food or water poisoning or had died violently at the hands of roving gangs or infected.

Had Moore discovered Jenny's subterfuge? Had he killed her to shut her up? Or was this pure chance? John preferred the latter of the two possibilities. If the soldier had found her out, then Martins might find himself in trouble. A lot of trouble.

Only hours before, the fake prostitute had alerted him to the discovery of the lost vial with its vital contents. John wanted that in his possession before anyone else could lay claim to it. Most notably, he wanted to keep it away from Terrence. That man had done enough, and it was Martins' turn to set policy and determine his own affairs for a change.

If Moore had realised that Jenny wasn't who she claimed, and had taken his retribution, then the woman had died in unnecessary and unearned shame. Just like the rest of the population, embedded with chips from the age of five, she'd had no idea of the back-access capabilities of the implants.

John had used this access to override her chip and control her actions. She'd had no clue of what he'd done nor any choice in the matter. The woman had simply been one of his many puppets. It was such a damn shame that the virus had taken everyone's chips offline eventually. Once the power grid failed, all the chips failed when the wearers couldn't plug in to recharge each night. Only those implants used on the army continued to function, using more advanced tech and auto-charging from the body's electrical currents.

From this remote distance, Martins couldn't override Special Moore's chip to bring him and the girl right back here to him. He needed him plugged in to a military mainframe portal within zone 1 to use the back-access.

Again, for about the hundredth time in recent months, John wondered what had possessed the president to take such drastic measures.

Sure, his age and brutality had both served to weaken his position. Rival factions dotted around Exxon 1 had arisen and begun to challenge his leadership. Even the other planets in the system had made noises of distrust and disgruntlement. But, with so much at his fingertips, the man could have chosen so many alternative ways of dealing with all of that. Why the virus?

Over and over, the only possible answer he could come up with came down to complete annihilation. Came down to the edict, *If you take me, I'll take you with me.* And, mimicking Terrence's uncompromising tones, John added, *You sons of bitches.*

Into his thoughts, his brain injected a way forward. Special Marino, the second soldier assigned to zone 9, could be used. Quickly, Martins pulled up the relevant screen and clicked on the communications link in Marino's chip. Despite not having the option of back-access, he could order him the old-fashioned way. As Terrence's second-in-command, he had that authority without having to go through Major Adams. After sending the special on a mission to apprehend Moore, John disabled Kaleb's personal portal code.

A few seconds later, he had a better idea. Instead of disabling it, he sabotaged it. If the wrong special tried to use the portal, it would explode. That way, if Marino failed in his mission, Moore would also fail. The vial wouldn't fall into the wrong hands. Far better that if Martins couldn't have it, then no one would. Amusement curled the corners of his lips a fraction. That sentiment sounded much like Denis's viewpoint.

Impatient, John tapped his fingers on the desk, waiting to see how things would unfold. The wait seemed to stretch for days. Then, after nothing for so long, all at once, the feed from Marino's chip blanked out. Shit. Make that fifteen remaining soldiers now.

What the hell had just happened? Had Special Marino perished while attempting to apprehend Kaleb Moore on Martins' orders? Or had his chip just failed?

On the second screen, the tag for Portal A09 flashed red. Bloody hell. This tiny bit of data alerted him to the fact that Kaleb Moore had used his code on the transporter, resulting in its destruction. What it didn't tell him was whether or not Moore had been in the portal at the time. And what about the girlfriend? It could have been Marino in the portal, for that matter.

John had one more trick up his sleeve. He

pulled up yet another screen, which tracked each and every soldier—both on active duty and retired. Kaleb Moore's blinked at him happily. Damn it. The man lived. What about the vial?

4

E90

With mixed feelings, Sasha closed the program, put the test sample in the fridge, and picked up the computer print out. She'd done it. They now had the key to the new virus that would prove so much worse than anything that had gone before. Trembling with both elation and fear, she secreted the sheet in her coat pocket and went back into the box room. There, she grabbed a dusty folder full of nonsense, slipped the printout into it, and carried it through to the main lab and Giles.

Though Sasha had achieved something great in developing this, she felt bad about it. Guilt plagued her every thought and action. Right up until she waved the file in front of Giles and said,

'I think I've found something,' she could have changed her mind. Backed out. But now that particular shuttle had left the station.

Giles smiled and reached out for the folder. Sasha handed it over, and lead filled her guts. No way but forward from here on in. And even if she did walk away from this, she had no way to take the information from Giles now, or from the lab computer. Only the professor had that level of access.

Aware of the surveillance on the lab, Sasha bowed her head and retreated back to the box room, where she made a show of continuing the fruitless search. She didn't believe the president would have had cameras installed in this storage space, but it paid to stay careful. And the noises she made might well pass beyond the door into the corridor, which did have monitoring.

While she did useless work, she wondered how some of the population hadn't yet succumbed to the original virus. The president had taken a hell of a risk by releasing the virus without an antidote in place already.

She'd worked on the original nanobots and

their delivery system. With the protein they'd used, nobody's immune systems should have failed to respond. So, how come some had done precisely that? Sasha worried that she still had too large a gap in her knowledge of the tech.

Then another thought struck her. It made her eyes go wide. This was a question she ought to have asked Giles well before now. And herself, for that matter. Without thinking, she dashed from the room and back into the central lab. She blurted out, 'You had an antidote for the president already, didn't you?'

Giles sat in a chair facing one of the work-benches. Her back stiffened, and her hands stilled. Sasha waited for her to turn around. Waited for the answer that might change everything. An affirmative would confirm that the president and John Martins had played Sasha right from the very beginning. That they hadn't ever needed her to work on an emergency antidote or send Eloise Martins in the helipod with it. But why?

A long sigh escaped the scientist. When she did turn around at long last, tears stained her cheeks. She held a memo in her hands and waved it toward Sasha, who dashed over and grabbed it. After reading it twice, disbelieving, she looked up at Giles and then pulled her in for a hug.

'He can't do this. You've come so far. Done so much.'

Giles shrugged and offered a sad smile. 'He can, and he has.'

Sasha clenched her fists, crumpling the paper. 'But your surgery is due next week.'

Giles shook her head. 'Not anymore.' Then her face hardened into resolve. Without seeming to worry about monitoring or censorship, she answered Sasha's dangerous question, 'Of course we had an antidote. What made you think we wouldn't?'

Sasha stood with dropped shoulders, head down, stunned. So, they'd set her up right from the get-go. Had used her to release the virus well away from zone 1 to keep them from suspicion. You couldn't get any more distant than zone 10 without going off-planet. Then they'd let her rush and panic to find an antidote, for the sole purpose of sending Eloise with it, knowing she'd never get there. They'd second-guessed Sasha. Had understood that she would sabotage the helipod. Even John. Willingly, and in full knowledge, he'd let her murder his wife. She cringed at the thought of them ever finding that vial, because then they'd know the rest of it.

Her head reeled.

She staggered and fell against a bench.

Giles caught her and helped her to a chair, hand on an elbow.

'Why?' Sasha murmured, distraught.

She no longer believed herself smart or superior. She'd been had in every way possible.

Giles twisted her lips and rubbed Sasha's knee. 'He likes me this way.'

It took Sasha a moment to catch up and work out that her friend had taken the 'why' to be about the cancelled sex-change op, rather than making an antidote. And when she thought about it, the why of the remedy was obvious, wasn't it? What a fool not to have seen that in the first place. Her greed for power had blinded her.

At a near whisper, Giles spoke again, 'He likes taking me up the arse, and having me do the same to him. Once I'm a woman, it only works one way, and I become no different to any other conquest.'

'What will you do?'

The scientist slipped from the high stool and stood facing Sasha. 'Time for a coffee. The food hall has a new bean in.'

In silence, the two women left the lab. Once they gained the fresh air, Sasha pressed, 'You can do it yourself with nanobots.'

Giles grabbed her arm and pulled her down a side alley, where she shoved her up against a wall and moved in close, as though the two embraced. She whispered, 'Nano-tech, yes. But not for me.'

Adrenaline coursing through her body, Sasha's breaths came in short pants. Her eyes went wide, and her jaw slackened. 'You're going to use the virus on the—'

'Shh.' Giles mashed her lips onto Sasha's mouth and kissed her thoroughly. Then she pulled her back into the main thoroughfare and to the food hall. Questions raced around in Sasha's head, chasing their own tails.

The breakthrough she'd had this morning had to do with programming the protein bots to target a specific chain. A precise part of the body's coding. What did Giles intend? What had Sasha just helped to develop?

The newfangled, trendy coffee slipped down her throat unnoticed. The conversation stalled, then died. Both women felt too distracted to give it the effort it needed. In a daze, Sasha got back to the lab on auto-pilot and went into the box room. Thankfully, she didn't have to wait overly long before Giles joined her, dirty file folder in hand. With the door to the corridor still open, she announced, 'This is useless. You'll have to keep looking.'

Once the door had whooshed shut, Giles and Sasha made their way to the other lab. An underground facility in more ways than one. As soon as they were securely ensconced, Sasha threw a barrage of questions at Giles, who held up her hands and said, 'It all comes down to you doing one thing. Just one tiny sacrifice. You've done it plenty of times, so it shouldn't be any hardship. And then we jump ahead in this sordid little power game.'

At first, Sasha balked at the plan her lover

outlined. At one point, she demanded, 'Why not you?'

Giles shook her head, 'He'll suspect me, now. After cancelling my change. I won't get anywhere near the man.'

After two orgasms, and professions of love and commitment, Sasha gave in and agreed. No sooner had they gone back upstairs than an armed escort arrived for Sasha. The president wanted to see her. If she'd needed evidence of surveillance, this would have offered an abundance. No doubt, he wanted to interrogate her about Giles. About what they might have spoken of. And, it went without saying, he would want to fuck her. Informants with benefits.

As always, he treated her roughly, with no tenderness or respect. He simply took what he wanted. Sasha used his vices against him. It worked to her advantage to give him everything he wanted, including supposedly dropping her friend in it. She let Terrence know how unhappy Giles felt, and even let slip that she suspected mutiny might be afoot.

All of this put the president off his guard and

allowed Sasha to get what she needed—a sample of his DNA. The most powerful man on the planet had no idea what was coming.

CHAPTER SEVEN

1

E90

To avoid as many people as possible, they travelled only by night, relying on the light of the moons. Manmade illumination would give them away to any watchers. They should reach the edges of zone 8 in an hour or so.

For the last twenty minutes, the roars of a raptor had dogged their heels. Kaleb prayed fervently that it hunted upwind of them. Over the long nights of their travel, rogue infected or gangs had troubled him. Now, he cursed himself for an idiot for not also worrying about the planet's natural predators. And in these days of chaos, even the cities weren't safe from them.

Unspoken, he and Priya increased their pace along the open road. It brought additional risk taking this route, but speed seemed of the essence right then. How had some of the native creatures survived the terraforming while others had died out to extinction? And why had just the meanest predators come through it? Sometimes, the world seemed like a crazy place with laws all its own.

Thirty minutes outside the next zone, just when he'd dared to believe the beast would leave them alone, it found them. The noise it made crashing through the dense undergrowth to the side of the road alerted them. Gave Kaleb time to go for his pulse-gun. Would its power take the animal down? Or did he need a bigger weapon?

'Run,' he yelled to Priya.

Mercifully, she set off at a sprint without offering any argument. Kaleb took a ready stance, feet and legs braced, and planted the stock at his shoulder. The raptor burst onto the neomac surface, an evil red-green in the moons' glow.

Its oval eyes, a vivid yellow in daylight,

looked muddy and brown but no less malevolent. More ominously still, it stopped growling. In complete silence, it stood and watched Kaleb. Studied him. The beast exuded a terrible intelligence.

Around the stock of his weapon, his hands sweated but didn't tremble. The army had trained him for this. And for things much worse. Kaleb closed one eye and lined up the raptor in his sights, aiming for the centre of its skull. The magnifier grew its eyes to the size of saucers. Though his heart thumped, his mind quieted, giving him the space he needed.

Then, without warning, the raptor glanced left and leapt in that direction. It had detected Priya. Knew her as the helpless prey. Kaleb battened down the hatches on his panic. Instead of dropping his aim and running after the animal, he stood his ground, panning the gun fast and far to the side. Jaw clenched, he took a blind shot through the trees.

Priya screamed in the distance. Then all sound ceased. All the creatures of the night waited with bated breath. Kaleb lowered the weapon and marched in the direction he had fired. The direction he had gambled his friend's life on. Had his educated guess paid up or down?

Panting, he broke through the thorny barrier and stood in a clearing. Despite the red-glow of the moons, the blood looked black. It gave the impression that a vast hole had opened up before him. The body lay on its side. Unmoving. And Priya stood frozen just a couple of feet from its gaping jaws.

Heart pounding at his ribs with relief, Kaleb strode to her and pulled her into his arms. Her paralysis broke, and she went limp. A loud sob burst free of her. Just the one. Then she stiffened and tugged herself free. 'I've never seen one … only on the telecast.'

Her voice shook, but otherwise, she seemed to have steadied herself. Satisfied she was okay, Kaleb nodded. 'We should go.'

Priya slipped her hand into his, and he led them through the trees and bushes and back to the road. With any luck, that would be the final predator of the night.

After that excitement, the remainder of the

walk passed in a blur. At long last, they reached zone 8. The place looked deserted. But then appearances could be deceiving.

Cautiously, they picked their way through empty streets, inhabited only by litter and signs of old violence. The low, mournful howls of wind around corners and through abandoned, open buildings made for their sole companion.

Where had everyone gone? Not that he wanted anyone to find them, particularly. A crack of thunder preceded the sky opening and pouring rain down upon them in sheets. The visibility dropped by about eighty percent. He and Priya huddled deeper into their collars and hurried on.

Soaked through and chilled to the bone, they rounded one final corner and came to a stop. Just like in zone 9, the area around zone 8's army portal stood derelict and deserted. It gave Kaleb all he needed to suspect that all was not as it should be.

Part of him had expected to find more soldiers waiting for him here. What had happened back in nine? Had Marino worked alone? Or had he gone there on orders? And if the latter, on whose?

Suspicious, Kaleb stayed Priya at the boundary and edged step by slow step toward the portal. In the middle of the open ground, he found a large stone, which he hefted in both hands. The heavy load had him stagger in big strides the rest of the way. At the entrance, he dropped the rock into the portal and stepped back. Then he keyed in his code and ran.

Once again, no hum and burst of white light came from the portal, it remained silent. Just like the last one, it erupted in a huge fireball and a blast of scorching air that lifted him off his feet and propelled him far through the air.

Kaleb landed with a thump and a grunt of pain. With a cry, Priya ran over to him and dropped to her knees by his side. He managed to get himself into a sitting position. Wetness trickled down his cheek, and when he put a hand to his temple, it came away bloody. A piece of flying debris must have struck him.

Priya asked the pertinent question, 'Why don't they want you to get to zone 1?'

He shook his head, trying to clear the daze. 'I

think they've rigged my personal code to trigger the explosions.'

'Who?'

Kaleb rubbed his bristly chin and sighed. 'I wish I knew. Someone wants to stop us. That's obvious. But who and why?'

Priya frowned. 'You have no idea? You didn't do anything? Are you lying to me again?'

Kaleb took heart from the fact that when he took her hand, she let him. 'I angered the major when I helped you, but I don't see that prompting him to this. And, at the end of the day, he wants the vial back more than anything else.' He shook his head. 'No. This is sabotage. And it's someone who has access to our personal codes. The radio channel too.'

2

E99

This night brought utter blackness, with not a single hint of red from the moons. A ferocious dust storm earlier in the afternoon had left the skies thick and full and unbreathable. Priya laboured to get air through her filter mask, unused to its suffocating bulk and the effort required to breathe through it.

Anyone interested in following their trail would have an easy time of it, for they left vivid footprints in the dust that lay thick on the ground. Every once in a while, she had to use her sleeve to wipe her visor clean so that she could see her way forward.

The heavy particles blanketed the world and brought a preternatural quiet, much like when it snowed. You could lay in bed and know that white surrounded you without even looking out of the window. You only had to listen.

A couple of times, from the corner of her eye, Priya had caught a glimpse of a fleeting shadow. Too small for another raptor. Too quick to catch. And obscured by the tree cover and poor visibility in the aftermath of the storm.

The hairs on her neck prickled, and goosebumps ran up and down her arms and spine. The trail of prints bothered her. As did the blanketing effect of the dust. That flitting shadow could be someone or merely a figment of her imagination.

Not wanting to add to Kaleb's cares, she stayed quiet. But five minutes later, he too straightened and glanced about them. Not needing to communicate, they picked up their pace. The drab buildings of zone 7 gradually encroached and killed off the trees, and soon a concrete jungle surrounded them instead of wild forest.

A blood-curdling scream pierced the air. Priya flinched and hunched her shoulders. She remembered that kind of cry coming from her neighbour back in five when the virus got hold of him. She hadn't imagined their tracker after all. An infected had followed them.

Kaleb reached out his hand to grab hers, but a ragged man burst from the shadows and barrelled into her, knocking her to the floor. The guy reminded her of a zombie of the ilk she'd seen in corny old movies.

She went sprawling on her back. Frantic, fearing another gang attack, she scrabbled to get away. The attacker showed incredible strength, and he pinned her down with ease. Terror paralysed her.

Then the man's weight lifted from her. Kaleb wrestled him to the ground. Because of his en-hanced strength, the infected overpowered even the army special with ease. The shock of seeing that broke her deep freeze, and Priya leapt to her feet, casting her gaze around for a weapon.

A large, serrated knife lay half covered in dust on the cracked concrete. Kaleb's knife belt hung empty. He'd lost it in the attack. Priya grabbed for it and dashed back to the grappling figures. Clearly, Kaleb fought on the losing end.

The infected had him by the throat, and Kaleb's face had mottled. Priya lunged and thrust the knife into the man's exposed back. Then she wrenched it out and stabbed him in the neck. Again, she withdrew and struck. Over and over in a frenzied and vicious attack. Only when Kaleb wrapped his arms around her from behind did she stop. The veil of rage dropped from her vision. A bloody corpse lay sprawled at her feet.

In a quiet voice, Kaleb said, 'He's in the final stages of meltdown from the virus. He's highly contagious.'

Mute, she stared at Kaleb. Then she raised her hands in front of her face. Cuts and scratches covered the two travellers. As did the infected's blood.

3

E111

Twelve thirty-hour moon cycles had passed since the attack. Priya and Kaleb had kept a close eye on each other for signs of change. So far, Priya seemed fine. Kaleb, however, had succumbed to the first stages of the virus. Nearly four months since the initial outbreak, she had hoped that its virulence would have lessened, if not died out altogether.

Not so.

At first, she had put Kaleb's withdrawn demeanour down to him still struggling to come to terms with the deranged violence she had exhibited back in zone seven. That night had changed things between them. It seemed that he treated her with kid gloves after that, worried she might lose it at any time.

He didn't know her at all. But then, how could he, when it shocked even Priya at how pleased she felt at her behaviour and strength. Maybe she had gone over the top, but it was a damn sight better than cowering on the ground and letting the guy have his way. She wouldn't do that ever again, not if she had any choice in the matter.

Despite the dangers of travelling by dark, they had continued. Unlike movie zombies, the daylight brought the infected to life and animated them beyond belief. And it remained a fact that the night guaranteed they would meet fewer people—ill or otherwise.

Tonight brought them to the outskirts of zone 6. She and Kaleb had agreed to leave the army portal here alone. Unless he could get hold of someone else's access code, the transporter would do them no good while also giving away their position. The plan was to skirt the city in an attempt to avoid any remnants of civilisation. They still had tube food and water enough, which meant they had no need to venture into the centre of the zone.

A lone neostil pod-house appeared out of the darkness, pink-topped in the light of the moons. When they neared, a low hum reached their ears. The pod had power.

By her side, Kaleb lifted a hand—signalling her to stay put. Fed up of that shenanigans, Priya strode forward with him. Hadn't she already proved she could hold her own? Though his expression said he didn't like it, he didn't try to stop her.

What he didn't realise was that Priya didn't trust him. She didn't recognise the danger as coming solely from 'out there'. His lies and deceits had her on edge already, and now he had the virus. What would it do to him when it matured fully? What changes would it bring? What havoc would it wreak? No, from now on, she would stick to him like everseal. Would watch and wait. Until he became too dangerous.

Up close, she noticed an open window. Soft sobs drifted on the still air. While Kaleb crept to the front door, Priya edged up to the window and looked in. A weeping man sat hunched up on the floor, knees to chin, rocking back and forth, the comforts of his furniture ignored. Discarded.

In his distress, he had missed the sound of the door admitting Kaleb. When the soldier strode into the room, the man flinched and threw his arms wide while a cry sprang from his lips. He scrabbled backward across the smooth floor, wailing 'no, no, no' as he did so.

Priya leaned through the open window and called to him in soothing tones, 'It's okay. We're friends.'

The man shook his head, wild in his panic. 'I can see it in his eyes.'

Priya could only agree. The virus left a faint violet tinge on the iris. 'He is infected, but he's still all right. Come and look at my eyes.'

The distraught man thought about it, still watching Kaleb with wariness, then he shuffled to his feet and came over to the window with a speed she hadn't expected. Up close, she saw that his eyes weren't as old as the rest of him looked. His grief and unkempt appearance added years to his silver hair and wrinkled skin. Something about him screamed middle-aged even while he appeared ancient.

Priya felt uncomfortable having him stare into her eyes the way he did, but eventually, he nodded and stepped back. He cast a glance of disgust over his shoulder and then looked back at her, 'You might as well come in.'

Intrigued yet cautious, Priya made her way to the front and entered. Kaleb remained standing near the exit, but Priya took one of the soft easy-chairs near the rear window. The stranger mopped at the tears still leaking down his cheeks and offered them coffee. Her mouth watered. She hadn't had coffee since before. The shock of all of this hit her. Just a few short months, yet it seemed like a whole other life. A whole other era.

The open-plan pod allowed her and Kaleb to keep an eye on him covertly while he prepared the brew. Tantalising aromas reached her far too long before the guy finally brought her a cup. Greedily, she sipped at the hot mug, eager to get her first taste of coffee in forever, and didn't mind the burnt tongue she received for her haste.

The man managed a watery chuckle and took a seat opposite her, keeping as far from Kaleb as he could. His next words shocked Priya, 'I have a virus too.'

She rocked back. No violet tint had warned her when she'd watched his eyes.

'It's okay.' He held up a hand. 'Not the one that's done all the damage. They gave me a different one.'

Still on edge but a little more relaxed, she leant forward. 'Tell me.'

The old guy, who didn't quite seem to fit his skin, shook his head. 'What brings you here? Where are you headed?'

By the door, Kaleb stiffened and crossed his arms. To buy time, Priya sipped at her coffee, now at safe drinking temperature. Right then, more than ever, she missed her implants, which could have told her whether or not to trust this stranger. On her own, all she could see for certain was his vulnerability. His pain.

The mug emptied and left her sucking air. She had to make a decision: Talk. Or leave. The man sat staring over her shoulder into the distance, looking more inward than outward. Tears continued to trickle down his face.

Priya took a chance. Told him her tale. Kaleb's too. The army special—ex special?—protested when she started talking, but soon shut up when he realised she would take no notice of him. Perhaps he saw something in the old man too.

All throughout her tale, wild as it was in places, the guy sat nodding here and there, taking it all in and showing no signs of doubt or disbelief. Priya finished talking, and then said, 'None of this surprises you.'

He shook his head. 'I can fill in a lot of the gaps for you.'

The empty mug fell from her hands and shattered on the floor. Priya leapt to her feet. 'Who are you?'

'All in good time. Sit down, and I'll tell you my story.'

Reluctant, but wanting to hear, she did as instructed. Before he began, he made them all fresh drinks—hers in another mug from the cupboard—and then resumed his place in the chair opposite Priya. Kaleb chose to sit on the floor by the door, but at least he'd ceased his overbearing standing vigil.

A pang of guilt hit her. That wasn't fair. All he had ever done was care for her. And his sole aim was to keep them safe. Get the vial where it belonged. He hadn't had to help her. Hadn't had to stay with her. He could have taken the bottle when she'd offered it to him. Or at any other time by force. And now that his secret was out, he no longer swung between the kind, caring, boyish guy and the impatient, indifferent man. He had landed somewhere in between, with the caring getting the upper-hand most times.

The old man began with a question, 'How old do you think I am?'

'Um …' Priya blushed.

'Go on.'

The smile that lit his sad eyes encouraged honesty. 'I'd guess in your eighties.'

His smile filled her with despair. How could a smile make you feel so sad? His next words gave her a partial answer, 'Forty-eight.'

Silence descended in the pod, so profound they could hear the cries of the various small animals from the nearby forest. After a couple of sips of coffee, the man spoke again, 'I used to have power. A great deal. Or so I thought. Now, I realise I held no use for those around me. It's a hard thing to realise you're a nobody. That all your efforts were for nothing.'

He paused, wiped away tears, and cleared his throat. 'I hold much of the responsibility for the virus getting out there.'

Kaleb interrupted, 'Welcome to karma. Now you're sick too.'

Priya and the not-old-guy ignored him. The man said, 'You can also blame me for hijacking your portal code.'

Kaleb leapt to his feet. Priya jumped up too, dashed over to the special, and placed her hands on his shoulders to restrain him. She whispered, 'Let's hear him out.'

Her friend stood and panted heavily for a moment or two, and then he slumped. With a curt nod, he eased back to the floor, where he propped himself against the wall. Then he made an impatient 'get on with it' gesture.

Heart thumping, Priya returned to her seat. The man finished his drink. Thick tension blanketed the room. 'I had to stop you from taking the vial to Terrence. We can't let him hold every single antidote—'

'Wait. There are more? Why haven't they used them?'

Another of those sad smiles. Then, 'He gives it to those who support him. Who can bolster him. The rest …' he shrugged. 'If the president has no use for people, he doesn't care for people.'

Priya gasped. 'He'll let them die?'

Once again, Kaleb rose to his feet, but less aggressively this time. 'We have to stop him.'

Their host laughed, a bitter bark of sound. 'Too late. They already did.'

Priya, tentative, said, 'That's good, then?'

At a near murmur, the man said, 'I'm not sure who's worse. Them or him.'

Kaleb demanded, 'Who are you?'

The old man looked up, weary. 'John Martins. Erstwhile second-in-command to the ex-president.'

Chaos erupted. Both Priya and Kaleb leapt to their feet once more. Both yelled 'What?' in high-pitched horror. Both believed instantly that they had walked straight into a trap.

Kaleb lunged forward and knocked the mug from Martins' grip with a back-handed slap. It shattered across the floor, spilling the small amount of liquid that had been left. John threw his arms wide and tried to defend himself, but too late. The army special had him in a headlock so fast that Priya hadn't had time to register the move.

Her heart hammered violently against her ribs and up into her throat. In an effort to calm down, she took great gulps of air, which eventually settled to regular deep breaths. Then his words penetrated the haze of panic and outrage. *Erstwhile. Ex-president.*

She bent her face near to John's, the man who had done so much damage alongside Terror. 'Who's in charge now?'

He shrugged, and a look of bitterness crossed his face. 'You wouldn't know them. Turns out I didn't either.'

Her threat alert dropped a notch. For good or ill, she believed him. Understood that he was a changed man, at least right then. With a long breath out, she deflated, adrenaline abating, and dropped back onto her chair.

Kaleb released Martins from his hold and moved back a couple of paces, but stood ready to react if needed. Then he said, 'How long?'

John and Priya looked at him, each needing clarification.

Annoyed, Kaleb said, 'The portal. How long?'

Martins answered, 'About a month.'

Priya pressed, 'Why?'

Instead of answering, John rose and went to the prep area. There, he set up the makings for a fresh brew and got busy cleaning up the mounting remnants of shattered ceramics. Impatient, Priya raised her voice a notch and repeated her interrogative.

John kept himself busy while he replied. 'I became suspicious. That, and I had an interesting conversation with Major Adams.' He cast a nod toward Kaleb. 'With the vial found, I realised I had to buy some time. See how things panned out.'

Priya nodded. 'Just as well.'

Kaleb surprised her when he nodded in agreement.

The two young people shared a long look. Wordless, Priya asked the question, *What now?*

Kaleb said, 'We keep going. Find out as much as we can on the way.' He glanced at Martins, hesitant. Priya could see when he dove into the deep end, committing fully. 'I've heard rumours of a rebel base deep in the centre of zone five.'

Priya wanted to know, 'How come the army has never found it?'

Martins grinned. 'The military—and the president—heard lots of differing rumours.'

A delighted grin spread across Priya's face. 'You made sure of it.'

Kaleb joined in the low-level hilarity. He accused John, 'You scheming bastard,' but his words sounded good-natured rather than accusatory.

Martins returned to the sitting area with fresh drinks, and they all sat around the small coffee table, the atmosphere much more amenable than previously. 'I'll come with you.'

Again, Priya and Kaleb shared a look.

John said, 'I have a lot of inside information. It could help.'

Before Kaleb's nod, Priya had agreed already. She said, 'Right. We'll head into zone five and see if we can't unearth the rebel base.'

4

E116

It seemed strange, travelling in a group of three, instead of just Kaleb and she. Priya missed the intimacy of walking for click upon click and sharing stories from their pasts. Since the last portal explosion, he had opened up to her more and more.

Still numb from the assault upon her arrival in zone 9, and wary of Kaleb's motives, she'd done more listening than talking and didn't let on how close, emotionally, she had grown to him. And that was okay because they shared something during their lonesome travels and travails.

Martins' presence changed all that.

The two men tended to walk together, talking. Well, not quite talking—more like interrogation and answers, with Kaleb doing the sharp questioning.

Martins didn't do himself any favours when he admitted, after some particularly brutal verbal pushing from Kaleb, that he hadn't changed allegiance until after the two usurpers had killed Terrence and turned on him.

Kaleb accused, 'You'd grab back any power you could just as quick as, wouldn't you?'

To which Martins nodded and gave a small shrug.

Over her shoulder, from a few feet ahead of the men, Priya said, 'Welcome to the world.' Which struck her as highly ironic, considering how much she'd loved her world until the virus had ripped it from her.

Out of all the conversions of the trio, though, Kaleb's had to signify the most significant shift. After speaking to various refugees on their journey, and comparing the many and differing rumours and assumptions, he had begun to waver in his firm convictions. The atrocities and deliberate release of the virus that Martins had admitted to, in cahoots with Terrence, seemed to have sealed the deal for Kaleb. When he'd agreed to search for the rebels, it had astounded and pleased Priya, whose own beliefs had started to metamorphose during her physical recovery.

Until it all went wrong, she hadn't held any strong beliefs about anything. She had just breezed from day to day, oblivious. If she could paint any kind of silver lining around all of this, it would be that, at least now, she had her eyes open. Wide open. And had begun to live. Truly live. Priya didn't have the words to describe her previous existence, but it hadn't been living, not really. Perhaps *existing.* Yes. That sounded more accurate.

From zones 7 and 6 onward, the buildings had huddled closer together, becoming crowded city streets, with one zone almost merging into the other. Zone 5 compounded that further, and it didn't have outskirts as such. Not much changed between 6 and 5 to say you'd crossed the border. Not this far across the continent. Only nearer the capital, closer to zone 1 would you see the more affluent properties, both commercial and residential, begin to pop up.

Despite the dense buildings, raptor cries still pierced the night air. The predators, ever more bold, came nearer to the cities with every passing moon cycle. She supposed that the soldiers had other, more important, animals to hunt these days.

Quite unconsciously, the three of them drew nearer together as they walked deeper into zone 5. The empty buildings had grown eyes. Unknown someones tracked their progress. As the sun burnt up the moon, blazing a new day, the air thickened and became heavy. Another storm was on the way. Priya's tongue tingled while her eyes smarted at the anticipatory dread of the dust that would come with the gale.

They reached City Square. A hanging scaffold stood in the centre. Blood splatters stained the once pristine slabs surrounding it. Priya shuddered. Had they just made a big mistake? Which side had caused all the bloodshed? The rebels or the regime?

As if by telepathic agreement, all three drew to a stop at the edges of the square. There they stood, watching and waiting. For what, Priya had no idea. But they each anticipated something.

The ambush came from behind. From the narrow street that approached the central area. The trio had nowhere to go but into the big open space. Exposed.

Priya counted ten armed men, all donned in dark grey jumpsuits—which used to represent manual labourers—around which they had cinched ammo and weapons belts. The newcomers surrounded them and held their guns at the ready. One by one, Priya, Kaleb, and Martins raised their hands in the universal sign of surrender.

One of the rebel soldiers, for that's what this group must be, lowered his pulse gun and stepped forward, fishing a device out of his chest pocket. He approached Priya first and shone the ultra-violet light into her eyes. With a nod, he moved on to Martins, who also seemed to pass the inspection. Then the guy got to Kaleb. It took only a fraction of a second for the rebel to startle, back away, and raise and aim his weapon. The rest of the team straightened to fresh alertness. They'd seen the infection. They meant to shoot him.

Without forethought, Priya leapt forward with a yell and placed herself between the guy and Kaleb. With a sinking heart, she understood that it wouldn't do any good. Any of the others could shoot him from where they stood, and she doubted they'd care overly much whether they hit her too or not. Then Martins stepped sideways and placed himself at Kaleb's back. He joined hands with Priya, the two of them trying to bracket Kaleb with their bodies.

The rebel with the device shook his head, spat off to one side, and said, 'Leave him. Take these two.' He gestured with his gun. Then he flipped the weapon end on end and, reaching through the gab above Priya and Martins' shoulders, whacked Kaleb on the side of the skull with the substantial stock of the pulse gun. The army special collapsed to his knees, and blood trickled from his temple, soon soaking his collar. Now Priya appreciated his choice of farmer green. Had the rebels suspected he was a soldier, they would never have left him alive. And thank everything in the universe she wasn't still dressed in the black suit he'd given her after Jenny died.

Another man separated himself from the group and tugged Priya's hands behind her back, where he—no, this was a woman—she secured cable ties around Priya's wrists. Martins received the same treatment. Another hit to the head left Kaleb on his side, bleeding heavily and unconscious. The rebels dragged Priya and Martins away, presumably toward their base. Tears poured down Priya's cheeks.

At the far side of the square, someone wrapped a blindfold over Priya's eyes. Terror engulfed her. Flashbacks of the assault rocked her on her feet. As well as the blood-soaked scaffolding they'd seen. Then someone pressed down the top of her head, making her bend at the neck, and said, 'Mind you don't crack your skull.' She stumbled over a step upward, and then different hands shoved her onto a narrow bench. Only when the craft lifted from the ground with a silent lurch did she recognise that they had loaded Martins and herself into a hover-shuttle.

Blind, Priya called out to anyone who might be near, 'I need to pee.' When no response came, she crossed her legs, leant forward, and said, 'Please. I won't make trouble.'

'No, just water.' A couple of guys laughed.

A woman tutted and said, 'I'll take her.'

Rough hands yanked Priya to her feet and dragged her down the narrow walkway between benches. Every couple of steps, she stumbled when one foot or the other nudged into the base of one of the seats or trod on someone's shoe.

The woman shoved her into a tight space—presumably the toilet stall. Then she undid the blindfold and shut the door, leaving Priya alone for a few brief minutes. She had to act fast.

Now or never.

When she tugged at the zipper of her jump-suit, her fingers shook, matching her erratic and speeding heartbeat. Before she shrugged out of the suit and dropped it to the floor, she retrieved the vial from her pocket. Then she freed one of her feet, listening for an impatient 'hurry up' from the guard.

Priya didn't want to do the next bit. Wasn't looking forward to it. Had never done anything like this before. She screwed up her mouth in distaste and raised one foot to rest on the closed toilet seat. Then she bent at her hips and waist, bringing the hand with the vial between her legs. She had to make sure she got it in far enough, or it would just fall out.

A mad vision of the bright-orange vial sliding down her leg and out of the cuff of her pants and onto the floor for all to see flitted through her panicked mind. While she had wanted to find the rebels, she had no intention of letting them get their hands on something as precious or vital as the antidote until she knew more of their motives and goals.

Loud knocking sounded at the flimsy door.

'Almost done,' Priya yelled.

'Hurry it up,' came the gruff reply.

Priya flipped up the seat lid, sat, and managed a quick pee. Then she stood, flushed, and dressed hurriedly. Cold water splashed her palms, and more irritable knocking sounded. The woman opened the door and peered in suspiciously. Priya made a show of drying her damp hands on her jumpsuit by wiping them over her stomach. With a tut of annoyance, the woman put the blindfold back in place and dragged Priya back to her position on the benches.

Unknown knees knocked hers when she re-took her seat. Martins? One of the guards? Another captive? Priya tried to calm her breathing. Tried to avoid wondering what they would do with her once they got her to their base. She couldn't care less about Martins. That evil prick deserved everything he got. Without the unwavering support from Martins and other men like him, Terror could never have gotten away with all those atrocities. Could never have used the virus in the way he had. Priya would make him pay for what had happened to her. She would make them all pay.

5

E117

The wind gusted and howled. The dust and

grit swirled and burned. Kaleb's head throbbed. The bleeding had stopped. The blood had dried to a tacky lump at his temple, matting his hair, which had grown way longer than the regulation two-finger measure. And now the storm threw red grit onto his wound, which stung and smarted.

Out of sight of the perimeter patrol, Kaleb crouched and watched, trying to work out their pattern. It unnerved him to see so many guards on patrol. He had to find a way through. A way to Priya. A way to the vial.

Doubts and confusion had plagued him ever since they had run into Martins. And Kaleb's unwavering loyalty and support of the president had shattered to pieces. He felt adrift, lost. Right then, Priya seemed like his port in the storm. Despite what she had gone through, she was tough. She had grit and determination and tenacity. He trusted that she would get the job done. What he didn't know was what that job now was. Who the bloody hell should they take the vial to? What should they do with it?

When he'd awoken to find himself alone and

Priya taken, he had felt heart sore. It no longer concerned him that he'd failed in his mission, but it did bother him that he'd failed her. That he'd missed the mark utterly when it came to protecting her and what she carried.

A strong gust rocked him on his feet, and he almost toppled over backward, having to grab the crumbling brick wall to steady himself. This area must have been one of the earliest builds when Exxon 1 was first settled. They didn't use brick anymore. The neostil worked much better.

A wall of grit blew his way, and Kaleb had to screw his eyes shut and duck his head to avoid the worst of the sandblast. His cheeks and nose burned and stung, and grit got between his teeth and on his tongue. Hell, it got everywhere, into every crack and crevice.

When the worst of it had passed, he raised his head and wiped at his face. Just as he opened his eyes, a heavy hand gripped his shoulder. A monotone male voice said, 'And who might you be?'

Kaleb startled, overbalanced, flopped onto his backside, and stared up at two armed, black-clad men. The pair of army specials assigned to zone 5. Had to be. He recovered his wits, cursing himself for a fool, and scrambled to a standing position, leaving his weapon where it rested against the wall.

On his feet, he raised his arms, palms outward, in surrender. 'I'm no rebel.'

The soldier who'd hung back rolled his eyes. 'No kidding.'

The lead special kept his gun trained at Kaleb's chest. He'd had more than enough of staring down the wrong end of the barrel for one day. Impatient, he snapped, 'I'm a special, like you. Zone 9.' With a strained smile, he extended a hand, inviting a shake. 'Kaleb Moore, ZN669900.'

The guys stiffened and shared a long look. What were they thinking? What did that stare communicate? Had the major put out a warrant for his apprehension when he'd gone off-radar?

A pair of hardened expressions, bracketing cold eyes, gave him his answer. Rear soldier levelled his weapon. Front soldier grabbed wrist ties from his jumpsuit and secured Kaleb's hands behind his back. He saw no point in protesting and risking further injury. The major would give him an opportunity to explain himself. And it would all work itself out then.

Kaleb walked with them amiably enough until he realised they had herded him to the portal square. He struggled free of the soldier who'd cable-tied his hands together. 'No way. Not in there. They can send a shuttle.'

The other special, the one who'd stayed quiet for most of their acquaintance, mocked, 'Fucking sissy. Want your mommy to hold your hand?'

Both men converged on him, guns at the ready position, and forced him forward. Kaleb gritted his teeth, determined that he wouldn't give them his code. If they insisted on sending him through that thing, it would be on their access, not his.

They marched him across the square. Pristine, unlike the ones in the other zones. Surprised, he glanced at the mouthier of the soldiers. 'This one gets a lot of use.'

The guy ignored him, and a few seconds later, the two men wrestled Kaleb into the slim tube. Head hung, he stood and waited for it to explode. It didn't. The regular hum sounded, and then his world obliterated into white light so blinding that he had to squeeze his eyes shut against it. When he could see again, a group of heavily-armed soldiers met his gaze.

Why all the fuss? What was he supposed to have done? Other than fail, that is. The major stepped forward and stared at him with a look of disgust contorting his roughened features into something grotesque. Something had changed since Major Adams had sent him out to zone 9 to retrieve the vial and confirm the death of some top scientist or other. He hadn't much cared about that part, just about securing the antidote. But when had it changed, and why?

Adams stepped close so that they stood nose to nose. Then he stiffened and leapt a step backward. Kaleb had to work hard to hold in his grin. Evidently, the major didn't like the new violet tint to the special's eyes. The two who'd escorted him here shared a look of consternation.

Bored and amused both at once, Kaleb offered a lazy shrug. 'You might have thought to send us out vaccinated.'

Adams blustered, 'Had you located the vial, we might have been able to.'

Kaleb gave him a cold grin and shook his head. When he spoke, he raised his voice to ensure the whole group would hear him. 'And what about you? Where did your vaccination come from? We both know that the story of losing the one existing vial is a complete fallacy.'

Mumblings and rumblings erupted around him. Adams slid his pulse-pistol from its holster and whipped Kaleb across the side of the head with it. His temple split open yet again, and his knees buckled. Dazed, he sank to the dirt floor at the major's feet. Despite his position, he glared up at the man in total defiance. If these were his last minutes alive, he would ensure that he sowed as much unrest amongst the ranks as possible.

Instead of ordering his death, though, Adams gestured two sergeants forward. 'Straw. Rennard. Take him to chamber three.'

Kaleb's guts chilled. Chamber three had one use and one use only. The torture chamber. The thought of a quick execution hadn't bothered him too much, but knowing what they did to people in there had his limbs quivering and his bowels twisting.

Chamber three was where they took dissidents to brainwash them.

CHAPTER EIGHT

1

E91

Sasha trotted into the lab, a triumphant grin splitting her features in two. Mindful of the surveillance cameras, she kept the sample tube—if not her exuberant mood—hidden until Giles followed her into the small box room and then into the underground lab.

Pleased with herself, and feeling as though she had achieved something, she handed her friend the president's DNA. The tiny clear tube, secured with a screw top, held a single pubic hair, spoils of war and her prize for pimping herself out yet again. *For the last time,* she told herself, grimly.

Inexplicably, Giles seemed subdued. And though she gave Sasha a brief hug, her body remained stiff and unyielding—distant. If this hadn't pleased the woman, what would?

Giles held the tube up to the light, where the single hair glinted ginger at each half-turn. Sasha tried to read her. Failed. Nervous and uncertain— feeling like a little girl again—she stood fidgeting, waiting for approval.

All at once, a small part of her felt glad at dropping her friend in it with Terror. Then guilt drowned the little bit of happy. They were in this together. Whatever this was.

Giles lowered her arm and clenched a fist around the tube. Then she fixed a hard gaze on Sasha. 'This is just the start. You know that, right?'

A hard lump grew in her throat, and she had to work hard to swallow it. Silent, she nodded, all the while attempting to calculate where this would lead next. Wondering what Giles would ask of her next. *Demand,* an unwelcome voice whispered behind her ear. And she had to agree, albeit reluctantly. For this had turned into a relationship of unequal parts. *Started out that way.* Annoyed at herself, she shook her head, trying to shake loose the unwelcome observer. Little Shura, however—the small girl who'd grown desperate for control in the end—knew better. Recognised truth when she heard it. Sasha had become blinded by emotion. A thing she had vowed never to fall victim to ever again. Fools in love and all that.

All of this processed within a second or two, and she reached out her palm to take the tube that Giles now held out to her. Mute and outwardly compliant, she agreed to extract the DNA and produce a working virus for the sole purpose of killing the president.

Timid now, unsure of herself and her judgement, she asked, 'How will we infect him?'

Sasha didn't like the smile that Giles gave. She shook her head and told the lead scientist, 'I won't sleep with him again. Not unless he forces me.' Unconsciously, she'd taken a step backward.

Giles held up a palm. 'I wouldn't ask you to.'

Her words left too much unsaid. Sasha pushed, 'Who, then? Who *will* you whore me with?'

'We need to have a little chat with Martins.'

Sasha nodded. She could cope with that much. So long as it was just this one final time. Just this one last sacrifice. But from now on, she would watch Giles closely. How much had changed in a single day. How much life could turn on a credit chip. No warning.

With her lips set in a line of grim determination—she'd come this far and resolved to see it through to its natural conclusion—she offered Giles another nod and then tried on a smile for size. It felt too small and constricted. As bad a fit as everything else just now.

Finished with the meagre discussion, she turned her back on her erstwhile girlfriend and got busy setting up the necessary equipment. With her recent breakthrough, and her obtaining the needed DNA, creating this version of a virus shouldn't take too long.

Nervous, she forced down the bile of regret and self-recrimination, which had risen up her throat, and concentrated. It made sense that Giles would want to involve Martins. He had the most access to the president. Was his closest confidant. Could get to him with far greater ease than could anyone else.

The work went quickly and without a hiccup. Despite her doubts, she felt pleased with her accomplishments. Everyone kept underestimating her. Well, one of these days, she would make them regret their easy dismissal of this lowly lab assistant.

Just as she transitioned from box room to main lab, two armed specials flung open the double doors and entered in tandem march-step, weapons held at the ready position. Sasha froze and watched.

Caught off-guard, Giles spun to face them. The dropper she'd held loosely in one hand fell to the floor with a soft clitter—too light to make a proper clatter.

'Wha—'

A rough arm around her bicep killed her question. Then wrist ties bowed her head and slumped her shoulders. Even before the second man spoke, both women knew what this was about.

'The president has ordered you detained on charges of treason.'

Other than her still-born question, Giles made no further protest. Soundless, expressionless, she allowed the officers to drag her from the room. None of them had taken any notice of Sasha. Hadn't even glanced her way. As ever, nobody saw her as a threat. Alone now, save for the surveillance cameras, she allowed a small smile to tug up the corners of her mouth. Let Terrence and his cronies make of that what they would.

The virus was complete. Ready. All Sasha had to do was implement the rest of the plan. She doubted that Terrence would let her anywhere near him just then, not until he'd had Giles thoroughly interrogated. Which left Martins. How to get him onside, though? She took the rest of the day thinking hard about that particular conundrum while pretending business within the dusty and useless box room.

Clocked off now and done with her official work day, Sasha took herself straight to Martins' rooms, where she made herself as inviting and alluring as she knew how, and then she undressed and lay on top of his bed. He wouldn't know what had hit him.

True to form, he entered his apartment grumpy and tired but soon brightened when he saw her waiting for him. John leant against the jamb, stopping the front door from sliding shut. 'Long time no see,' he told her, arms crossed. But his smile and the glint in his eyes gave her a different message. As did the bulge in his trousers.

Sasha grinned. 'I missed you too.' With that, she trailed her fingers down her naked torso and licked her lips.

Not bothering to disrobe just yet, he crossed the room in three quick strides and fell on top of her. While his lips sought hers, his fingers got straight down to business and slipped between her thighs before pushing inside her. When he found Sasha wet for him, he grunted with pleased surprise. It had taken her nothing to keep herself primed while she'd waited for him to arrive.

Unlike their usual encounters, she kept him going for the best part of an hour, backing off and teasing him whenever his orgasm came too near. By the time she let him go, he lay sated and cuddly—open to pillow talk and suggestion.

For now, her confidence had returned, and she felt that she had regained some control of circumstances. Her many encounters with Martins assured that she knew how to play him. Sasha began by reminding him how much she had missed him, then she went on to talk about how lonely she felt, especially now that her mentor had been arrested. The news of Giles's detention seemed to startle John. Terrence hadn't included him. This just got better and better.

Sasha grabbed the opportunity, 'She was his top scientist. One of his closest allies. What's he doing, John?' She stared up at him with worried eyes.

Though he lay with pursed lips, his fingers caressed her erect nipple idly. Finally, after long seconds, John said, 'He's been getting more and more paranoid of late.'

'So, none of us are safe?'

That stilled his hand. He glanced at her, looking dismayed and appalled.

Sasha pressed the advantage, 'He's already taken Giles. Who's next?'

His body tensed. She raised a hand to his chin and stroked it gently. At a whisper, she said, 'We have to stick together.'

His gaze softened a little.

She continued, 'Will you protect me?'

Will not *can.* Oh, she knew just how to play him.

Still watching him, with a mixture of concern and sexual wantonness on her face, she shifted so that her breast rested beneath his hand once again. Then she moved her hips against his groin. He smiled. 'Of course I will, little Shura.'

His arrogance would never allow him to admit his doubts about his own safety amidst the unstable regime and its megalomaniac leader. From here on in, she had to tread with extra care.

'A man like you should have had more power a long time ago.' She paused, gauging his response.

He bent and sucked on a nipple, and one of his hands grabbed a buttock. Beneath him, she groaned. Only when he lifted his head and looked at her, did she speak again.

'Do you remember when I got here? When I told you I could be of assistance?'

Here came one of the most treacherous bits. Either he would welcome any suggestions or he wouldn't. Whichever, she had to press on now. His hand stilled at her backside but stayed in place. He watched her, waiting, giving just the one minute nod to tell her she could go on.

'I might have a way.'

His eyebrows rose, lifting his brow. 'A way?'

Before answering, she lifted her neck and shoulders so that she could kiss him on the end of his nose, then she lay back, her sexiest smile on her lips. 'A way to put the power where it belongs.'

For long moments, he lay propped on an elbow, watching her. No need to ask had she gone too far, for his musing expression showed his greed. His eagerness. All that stopped him from agreeing right away was his usual calculating demeanour, interested only in self-preservation. He would remain wary of a trap and manipulation.

Softly, softly. 'The regime needs stability. A strong leader. Credit where credit's due.'

At last. At long last, he nodded, giving her permission without needing to know her exact plans.

'It needs you for it to work.'

That had him looking concerned. Sasha hurried to reassure him. 'Well, it needs your nose drops.'

Intrigue replaced worry.

'Go on,' he said.

Here, she took in a deep breath. Held it. Once she told him the rest, there was no going back. She would be totally at his mercy. He could destroy her if he wanted. She hedged and spoke only part of the truth, 'The lab has a different virus. One that's DNA specific. You … we would be perfectly safe.'

When he shook his head, her heart almost failed. Then, with a sudden thud, it began racing. 'Everyone would know. I'd be the last one with him before he died.'

Sasha relaxed and let out the air she'd held in her lungs. 'It wouldn't take effect for a few hours. That would put you in the clear. You know how many appointments he has in a day.'

The silence that fell then lasted for an eon, or so it seemed. In all honesty, she had no clue which way he would lean. Whether he would take her up on her offer or drop her in it.

Just when she'd begun to give in to despair, thinking everything lost, he nodded, and a broad smile stretched his features and bunched up his cheeks, which had grown rosy. An excited glint lit his eyes.

'It's the only way,' he told her.

She nodded and stroked his chin. 'We'll be next, if not. Both of us.' Then, cleverly, she echoed his words, 'It's the only way.'

'I'll do it in the morning.' Then he pushed his knees between her legs and took her hard and fast, reasserting his control. Like she bore every-thing else, Sasha closed her eyes and thought back to her childhood, to before her parents had died. More accurately, to before she'd murdered them. It had been easy enough to research which cable to loosen so it would snap en-route. Really, she couldn't have planned it any better. The brakes had failed spectacularly, smashing the hover-car into the control tower, where it exploded in a huge fireball, obliterating the two people within. Well, they'd survived for a further three days, neither regaining consciousness. That success had fed her sabotage of Eloise, which had also worked out flawlessly.

John finished fucking her and rolled off to one side. Within seconds, his guttural snores rattled throughout the room. Sasha lay there, grinning and planning. Giles under arrest, and tomorrow, Martins would kill the president. *Which leaves little ole me.* Little Shura, whom everybody had dismissed and discounted. With endless possibilities all around her.

While John slept, Sasha crept from the bed. When she'd last searched his apartment, she'd rushed, nervous of discovery. Since then, a certain smooth stretch of bland wall—too bland— had nagged at her. Now, she tiptoed from the bedroom to the study. In the doorway, she hesitated. Did he have his cameras activated when he was at home? She shrugged. That was a chance she felt willing to take.

Quietly, breath held, she eased the study door closed behind her. The lights came on automatically as soon as she set foot into the room. Sasha gasped at the sudden brightness. Alert, she listened for sounds of John rousing. None reached her. Okay, then, down to business.

Sure enough, her fingers found the slightest of seams, invisible to the idle eye. But she had come looking for it. She ran her smooth fingertips over it, along it, tracing its path. A perfect square. How to get in, though? A soft noise startled her.

Alarmed, she spun away from the wall and edged to the closed door, where she stood and listened intently. Nothing. With a sharp exhalation, she eased open the door and peeked through the small gap. Again, nothing. Too strung tight, she made her way back to bed and slid beneath the covers, careful not to wake John. She would come back and examine that hidden chamber another time.

That night, she got little sleep. Far too keyed up. What she hadn't expected the next morning, was for John to leave his comms turned on when he breakfasted with Terrence. He'd done that for her. So that she could listen in. She paused, cereal spoon halfway to her lips and concentrated, wishing she could see as well as hear.

Ceramic tinkled, a drink being stirred. ...

Had he put in the drops already? Sasha bit her bottom lip.

Creaks of leather furnishings as two heavyset men took their seats. Silence ...

Comfortable for them (well, at least for the president, likely not so much so for John this morning, and most definitely uncomfortable for her). Would John go through with it?

Martins spoke, 'You have Professor Stephenson in custody, I hear.'

A low chuckle answered. But then came bitter words, 'Ungrateful bitch. Without me, she would have had nothing. Nothing.'

Caution wrapped around every one of John's next words, 'We all owe you. I, for one, will make sure you get what you deserve.'

The pause that followed wasn't just pregnant, it was at full-term with the baby's head poking out. Sasha held her breath, waiting for the contraction to hit, pushing it out the rest of the way. Instead, the President sighed heavily. He'd missed the innuendo. What the hell was Martins playing at? Did he want finding out?

'You're a good man, John. One of the best. All these years, you've been the only true friend to me. On you, I can rely a hundred percent.'

'Thanks.' Martins' voice sounded strangled.

Sasha leapt to her feet. Was he overcome with regret? Had he swallowed the president's words? Would he now drop her in it? But he couldn't, not without also jeopardising himself. She chewed on a thumbnail, already short and jagged.

John's next words had her screech and hug her arms around her torso.

'Yet you've never once rewarded my loyalty.'

Anger and threat replied with deceptively mild words, 'Yet here you sit, breakfasting with the most powerful man on the planet.'

John wasted no time. 'Just once, I'd like for you to share more than your coffee with me.'

Again, Sasha fretted that he hadn't used the drops yet. That he had no intention of going through with it. Was that why he'd left on the comms? So that she could listen to her own doom as it unfolded?

More creaking and shuffling indicated that one of the men had stood.

The president said, 'Resentment makes for a dangerous bedfellow. I should be careful.'

From the sound of it, the other man also now rose from his chair. 'Perhaps I just need a break. I lost my wife to all this.' Slow, soft footsteps padded across the plush carpet.

They didn't diminish, which told Sasha that these must belong to John. He'd dared to walk away from the president without leave. Most likely at the door by now, he said one last thing …

'I'm sorry, Denis.'

The swoosh-swish of the door opening and then closing again preceded heavier, quicker steps on hard tile. A click broke the connection.

With one arm still wrapped around her body at sternum level, Sasha mashed a fist into her mouth and chewed on the knuckles while she paced up and down. What had just happened?

How had Terrence taken those final three words? Had John set off alarm bells? If he'd blown it, the president would have him and everyone around him executed.

In vain, she tried to calm her nerves. If Martins had infected Terrence, she had only to wait for another few hours, and then he would die. Painfully. Horrifically. At first, the haemorrhage would start small, a mere trickle. Then the damn would burst spectacularly.

However, had John not administered the virus, he had just condemned them both to death. Whether he realised that or not.

2

E92

Déjà vu. Sasha lay in bed with Martins. Post sex. Again. Only now, it was different. It had all changed.

In the drowsy voice of a man on the edge of sleep, John joked, 'Missed you. Long time no see.'

She laughed. 'I've been a bit busy.' After rolling onto her side to face him, she said, 'John, why did you leave the comms on?'

His heavy breathing stilled, and his eyes opened slowly. More alert now, he pierced her with his gaze. 'You and I both want Terror out of the way.'

Sasha laughed humourlessly. 'Why should I trust you? After everything.'

He shrugged. 'We two can argue about who gets the top seat later.'

With a grin, she straddled him. 'That would be me.'

Instead of joining her bit of fun, he went rigid, but not in the right place. That remained as flaccid as a limp lettuce leaf. John pushed her off him, and she bounced on the mattress with a grunt of outraged surprise.

'What the hell?'

His focus stayed somewhere at ceiling level. 'You little bitch. You killed my wife.'

Shock had her gasp.

He couldn't know.

He did know.

'How?' It was all she could manage.

'Silly little girl. You honestly thought the president didn't anticipate your every move.'

Her whole body went cold. Goose-bumps broke out along both arms, and the hairs on her neck stood on end. Desperate to get up and dress, she restrained herself, sitting still and waiting for what more he had to dump on her from on high.

'We know all about your parents. Your aunt.'

Now, she did leap from the bed, convinced that Martins hadn't put the drops in the president's coffee. The two men had set her up. Panic tunnelled her vision, and she stubbed a toe at the foot of the bed. Cursing, she grabbed her crumpled garments and dashed to the bathroom.

Dressed, she sat on the toilet lid, contemplating. The alarm should have sounded by now. Someone should have discovered Terrence dead in his quarters. Why hadn't any alert gone out? Sure that John had double-crossed her, furious, she marched back into the bedroom. Martins sat on the edge of the bed, clothed and smoking. The disposal unit hovered nearby, ready to swallow the discards.

Sasha felt like that unit, swallowing discards her whole life. She should have understood that someone like her could never climb to the top. Could never succeed. Men like her father, like Terrence, like Martins, would keep her down. Keep her in her place.

John spoke, and it all changed again. 'I infected Denis.' He glanced at his watch—an ancient timepiece handed down in his family through uncountable generations. Who needed a worthless antique when implants told you the time and so much more?

While Terrence had decreed that all alerts be turned off within the presidential zone, to ensure you couldn't read a person's intentions (ominous in itself), he had allowed the implants to continue performing the more mundane functions.

Sasha brought her spinning thoughts to an abrupt halt. What did it matter what bloody watch the man wore? He'd just said he'd infected the president. She opened her mouth to query the lack of alarm and, right then, the lights in John's suite complex flashed red, and a high-pitched beep-beep-beep rang throughout the apartment.

John flashed her a grin full of malice. 'Time to put your game face on.' Then he left the apartment. As the second in command, he would become the automatic temporary leader in the immediate aftermath of the president's demise. Now that she knew what he knew about her, Sasha could not let that happen.

From the start, Giles had planned to remove Martins from the equation. Sasha had balked. Not now. Not anymore. He held too much over her. Had become far too dangerous an entity. She would put the professor's designs to good use. To that end, she searched his pillow until she uncovered a stray hair. Though only half an inch in length, it gave her plenty.

The virus she had in mind wouldn't kill him. It would do something far worse. The man should suffer, and he would. She'd make sure of that.

3

E93

The fight came in a flood of inevitability. The woman would never let up. For Exxon's sake. John shook his head. He'd killed his long-time friend for her. Had committed the ultimate act of treason in murdering the president. And now she wanted more. Did she not realise that his actions gave him the top seat? Did she not recall what he'd said when she'd first arrived in zone 1? Sasha owed him. He owned her.

Reluctantly, and against his better judgement, he'd agreed to free Professor Stephenson from the interrogation cell. And here his little Shura stood, assuming that she had any modicum of control, any kind of a say in matters.

Furious, he levelled a finger at her nose. 'I don't appreciate your trying to manipulate me.'

She balked. 'After everything I've done—'

John lost it and yelled, 'You killed my fucking wife!' Disgusted—with the slut before him, and with himself—he spun away, intending to put distance between them. A sharp sting pierced his neck. He put up a hand to hold the hurt and found a syringe sticking out of his skin, quivering.

Appalled, disbelieving, he turned on her. The bitch had stabbed him in the neck. Might as well have been in the back. Slowly, with great care, he eased the needle out and held the vile thing in his palm. The syringe sat there, empty, winking in the strong overhead lights.

'You treacherous bitch.' John took a threatening step toward her.

She backed up. 'You have no power, Martins. Never did. Giles and I are in charge now.'

The door opened, and the professor stood there with Major Adams. As the new de facto president, John held the position of General Supreme. The major had no choice but to obey his every command, no matter what. All at once, the strength returned to his locked knees.

'Adams. Good. Take these two traitors down to level eight.'

The soldier freed a wrist tie from his belt pouch and strode into the room, leaving Giles behind him. What was the man thinking? Instead of apprehending Novikov or the professor, he grabbed John's wrists and secured his hands behind his back.

Too late, he tried to resist, having wasted vital seconds frozen with shock and disbelief. Stephenson oozed into the room, wearing a gleeful expression. Sasha crossed her arms, and despite her smile, her eyes showed nothing but pure hatred and loathing. 'Like I said, you have no power. You're nothing.' She studied him. Then, to his surprise, she said, 'Get out.'

John wasted no time in complying. Convinced she'd infected him with the same deadly concoction as he'd given Terrence, he wanted to get as far away from the capital as he could. No way would he leave his earthly remains here for the harlots to do with as they would. In utter panic and disarray, he fled.

You're a nobody. All your efforts for nothing. You failed. Soon, you'll die the same horrific death as Denis. What do you think you're going to do now? You bloody idiot. John blocked out the tormenting voice in his head. He would make a comeback. Somehow. He would show them. First, though, he had to get away. And then he had to come up with an antidote to whatever they'd given him. After that, he had to come up with a plan.

Unbeknownst to anyone except Martins, as yet, Denis had kept his personal portal open. After grabbing a few essentials, Martins jogged down eerily empty corridors to the presidential transportation room. Everyone had gone to ground until the dust settled. Cowards. At the portal, he used Terrence's unique personal access code to activate the machine, not trusting his own to have remained uncompromised. The major could have pulled the same stunt John had played on Kaleb. He didn't want to risk it.

Still, when he stepped inside, his heart ratcheted up a few notches, and sweat pooled in his palms. Worried but desperate, he shut his eyes and waited. The expected hum started, and then bright white light assaulted his closed lids. This was it. Now or never.

4

E93

From across the room, Sasha studied Giles. Had she done the right thing in freeing the woman? Or was this more of her naiveté? She shook her head. They needed one another. Major Adams' sudden switch alarmed her, though. Giles had kept that one quiet. It put Sasha at a distinct disadvantage.

From the beginning, she had pursued power. Control. Safety. Had assumed that she and the professor would share equal status once all the pieces fell into place. But, already, she saw things wouldn't pan out that way.

A small smile tugged at her lips, and she had to work hard to hold it back. She knew how to get rid of people. Yes, she'd learned that much. That same thought also unnerved her. Giles held identical cards when it came to making trouble-some folks disappear. Time to tread extra careful-ly. For now.

Her caution hurt and rubbed against the overwhelming love she felt for the other woman. The planet had now reached a pivot point. In the power vacuum, the two of them could seize the reins. They could work together. Again, Adams' presence unnerved her. She didn't trust the man. Not one iota. Giles may believe she had him wrapped around her little finger, but he would have his own agenda—of that, she had no doubt.

A notification beep broke into her thoughts. All three of them glanced toward the president's desk, where a red light flashed rhythmically. Giles dashed over to it. Then she looked up. 'It says someone's accessed the transportation room.'

The major's spine stiffened, and he frowned. 'The president's portal shut down along with everyone else's. Only select army access points remain operative.' He cast a worried glance toward Giles. 'I took care of it, I swear.'

The professor crossed her arms, annoyance darkening her features. 'You stupid man. If you've let Martins leave the zone …' Her threat sounded all the worse for staying unsaid.

Adams' features settled into an unreadable mask. Stiffly, he said, 'With your leave, I'll go and check the room.'

Giles gave a curt nod and turned away. The major strode from the office. Fascinated by the subsurface power-play, Sasha watched. How long would he tolerate some little woman speaking to him that way? Could Giles not see that?

Alone, at last, Sasha ran to her friend and flung her arms around her. 'We did it.'

'So far, so good.' Giles pulled away and studied Sasha. 'We have a lot of work to do yet.'

Eager, Sasha nodded. 'Right. The antidote. We can mass produce it now and distribute it wherever it needs to go.'

Giles' eyes shuttered, and she stood tall. Sadness dulled her features. 'Oh, little Shura. You really have no idea, do you?'

Stunned, Sasha stared up at her. 'What now? I did everything you wanted. I even got rid of John for you.'

Giles shook her head. 'Don't lie to me. What you gave him will make him age prematurely, but it won't finish him off. When it came right down to it, you couldn't kill him, could you?' Her gaze sent daggers spinning toward Sasha, who flinched. 'Why not?' Now her expression filled with cold mockery. 'Don't tell me you love ickle Johnny too.'

Unbidden, Sasha's palm covered her open mouth, which worked like the maw of a dying fish. Well, now she knew.

You knew all along.

Horrified, still in vehement denial, she shut her eyes and shook her head. Then, inevitably, fury rose up and eclipsed hurt and self-recrimination. Giles had used her. Had never cared for her. Would pay for it. In blood.

The silence stretched too thin and snapped. Giles filled the void, 'You could have been second in command with me. Your problem is you never know when you've got it good. Nothing's ever enough for you.'

Sasha stood tall, which still left her well below the other woman's eye level. 'Shame on you.' Both her voice and her eyes blazed.

Giles stumbled backward. Not expecting this show of strength. She opened her mouth to cut

Sasha with her words, but the younger woman beat her to it. 'You're not the person I thought you were. The whole point of deposing Terrence was to make things right. You said we'd give people the cure. But now you want to withhold it. You're no better than him.' She shook her head. 'No. You're worse.' With that parting shot, she turned and marched from the room, daring Giles to try and stop her.

As soon as the door slid shut behind her, the trembling started and her kidneys turned to liquid. For a moment, she stood there frozen, clueless as to her next steps. No longer able to invest in her denials, she had to admit that she had known all along. She just hadn't wanted to see it.

Her legs started taking her toward her rooms, but then she had second thoughts. That hidden cubby hole in John's suite. She turned around and dashed the other way. Time was short. She had to access that cubby hole and then get out of here. Away from zone 1.

As she trotted through the corridors, her outrage at his dismissal of her, and his intent to imprison her and Giles, left her furious.

An open door on her left caught her attention. It led to a tiny utility cupboard, which held cleaning items and tools. Sasha grabbed a screwdriver and continued on her way. As she'd hoped, someone had been through John's apartment already, and they had left the door unsecured after they'd finished.

Someone had ransacked the rooms, and the furniture and furnishings showed disarray. Sasha wasted no time and headed straight for the study and that extra-smooth bit of wall. A rage impelled her to work with determination and brute force. The screwdriver she'd grabbed on impulse came in handy, and she had the compartment pried open within minutes with no need to take the trouble to override its basic security features.

The small square space held two things: a manilla folder and a flash drive. Sasha grabbed both and fled.

Unsure of where she would go, of where she could go to escape Giles and the soldiers, Sasha strode down the corridor toward her quarters. As well as packing her bag, she also stuffed away any and every emotion, except for the one that would see her through this. Her rage she would carry on her shoulders until she could put it to good use. The same with the folder and the drive. She felt certain both would prove useful later on.

Of pressing importance right then was getting out of here. Away from the capital. Away from Giles. Away from her self-blame—anger turned inward. *What have you done?* Sasha hunched her shoulders, trying to ward off the unwelcome question and its natural epilogue: *Can you fix it?*

'Never mind all that,' she yelled into the empty room. Then, at a near whisper, she told herself, 'You have to get out of here. Now. Right now. Go on. Go.'

A sudden intuition had her pause. Unsure why, she retrieved her new finds from her bag and thought hard. Where to hide them? Then she shook her head. She knew just the place. She shoved the items back into her bag.

Even though she didn't know where to flee to, where to hide, she zipped shut her bag and strode to the door, which whooshed open for her.

At a run, heart pounding, she went to the lab,

into the box room, and down into the secret place. There, she pushed up a loose panel in the ceiling near the back of the room. She secreted the folder and drive in the dusty space, and then she secured the panel once more. Terrified she'd taken too much time messing about with this, she trotted back through the rooms and up into the main lab.

Sasha pushed through the double doors and into the corridor. Giles stood there waiting, arms crossed and a grin on her twisted face.

'Just where do you think you're going?'

CHAPTER NINE

1

E117

Priya screamed and struggled, but it made no difference. The men pinned her down. Took her blood. Soaked through with sweat and stinking of fear, she lay on the floor, half-sobbing, half-gasping. Her wrists and ankles smarted, and she rubbed at the bruises, vainly trying to ease the discomfort.

The next hour trickled by, drip by infuriating drip. When the Reverend Leopold Canmore, self-appointed rebel leader, eased into her tiny cell, it almost came as a relief. For a while, he stood and stared down at her where she sat on the floor, a thoughtful expression crinkling his features. 'You're a natural immune. Did you realise that?'

Stunned, Priya shook her head, momentarily mute. At last, she managed, 'No. I had no idea. What's that mean?'

Again, Canmore watched her in silence. She didn't like the look in his eyes. 'We could use you. Or, rather, your immunity.'

Taut with nerves, she edged to her feet, ready to flee or fight. He'd left the door open. Angry as well as scared, she shook her head. 'I came to find you. Your group. You understand that? You don't have to keep me like an animal in a zoo.'

Inexplicably, he smiled.

She waited.

'So, you're inclined to help us?'

Priya spread her arms wide. 'Take all the blood you need. So long as you leave me with enough.'

The rebel leader shook his head, and his eyes darkened with sadness. Now what? He took a step toward her, and she cringed against the cold wall, ignoring the dampness.

'The planet needs all the immunes it can get. All six planets, I would assume.'

She echoed his head shake, but for entirely different reasons.

Canmore took a further step forward. Priya bolted. She shot past him before he could react. Made it as far as the corridor outside her cell. Ran smack into the solid chest of a guard. Dammit. Sod it all to hell and back.

Exhausted and defeated, she slumped and allowed the man to lead her back into her tiny prison. She shot a glance of defiance at the so-called reverend. At last, she found the voice to put her suspicion into words, 'You want to breed from me.' Just getting that nastiness past her vocal cords and slithering over her tongue made her want to gag. Wash out her mouth.

Canmore nodded, watching her, trying to gauge her reaction. She laughed and spat at him. He slapped her. 'A successful pregnancy would bolster our position. Of course, we want your blood too. We can work on developing a cure from it. But we need clean babies as well.'

Priya rubbed her reddened cheek. 'Over my

dead body.' Getting raped once was more than enough, thank you very much. Suddenly chilled to the bone, she massaged her arms and shrank down onto the single cot, wishing everyone would leave her alone. Why had she assumed the rebels would help? That they were good people? Would she never learn? She should bugger off alone and leave them all to destroy themselves.

The reverend turned and marched from the cell, leaving her alone and shocked. She'd expected retaliation or, at least, some response from him. His lack of reaction unnerved her more than the rest of the conversation. Ironically, she sat there wishing she *had* been infected. Even if that would have meant they'd shoot her dead, as she felt sure they had Kaleb.

A cold draft blew her hair back from her face, and she glanced up. Leopold had left the door open. Footsteps approached. A lot of them. Hardly breathing, she waited for the worst. She wasn't wrong. Five men stomped into the room, making the space even more claustrophobic. Uselessly, Priya shot to her feet. When she tried to protest, her voice came out hoarse and in a squeaky whisper, 'No. Please. Don't. Not again.'

Flashbacks of her gang rape froze her in place …

(Jimmy showed her into a large kitchen with a range cooker lining one wall.

The occupants fell silent and stared at her while she stood cowering behind Jimmy. He'd said nothing about his group being all men.)

The guy in the middle, the only one without a gun, stood staring at her. Not much more than a boy, really, but capable of raping her if it came to that. He looked torn. Dare she hope? It seemed not. 'Don't resist, and it'll go easier for you. We don't want to hurt anyone.'

'Then don't do this.'

(Dazed and helpless, she shivered when rough hands ripped her clothes from her. Then she heard the ugly clang of metal on metal and forced her eyes open all the way. Hank stood unfastening his belt.)

The men closed in. Grabbed a wrist or an ankle each. Held her. She closed her eyes. Shut down. She couldn't go through an assault again.

(In and out of consciousness. On her back.

One man then another shoving and grunting on top of her. Pain. So much hurt. Rough hands forcing her onto her front and pushing himself into the wrong hole. Another engorged penis coming for her broken jaw. Oh God.)

Let them kill her. Yes. If she fought hard enough, maybe one of them would shoot her inadvertently or break her neck or something. Anything but this.

Priya broke free of the post-traumatic prison, sucked in a deep breath, and let it out on an ear-splitting yell, 'No!' She bucked and writhed and kicked and twisted. One of her arms came free. Wasting not a second, she grabbed for the nearest crotch and squeezed for all she was worth, digging her nails deep into the soft tissue beneath the pants.

Her victim squealed and leapt back. Someone aimed a kick at her head, another into her abdomen, leaving her winded and gasping. The others let go and stepped back, guns raised. Now or never. They wouldn't give her another chance to hurt them.

In the doorway, a shadowy figure moved—

believing it to be Canmore, Priya grunted out, 'I told you. Over my dead body.'

To her surprise, a female voice spoke up, 'What's going on here? What is this?'

Tension thickened the room, and booted feet shuffled uncomfortably. The figure stepped into the cell, away from the corridor's gloom. She wore the white of a lab tech or scientist. The woman stood with her legs braced apart and her arms crossed. Her foreboding expression promised pain and retribution.

From behind her, Canmore said, 'This has nothing to do with you. It's compound business.'

Priya's soft-spoken saviour spun on the reverend, brows raised. Priya remained curled in a ball but lifted her gaze to watch how this would play out. 'What's this poor child done?'

Ouch. No one had called her a child in a long while. She didn't have the leisure to smart at the diminutive term, however, as Canmore took a couple of steps so that he stood nose to nose with the woman. 'This is not your place.'

Priya flinched from his venom, but the female stood her ground. 'If you want my help, it is.'

The two faced off, glaring at one another. His eyes gave away his submission before he spoke. Priya breathed a silent sigh of relief. Canmore stepped away until he backed up against the door frame, where he stopped and waited, surveying the scene.

In one swift glance, the woman took in the situation. She cast an accusing glance to Leopold. 'How could you even contemplate this? You're no better than them.' Then she crouched by Priya and offered a hand to help her to her feet. 'I'm sorry. This should never have happened.'

As Priya dusted herself off, she ventured, 'Who are you?' Which, of course, encompassed so many other questions such as, *Why are you so important? What do you want? Why did you help?*

The lady smiled. 'My name is Ellie. Eloise Martins. And you?'

'Priya. Priya Shaw.'

The two studied one another. Ellie spoke first, 'Where do you come from, Ms Shaw?'

Priya took a chance, 'I—I found a vial … the

missing vial.' Her words finished in a rush.

Ellie's whole posture changed. Her voice faltered and cracked. She cleared her throat. Tried again. 'How do you know about the vial?'

2

E117

On numb feet, still not wholly believing she'd avoided another rape, Priya followed Ellie down a bare corridor and into what appeared to be her private rooms. Despite the woman saving her, she remained suspicious of her, and of her motives. Why had she reacted so strongly when Priya had blurted out about the vial? Just who was Eloise Martins? Could she be related to Terror's second in command? Priya shook her head. It didn't bear thinking about. She had enough on her plate. Like cutting herself up for her stupidity in yammering about the antidote for all to hear and take advantage of.

Ellie didn't mention anything of import, though. At least, not yet. Priya adopted her watch-and-wait stance, which seemed the best way to proceed for the moment. Instead, the scientist settled her in a comfy chair and made a pot of fresh coffee. *Martins ... John Martins made Kaleb and me coffee too. Coincidence? Where do these people keep finding the good stuff?* Her misgivings ratcheted up a few notches.

Grateful, she took the steaming mug and wrapped both palms around it. Eloise fixed herself a drink too and took the seat perpendicular to Priya's. The proximity left her uncomfortable, but she refrained from flinching away or fidgeting. She wanted to put the other woman at her ease and hear whatever she might let slip or decide to divulge.

Ellie sat and stared off into space, or deeply inward, lost in thought. It took her five minutes to speak, and when she did, it was to ask a question. 'Are they looking for me too?'

Her sharp gaze pierced Priya, who'd startled at the unexpected shift from near-trance to interrogative. Wide-eyed, she shook her head. 'No. I didn't even know about the vial until Kaleb. And I still don't know who you are.'

Ellie relaxed. 'And you don't know much about anything still.'

Priya took that as a statement rather than another question. The woman's cool assumption annoyed her for some reason. 'The vial holds a cure. I don't need to understand much more to appreciate what it could mean.'

Inexplicably, Ellie smiled and leant forward. 'I was taking the antidote to zone 1 when the helipod crashed. Leo pulled me from the wreckage and brought me here. By the time I regained consciousness, I learnt that the people who wanted me out of the way believed I'd perished. My monitor got damaged in the accident and transmitted failed vital signs. Unfortunately, no one in this group knew of the vial, and it got lost.' She gazed at Priya. 'Where did you find it?'

Priya saw no point in lying. 'Zone nine. … In a shit-house.' After a couple of seconds of silence, weighing her options, she told Ellie the rest of her tale, omitting nothing, not even the awful beginnings.

The woman gave nothing away, all emotion and response hidden behind a mask of detached stoicism. When Priya had finished her sorry tale, Ellie surprised her further by sharing her own story, explaining about the plot hatched by Terrence and her husband. So, Priya's assumption had proven correct: The two Martins were related. By marriage. *Did I do the right thing in trusting her?*

Of course, you idiot, they wanted her dead, so she must be different. Kinder.

She squashed the arguing voices in her head and tried to pay attention. Ellie moved on to her time with the rebels, 'They took me in. Cared for me. It could have been my white garb, I don't know, and frankly, I no longer care. It turned out we could help one another. I've been working on developing a cure here with little success.' She stared at Priya. 'You bringing the vial will make all the difference.'

Priya squirmed. While she'd admitted to possessing the tiny container, she hadn't yet let on what she'd done with it. Embarrassment flooded her face with crimson heat. Perhaps she could come up with a way of avoiding that particular little nugget. And thank the heavens they hadn't raped her with that still stuck inside her.

Ellie finished her brew. 'Did you see the holding area for the infected?'

'No.'

'Would you like to?'

'I'm not sure *like* is the word I'd use, but … sure.'

The two women rose to their feet. Ellie talked while they walked, 'We gave them shelter, or as much as we could, in the hope we'd have a chance to cure them.' She shrugged. 'With the lack of space, we couldn't segregate them from one another. And, well, some fatalities were inevitable.'

Priya blanched, understanding the violence left unsaid. Experience had shown her all too well how far people fell once the virus had them. The smell reached her first. Then the cacophony —moans and groans, yells and screams, and more animalistic noises such as growls and snarls. The hairs on her neck prickled. Worst of all, though, was the sight. Not a single thing so far could have prepared her for the appalling spectacle that waited just around the corner.

She stumbled to a halt, staring aghast at the crowded cell. So many infected packed the old warehouse that it appeared no more than a few feet square. Priya glared at Ellie. 'How could you keep them like ... like ...'

Ellie rested a hand on Priya's elbow and spoke in soft tones, 'Like animals? You must see that's what they are. What they've become.' She indicated a man standing near the front bars, who appeared to be in the early stages. 'Or what they will become.' When she felt she'd made her point, she turned her hard gaze upon Priya. 'Where do you have the vial?'

'It's safe. I can get it.'

With her arms crossed and a stern expression, she pushed, 'We need it. You must see that.'

Priya did. How could she not? 'I—I need to use the bathroom.' On those words, she bolted. She had to get out of there. Even more urgently, she needed to remove the vial from where she'd secreted it.

Thankfully, nobody followed or tried to interfere. Not knowing where else to flee to, Priya dashed back to Ellie's quarters and found the bathroom. Locked in, she undressed hurriedly, dropped into a squat, and reached trembling fingers inside herself.

For a horrifying second, she couldn't find it. Could feel nothing but slippery disgust. Then her fingers brushed a hard lump. After a couple of failed fumbles, she managed to snag the thing and ease it out. Pulse racing, she dashed to the small sink and pressed down the plunger to block the plug hole. It would do no good losing the bloody thing after everything she and Kaleb had gone through.

On autopilot, she held her hands in front of the sensor. Of course, the tap stayed off. No water flowed. *No power, idiot.* With a tut of frustration, Priya scanned the small room. A bucket stood just beneath the sink pedestal, and fresh water glistened in its depths, cool and inviting.

Hurrying now, aware of how much time had sprinted by already, she dropped the vial into the sealed sink and grabbed the bucket. Hands trembling, she sloshed some but managed to pour enough water into the basin to do the job. A lovely new bottle of liquid cleanser stood on the shelf. And there she'd been, making do with crappy rough bar soap made from foraged herbs all this time. The rebels ... or Ellie, must have connections in high places. Otherwise, how would they know where to find this stuff?

While her thoughts meandered, her hands scrubbed, and she soon had the little container acceptably clean. Relieved, she wiped it dry on the tattered towel hanging from the rail—huh, not everything was new and pretty here, then. All done, she dashed from the bathroom, intending to take the antidote straight to Ellie.

Back in the main quarters, she stopped short, jaw hanging open. Mrs Martins sat in one of the easy chairs, seemingly waiting for her. Priya shook her head. No way could she have known. No, it was a lucky guess was all. Ellie's next words soothed Priya a little, 'Ah, good. I wondered if you were all right.'

Of course. Silly me. Jumping at shadows and phantoms. Gotta pull myself together. Her hands shook when she held out the precious container. Ellie seemed almost reluctant to take hold of it. After about three seconds, she closed her fingers around it, securely but gently. Then she gazed at Priya. 'This is the antidote?'

Priya nodded. 'Well, I only know what Kaleb told me.' She shrugged and then dropped into a chair, suddenly exhausted. But then, it *had* been a bit of a day.

Ellie chewed her bottom lip, thinking. Priya let the silence roll on, welcoming the chance to slow down for a moment. A few minutes passed, then Eloise spoke, 'We need to take this to Canmore.'

'What? No. He tried to have me raped.'

The scientist smiled and shook her head. 'Men can be such lumps sometimes. He saw an opportunity and pursued it without thinking about the ramifications.' She glanced at Priya. 'He's not a bad man, not really.'

Priya came to a decision. Despite the orders he'd given, he had seemed saddened at the necessity. 'Okay. Yes. Let's do it.'

Ellie eased back in her chair, relaxing. Even before Priya spoke, the other woman tensed right back up, nearly—but not quite—stopping her from saying what she'd intended. 'I didn't come here alone.'

Ellie said, 'I know.'

Priya pushed, 'Yes, but do you know who?'

Ellie waited.

Priya took a deep breath. 'Your husband. John Martins.'

3

E118

Ellie stormed into John's cell, gun in hand, intending to shoot him. Calm, he looked up from where he lay on his cot. A sardonic grin lit his face at her explosive entrance. 'You found me, I see.'

'I knew you were here already. I tried to calm down first. But, well ...' She waved the weapon vaguely from side to side.

'Tut. Tut.' Martins shook his head slowly from left to right and back again, mocking her. 'This is so unlike you, my dear.' He spoke in a lazy drawl. 'So out of character.'

She returned a bitter smile. 'Oh, you have no

idea.'

Ellie wanted to kill him, but too many witnesses lingered in the vicinity. Her traitorous husband was far too clever and had ensured, already, that the rebels knew his identity and what he could do for the cause. If she murdered him now, a whole planet-load of hurt would fall down on her head.

John patted the thin mattress by his leg. 'Why don't you come and listen to me?'

She crossed her arms. 'I can hear you plenty from here, thank you.'

Stubborn as ever, he repeated the gesture. Ellie sighed. 'The last time I listened to you, you betrayed me. Explain why I shouldn't just shoot you now.'

'I'm useful.' He stared at her. 'Let's cut the crap. I can help, and you know it. … Canmore knows it.'

Against her better judgement, Ellie lowered the weapon and dropped onto the end of the cot, agreeing to hear him out. 'What happened to you?' She circled a finger around her face to indicate the direction of her question.

John smiled, but his eyes grew pained. 'Karma. What goes around …' He shook his head again, staring at the pitted, damp floor. 'I betrayed you. My bit on the side betrayed me. So, there you have it.' In the pause, he raised tortured eyes to her. 'I'm sorry.'

Ellie didn't believe him. The man could fool even the best lie detector, and he had no clue what genuine remorse felt like. Undoubtedly, Sasha had turned on him—that seemed true to the girl's character. But no way had John turned the corner onto Good Street.

Tired, she rose to her feet and leant against the wall by the exit, arms crossed once more. 'What are you offering?'

He stared at her, mute.

'In return for your life, what can you do that we can't do for ourselves as is?'

'Ellie, I *am* so sorry. Truly. I'd tell you I repent all my sins and all that mush, but you'd only mock.' He shrugged. 'I'll have to show you instead.'

She laughed, short and harsh. 'Right, actions speaking louder than words and all that rot.'

'Sweetheart, please.'

'What did you expect, John? I'm not your little dumb, blonde bimbo.'

Martins rubbed his chin. 'And with your fiery red hair, I should've known better.' A small smile stretched the corners of his lips.

In spite of herself, she chuckled, warming to him. He always had known how to get around her. 'I'll forgive you if you'll help us. Tit for tat.'

John eased to his feet but kept his distance from her. 'That's not true forgiveness. It doesn't work like that.'

'It does now. In the world you created. You and your buddy.'

John paled. 'He's dead. Denis.'

Ellie straightened, leaving the support of the wall. 'Yes.'

His eyes went wide. 'You knew? How?'

Ellie gave nothing away but a cynical grin. Then, stiffening her spine and hardening her heart, she pushed, 'What can you give us?'

A significant pause ensued, and Ellie thought John would refuse to negotiate with her any further, but then he spoke, 'The capital. I can give you the capital.'

4

E119

The clatter and chatter of communal lunch in the dining hall wrapped around Ellie's isolation and invaded her space. Deliberately, she'd chosen the smallest table she could; one that seated just two people. Folks had taken the hint and stayed away. Not that many socialised with her at any rate. Her position offered a natural buffer. That and her dedicated aloofness. She'd had enough of relationships and friends, who would only betray you in the end.

The bland mush on her plate almost finished, she shoved it around with her fork, knowing she should eat but having little appetite. The paltry fare didn't help: soggy cauliflower cheese with synthetic protein mixed into the thin sauce. Amidst the noise of a busy room, footsteps approached. Cautious, she looked up.

The bastard who'd lied to her, used her position against her, and then fucked her young protege, stood just out of arm's reach, waiting for an invitation. Ellie almost didn't extend one. Wanted to leave him standing uselessly in no-man's land. But people had started to notice. The last thing she wanted at this juncture was the wrong kind of attention.

Annoyed, resentful, she nodded. John strode up to the table. The chair scraped across the floor when he pulled it out. The high-pitched squeal made her cringe, and her shoulders hunched up to her ears. She glared at him, sure he'd done that on purpose.

In silence, he sat and watched her. Or, rather, an old man did. One in his sunset years, with darkness threatening from every angle. Guilt wracked her. No matter what he'd done, he didn't deserve that. Her old feelings of love and caring rose, and she tried to push them down. Such affection would only get in the way. But still, she couldn't budge the guilt. Ridiculous, really, as she'd done nothing herself to earn it. Other people had put him in his current position. Including himself, of course.

When he spoke, even his voice sounded old. 'You're planning to invade soon.'

Statement. Not a question. Who had blabbed? She shrugged. Played nonchalant. 'Of course.'

'Take me with you.'

Carefully, Ellie settled her fork on her plate and stared at him, aghast. 'What makes you think I'd take such a risk? The last place I want you is anywhere near the seat of power.'

He held up his hands, palms out, all affable and innocent. 'I only want to help.'

She didn't buy it. His eyes moved too much, and he looked down and to the left. Classic signs that he had something to hide. How had she never realised what a fool he could be before now?

And, of course, he didn't know what she knew.

Ellie came to a decision, startling in its simplicity. John would never see it until it was too late. She smiled. 'Take it to Canmore. The decision lays with him.'

John studied her. 'I thought you held all the power around here.'

Ellie shook her head. 'You never did understand about sharing, did you? Most relationships are a two-way thing, you know.'

On those words, she stood, ending the conversation. John sat and watched her. She saw the calculation behind his eyes. For now, she'd thrown him, but it wouldn't last for long. Ellie had no doubts at all that he planned, somehow, to take the power back for himself. He would bear some watching.

5

E120

True to her word, Ellie had gained John access to an early morning planning and strategy meeting. He and Leopold faced one another across the vast table. A holomap hung in the middle of the space, semi-transparent and going some way to hiding both the rebel leader's face and John's. Which, right then, worked in Martins' favour.

While Ellie stood to the left of Canmore, looking unhappy, John took over the narrative.

He kept it short and salient, listing verbal bullet points, and telling Leopold of the evil women who had stolen the power, having killed the president and maimed himself. The two evil creatures who had turned out not only to be as bad as Terrence had been but so much worse again. To emphasise his closing words, he held his arms wide, palms outward, and planted an outraged expression on his face. 'They lied to everyone and tried to kill me.'

Much to John's chagrin, Canmore stood and stared across the space to Ellie, who met and held his gaze. Eventually, he nodded. 'We'll attack today.'

John worked hard to hold in his grin, but when Ellie's outburst came at the leader's next words, he failed miserably.

'Eloise, you should stay here.' Then he nodded to the girl by Ellie's side, Priya. The foolish girl who had helped bring him here. 'You too.'

While Ellie objected, Priya took it on the chin and didn't so much as murmur in protest. She and his wife did glance at one another, though. All this silent communication left him on the outside, and he didn't like that. Not one bit.

Before Ellie could raise more objections, Leopold addressed her, 'It's far more dangerous than we'd believed. With Terror out of the way, it should have proven much easier, especially as Mr Martins has Major Adams on side.' He paused and rubbed his chin, still—bravely, in John's mind—holding Eloise's gaze. 'From what we've just heard, I have to rethink the whole plan. We now have not one despot holding the reins but two. We can't risk you. Not now. Not when we're so close.'

That caught John's attention. What did the man mean by that? What did they have up their sleeves that John didn't know about? Again, he felt left out and annoyed. Everyone kept discounting him. His value. He would show them all.

'I can take care of Sasha Novikov.' He glanced around the assembly. 'She and I have history.'

Leopold nodded, apparently having taken it as read that John would accompany the rebel forces.

Ellie hadn't. 'What? No. We should keep him as far away from zone one as possible.'

The little bitch. Yesterday, she'd let him believe she was on his side. That she would support him in joining the invading troops. And now she stood there working against him. With his mounting temper firmly suppressed, he shook his head.

John took care to look at no one but Canmore. He was the man Martins had to convince. He saw, now, that Eloise didn't pack the punching power he'd assumed. 'I know the women. I know the sector. And Major Adams will work with me.'

To his surprise—and then chagrin—Priya spoke up, 'We know you, Mr Martins. Ellie and I.' She flicked her hard stare to Leopold. 'And if he's going to zone one, he needs watching.'

Canmore stood quietly, thinking about it. Under his breath, John swore. Two little bitches together. It seemed he now had four women who he needed to teach lessons to. Despite his annoyance, his grin widened but left his eyes cold. The prospect of having the four females subjugated beneath him was a pleasant one. The leader spoke again, catapulting John from his mixed thoughts and back into the room.

'Okay, we all go.' He glanced from one to the other. 'John, you join the ranks. Svenson will provide you with arms.'

Martins nodded. And then bristled when he realised they all expected him to go with the rebel troop right then and there. Flushed and furious, he turned on his heel.

Behind him, Leopold outlined the rest of his decision, 'Ellie, you and Priya will stay with me.'

John slowed his pace so that he could linger as long as possible, but no one else spoke until the door had whooshed shut behind his stiff spine.

He had no choice but to go through the motions and follow Svenson to the armoury, where he received a pulse repeater gun and spare charge packs. 'No armour?'

The guy shrugged, not giving a fuck. 'We need what we have for the men.'

Of which John wasn't, evidently. The bastards would learn better by the end of the day.

From him leaving the meeting and going to

get outfitted, things moved quickly. When Svenson led John to the flight bay, orderly lines of troops stretched from end to end in the cavernous area, and Canmore stood giving final commands and instructions. When he spotted John, he allocated him to C section, along with Svenson, who he now realised would act as his minder.

Five bays across, Eloise and Priya ran to a waiting helipod, along with Leopold and half-a-dozen hand-picked rebel troops. Martins grinned. It wouldn't prove challenging to elude Svenson and the others once they landed and the fighting began.

For it would begin. Major Adams knew they were coming. John had made sure of it.

CHAPTER TEN

1

E119

Zone 1.

The infamous chamber 3.

Stark white walls, floor, and ceiling.

Crimson blood splattered in gory contrast to the sterile cell.

Kaleb fought hard. Beads of sweat blossomed on his torso, ran down his back, and soaked his forehead, stinging his pinned-open eyes. Desperate to blink, he bit down on his tongue, repressing his need to scream. The forceps held his lids firm, preventing him from bringing the much-needed relief to his moisture-less eyes. An old method of torture but effective.

Meanwhile, the impassive lights blazed down upon him, blinding in their awful brilliance. For two days, they had burned and burned and burned. Not even for a second did they dim or flicker, offering no relief whatsoever.

His head pounded, and his tongue and throat had grown thick and furry with dehydration. What he'd give for just a drop of water. Sick, he couldn't stop himself from glancing to the cold glass sitting mere inches out of arm's reach. Condensation misted and formed rivulets, which ran seductively down the tumbler. Kaleb licked his lips, and his dry tongue rasped over his rough and equally parched lips.

In vain, he shook his head, trying to dislodge the holo-glasses strapped tightly around his skull. They didn't budge. The band dug into his scalp, bringing its own form of torture. Their lenses delivered a constant stream of input on a repeat loop, assaulting his sleep-deprived and punished brain.

Even when he cast desperate glances to the

out-of-reach water, the images burned themselves on his retinas, overlaying the physical, and audio blared into his eardrums. On and on and on.

And on.

And still, Kaleb fought. Resisted. Tried everything he could to avoid succumbing. Had they not interspersed the monotony with beatings, they might well have succeeded. That extra cruelty became their downfall.

Hour after hour, the brutal assaults came. But at least they brought respite, even if only briefly, from the audio-visuals of the holo-glasses. Each time, a different soldier came to him. Every time, he punched the prisoner unconscious, so he hung limply from the wrist chains suspended from the ceiling.

Electric shocks would bring him around once more, only to face connectors zapping his nipples, his buttocks, and his bollocks. At those times, he did scream. Unabashedly. He yelled and yelled and yelled.

His attacker would wait until he passed out again, and when he roused, the man would start in with the knives. Cuts of varying ages and depths crisscrossed his back, his abdomen, his arms, thighs, and the soles of his feet.

By far the worst, however, were the pins. Such tiny, inconsequential things. But, oh, the pain. The horror of it. Kaleb had always had a thing about eyes. Did the major know that? Or was this simply standard? And with the forceps forcing his eyes wide open, he could only hang there and watch the needle approach, glinting beneath the fierce interrogation beams.

For that part, a clamp would descend and lock in a vice around his skull, holding him still and preventing him from shaking his head side to side to avoid the needle.

Finished, the soldier would leave. That's when Major Adams made his appearance. They shouldn't be so predictable.

This time, the major studied him with a look of satisfaction, failing to see his lack of full success. Despite what they had shown him, and what he now believed because of that exposure, something within him continued to resist. To not entirely fall over the edge.

Before they'd taken him, he never would

have felt grateful for the virus. He did now. Somehow, it seemed to help him withstand the physical blows and cuts and shocks. Little by little, he came to believe that it might have given him super strength, or stamina, or something.

Something the nanobots had done to him, something in the changes they had wrought in his personality and character, limited the effectiveness of the brainwashing. Or so he thought. And could he trust his perceptions after all that had been done to him?

Adams slipped a pistol from his waist holster and levelled the barrel at Kaleb. Dumbfounded and befuddled, he swung at the end of the chains, arms screaming in protest, and gaped. Why would they put him through all this just to shoot him now?

Time slowed. Every minor movement became magnified. Kaleb watched the major's finger first twitch and then flex. Swore he even saw the flash. Could see the bullet headed for him. Heard the report.

He blinked. If he'd heard the report, he was still alive. Through blurred vision, he scanned his torso. No blood. No extra pain, except for a feeling of having just received another punch to the gut. No new absence of pain. Stunned, he raised his strained gaze to the major, who nodded and re-holstered his weapon.

'Just as I thought.'

Kaleb watched him.

At the door, Adams turned to face him. 'The bullets won't pierce your skin. I'd heard of that particular side-effect. Interesting that the sharp knives will. Mmm, something for us to look at. It's a bonus for you that you have the virus.' Then he turned and left.

2

E120

Adams sauntered into Kaleb's cell, where—mercifully—he now sat on a narrow cot, head in his hands. No chains or torture instruments lay anywhere in sight. They'd even fed and watered him. At the intrusion, he raised his eyes and stared at the major.

The man stood there, swinging the keys to Kaleb's freedom. In the distance, booms sounded, indicating explosions and fighting. The rebels had come. Adams had said they would. Dimly, Kaleb wondered how the man had known of the attack so far ahead of time. Who did he have on the other side? Were there more like Kaleb, who had been brainwashed and sent out as spies? Or was it just somebody happy to play for both teams?

Silent, Kaleb continued to sit and stare at the prematurely grey-haired man. He would make him speak first. Would force him to tell Kaleb what he wanted and why he'd had him tortured and brainwashed. For he did recognise what had happened. Somewhere, in the depths of his damaged mind, he understood, even if he no longer had perfect recall of the during or the before. What mattered now was now.

At length, Adams stilled his hand and the jangling keys and took in a deep breath. Here it came. 'As I'm sure you can hear, the rebels are here.' He paused.

Kaleb nodded.

'We'll let them win their little game. And then we push for elections. It's about time we aligned ourselves with the rest of the democratic system, don't you think?' He studied Kaleb.

Evidently, he expected some sort of response from his prisoner. Again, Kaleb nodded.

Satisfied, the major grunted then took another breath. 'You'll put yourself forward as one of the presidential candidates.'

Ah, so that was his game. That was why he'd wanted Kaleb. But why him? Why not just any special? Priya. Somehow, he had found out about Priya and the vial and Kaleb's changed priorities and loyalties. Realisation sank in: whoever had forewarned Adams of the rebel attack had also given him information on the vial and Kaleb's travelling companion, as well as their where-abouts. And then he had it: Martins. Had to be. No one else could have known so much. They'd been fools to trust the man.

The only way the major could have known where to apprehend Kaleb was via John Martins. He'd given them away, but why? Unhappy, Kaleb once again met Adams' gaze. Mute, he chose to imply consent with another nod. Best to sit quietly and let the major talk.

Adams eased down onto the end of the cot, and Kaleb twisted so that he could still observe his captor. 'Of course, you will work for me. For the good of the planet. Together, we can ring the changes needed.'

Another nod from Kaleb, encouraging without committing.

'Good. They all think they are owed something. That they have a right to hold power. Yet every single one of them needs me. Or a man in my position. Without the army, and a major to run it, they have nothing. Are nothing.'

A grunt of acknowledgment seemed in order, so Kaleb offered one.

The major nodded. 'They all want to use me. Think they can control me.' He gave a short bark of a laugh. 'But what are they without me?' Adams pierced Kaleb with a hard stare. 'Without us. As a team, we can take it all. You and me. I have the army. You have the trust of the troops and the rebels.'

For the first time during that whole interview,

Kaleb spoke up, 'Yes, sir.'

This time, a tacit agreement. But still, he'd given nothing away. Made no true commitment. Adams believed he had Kaleb under his control. And while Kaleb had changed his mind on a lot of things this last couple of days after his torture, he didn't necessarily want to live as someone else's puppet, not any more. He'd had enough of that ever since the academy had taken him.

Regardless, he would do the major's bidding. But as to which way he would go, even Kaleb would have to wait and see.

CHAPTER ELEVEN

1

E120

The zone-1 soldiers attacked as soon as the rebel helipods landed. The army executed the ambush perfectly. But, of course, Major Adams had known they were coming. John Martins had made sure of that.

In the initial confusion of the fighting, Martins slipped away, leaving the transport and the troops behind. Twice, bullets missed him by mere inches. Then a third one grazed his cheek, drawing a line of blood that burned.

Hand up to his face, John ducked and ran,

seeking cover wherever he could. His heart hammered. When he'd fought for inclusion on this raid, he hadn't allowed for getting caught in the ambush himself. His obsession with killing the women had buried such common sense.

Another bullet pinged off the stack of metal crates behind which he hid. Then the white printing on the cases impressed itself upon him: Munitions. If a stray shot pierced an outer shell, the whole pile would explode, sending deadly shrapnel in all directions. He had to move.

While he alternated running and ducking for cover, John calculated where best to search for Sasha. She would die first, and then he would kill the other bitch. They would rue the day they had crossed him. A malice-filled grin lit his features. Little Shura shouldn't have been so soft. By keeping him alive, she'd ensured an early and brutal demisc for herself and her twisted lover.

He would rape her first, then kill her slowly. With all her lies and manipulations, she'd earned it. John shook his head—it would hurt Sasha far more if she had to witness his treatment of Giles before meeting her own fate. In total defiance of his early and engineered ageing, an erection strained at his zip, eager for release.

Where would the two women have gone upon the invasion beginning? He couldn't imagine that either one would have remained in such a prominent place as the presidential offices or private suites. What place offered the most security—familiarity—to the two bitches?

The lab.

Their lives and work had centred around one scientific instalment or another for years.

Martins headed there.

When he'd fled the capital, he hadn't had time to check his little hiding place. He would have to take care of that later. After he'd taken care of Sasha and Giles. However, he *had* managed to keep his executive general-access pass, which would grant him entry to the lab complex.

As his legs pumped, his brain ran. A plan formed quickly. Oh God, it would be so easy. Canmore also had a general-access pass, courtesy of Martins himself. Which meant that John wouldn't be giving away the killer's identity by using his pass to corner the two women. With his seeming generosity, he had the other man nicely positioned to take the fall.

Perfect.

The corridor leading to the labs was, expectedly, deserted. Its fluorescents shone as brightly as ever and brought the stark white walls, floor, and ceiling to an almost blinding gleam. Up ahead, though, things looked quite different.

The glass set in the tops of the double doors showed up as black squares. No illumination came from within. To all intents and purposes, the place appeared empty. Martins didn't buy it.

Without pause or hesitation, he swiped his card and pushed through the doors on the opening beep. With purpose, he strode into the darkness. The motion-activated sensors picked up his presence, and the overheads flickered to bright brilliance, exposing the empty benches around him. No activity had taken place in here in a while.

John cursed.

Perhaps he *had* misjudged.

Maybe they weren't here.

He shook his head.

No. He couldn't be that wrong. Determined, he straightened his spine, dropped his shoulders, and got busy searching the massive complex. Fifteen sweaty minutes later, he returned to the central lab and stared around, frustrated.

The door to the dusty storage cupboard pulled at him. That had been one of the first rooms he'd glanced into. A cursory perusal had shown him boxes stacked haphazardly—nothing of interest in there—and he'd dismissed it quickly and exited. Now, however …

What had he seen subconsciously? In his haste, what had he missed? Dismissed? Jaw set, he strode back to the small, plain door and shoved it open. The same bland, dusty, cluttered space met him as it had earlier. Only … not all of the stacked boxes held a random pattern. He felt sure of it. John switched on the dim room lights. How could anyone find anything in here?

Slowly, the room's true purpose revealed itself to his steady but penetrating gaze. The three rear cartons stood a few inches away from the wall and had been arranged more neatly than those in the rest of the tight space.

Martins edged up to them, one careful step at a time. A couple of feet away, he stopped. The shadows cast by the inadequate bulb hid a patch of wall worn smooth and shiny from use, barely visible behind the end row of boxes.

Sweat broke out on his brow. Anticipation had his heart thump and thud at speed. His erection throbbed and hardened, making him most uncomfortable. Just like the abhorrent raptors, he knew precisely where he would find his prey.

John reached out his arm and pressed the flat of his palm over the shiny patch. Within the wall, something clicked and released. The fake partition slid to the left, concealed by the stacks. Now he understood why they had been placed so far away from the wall, eating up much-needed space. For a second, he stood staring at the dark passage the concealed entrance had revealed, and then he strode into the blackness.

This time, no sensors reacted. No lights blazed. The impenetrable dark persisted. John backtracked. Behind him, the fake wall slid shut, blocking the meagre light from the box room. His fingers fumbled in the darkness, searching for a switch. After a couple of seconds, they found what they wanted. He flipped the button, and subdued overhead beams shone down, much like the emergency lighting throughout the zone 1 presidential complex. He gasped. Had he taken another couple of steps in the impenetrable darkness, he would have tumbled down many flights of unforgiving concrete stairs. With the lights to guide him, he descended.

Every step forward brought more excitement. First, he would incapacitate Giles. Next, he would corner Sasha and use her body one last time. Only this time, it wouldn't be her choice, and she wouldn't glean any benefit. This one was all for him. When he'd finished with her, he would make her watch while he mutilated Giles—a fitting end for such a warped soul.

At the next barrier, he paused and listened. No sounds came from behind the closed door. Martins scanned the adjoining walls. No security measures showed. No card readers, no fingerprint scanners, no nothing. He rubbed damp palms along his thighs and stepped forward. The door slid open soundlessly on well-greased tracks.

Within, lights blazed. Another, better equipped, lab space met his astonished eyes. How the hell had Ms Stephenson kept this so quiet? The scheming little bitches. Who would have known? Was this where they'd developed their little side viruses? The special ones for him and the president? Oh, such sweet, ironic, justice. To take them here. In their sanctuary. And being so secret, no one would find them down here.

At the far end of the room, pressed against a gleaming counter, stood Giles. Her taut fingers dug into the solid bench surface in vain. As if she could hide from him now. Wide-eyed with horror, she watched him advance.

John grabbed her by the throat. 'Where is she?'

Inexplicably, Giles smiled.

The dazzling lights glinted off her prominent cheekbones. Her square jaw mocked him. He tightened his grip and shoved her harder against the unforgiving workbench. A laugh bubbled up from her constricted throat. She tried to speak, but his punishing grip prevented her from getting her words out. Martins let go and grabbed a fist-ful of hair instead, yanking her head back cruelly.

Giles held his gaze, her eyes taunting. 'I put her in the cells. By all means …' She spread her arms wide. '… Go and find her.'

Disgusted, John spat in her upturned face. Well, *his*—not *her*—not really. Giles had never finished his sex change. Intending to cause pain, Martins reached between her legs with his free hand and grabbed for the expected male genitals, his fingers flexing, ready to squeeze.

The small, flat mound of a female's anatomy met his questing digits instead. The bitch had gone and done it for herself after killing Terrence. Bloody hell. In his pants, his erection throbbed. Frustration flared into hot, red rage.

With Sasha safe in the cells, he would never reach her undetected. People would know where he'd been. What he'd done. Fuck it. He would have to make do with Giles. For now.

Still gripping her hair relentlessly, he moved his free hand up to her breasts and pinched, hard. Giles squealed. Just like a fucking girl. John leered at her. 'You want to be a woman so much.

I'll show you what it's really like.'

He ripped her zip down and bent her further back over the bench, straining her spine. Her breasts thrust out toward him. She wore no bra. Well, more fool her. John lunged, clamping his teeth around one of her nipples, biting down and drawing blood along with desperate screams from his victim. If he couldn't have Sasha, he would have her.

Blind rage descended.

Afterward, staring down at Giles' mutilated, well-used body, he felt mildly disgusted at his animal brutality. But she'd asked for it. She'd done this to herself. In one final fit of temper, he kicked his booted foot into her abdomen. She didn't respond, just lay crumpled on the cold, unforgiving floor. The bruises ringing her throat stood out in grotesque lividity.

John spat on her corpse and strode to the door. Then he retraced his steps up the stairs, down the concealed passage, and out into the box room, turning off lights as he went. With any luck, no one would find her body for a while. On his way out of the fake partition, his shoulder nudged the top two boxes of the third stack, and he stumbled. Annoyed, and drained after his recent exertions, he rubbed the sting away and exited that room too. In his distraction, he forgot to reset the boxes. Neither did he turn out the light.

With his thoughts set on reaching his apartments, and his hiding place undetected, he moved stealthily through the complex. At each corner, he stopped and listened. His knowledge of the camera placements came in handy, and he took pains to avoid positions that would give away his movements to anyone looking.

Instead of just minutes, it took John a little over a quarter of an hour to reach his suite. With each step along open corridor that he took, his heart settled back into its normal rhythm, only to accelerate alarmingly each time he approached a corner and peered around it cautiously. At any moment, he expected a heavy hand to fall upon his shoulder. Kept imagining a hard voice demanding to know his business.

The difficulty he encountered en route to his apartments reiterated how much more dangerous it would have proven had he risked seeking Sasha in the cells. Even with the rebel invasion, those levels would retain an armed guard—all the more vigilant because of the fighting.

At his door, his thumping heart missed a beat when the card swipe failed to open the entrance. Then he laughed at himself. He'd been away too long. Rueful, he shook his head and looked up at the overhead scanner. It beeped once, and the light turned green. His door slid open, revealing a dark and empty room beyond.

John stepped in. Disarray met his dismayed gaze. In his absence, someone had trashed his place. Had they found his hidden cubby? Suddenly frantic, he ignored the mess and dashed through to his study, which also boasted overturned furniture and smashed fittings.

Where blank wall should have deceived, much like the fake lab portal, a black hole glared at him, rimmed with tattered neostil. A great rage had impelled someone to work with determination to not only find his hiding place but to rip it open like this. It would have taken little for them to override the security mechanism once they'd found it.

Already despairing, nevertheless, he reached shaking fingers into the hole. As he'd expected, they found only grit and disappointment. Empty of his treasures, the compartment offered no clue as to the whereabouts of the drive or the folders filled with potential blackmail material.

Furious, John yelled and punched the wall. Pain lanced up through his wrist, and his knees buckled, sending him to the floor. There, he eased back to his feet on stiff legs and sucked at his middle knuckle. Already, it had swollen to twice its size and glowed a sullen red. Gingerly, he rubbed the joint, and then he cried out in agony, sure he'd broken the bloody thing.

His watering eyes found the useless hidey-hole, which mocked him and all his plans. Who had the files? And what about the drive? The missing credit chips didn't bother him anywhere nearly as much as the papers and data. Without those, he had no power. Without anything with which to bargain, he was finished.

2

E120

Martins crept from his suite and found a platoon of rebel troops. They seemed to be on the winning side, so—for the time being—John aligned himself with them. For his troubles, he received a bashing when thrown into hand-to-hand combat with an army special. All to the good—he could blame his other injuries from assaulting Giles on heroics aimed at helping the invaders.

To aid his cover, John stayed with the victorious rebels and assisted in the clean-up operations. While he felt confident that Gile's body wouldn't be found anytime soon, he also didn't want to take any chances. To that end, he kept his head down.

It took a couple of hours for the search for Professor Giles Stephenson to begin. Before Eloise and Leopold realised that the scientist hadn't simply gone into hiding. John stayed silent, even while the witch hunt raged. He'd known they would find her body eventually, but because of its location in the subterranean and unofficial lab, he'd assumed it might take a day or two.

Not so.

They discovered her within the hour. The lights in the storage room had led searchers in that direction, and a stack of disturbed crates had shown them the secret access panel. In silence, John cursed his stupidity and continued to play his part.

Because of where they found her body, the troops didn't come under suspicion. None of them had access to the main lab, let alone its deeper rooms. Until the search commenced, not one of them had high-level access anywhere.

The net closed in.

Currently, only two men in zone 1 had the necessary access pass: Martins and Canmore. John had made a mistake in killing Giles in the lab. Another in using his own access card. But he couldn't very well have dragged her through the complex to rape and murder her elsewhere, could he? Even though that would have thrown the web of suspicion wide open, it would have incurred far too much risk in the execution.

John believed that he still had Ellie under his thumb and that things were as they always used to be. Without the information stolen from his safe place, he had little else to go on. Any power he retained lay solely on Eloise's shoulders. Based upon that supposition, he blamed Canmore for the crime. Indirectly, of course. He said he'd seen the man headed that way while everyone else remained distracted, engaging in the fight for life and liberty.

With all the indignant outrage he could muster, Martins called for Leopold Canmore's arrest, reiterating that a man like him couldn't possibly hold any position of responsibility.

All the leading players stood in the room: Ellie, Leo, Priya, and John. The girl's companion, Kaleb, remained missing. And, of course, Sasha languished in one of the cells. Until, that is, John could get to her undetected. He'd come this far and didn't intend to leave any loose threads.

Once more, Ellie paced the room and murmured, 'Which one of you could commit such an atrocity?'

Martins and Canmore glared at one another in a mute battle of wills. Both men knew who'd done it. And each now relied on Eloise to make the right decision. No amount of protestations would prove their innocence. Only forensics could pin it on the guilty man. And that would take valuable time.

Priya spoke in timid tones, 'Canmore was going to have his men rape me, remember?' Her gaze pleaded with Ellie.

Leo objected, 'I had no choice. The survival of the human species was on the line. You must understand. Until we had the vial, all was lost.' He dropped to a knee and clutched one of Priya's hands. 'I never wanted to hurt you. Please.'

Priya pulled her hand away but not before a slight hesitation. Could the girl actually like the man? John hid a chuckle. After he'd given Eloise one more little nudge, the pair's blossoming friendship would end up shot to shreds.

Martins said, 'Come on now, dear. How

could you ever doubt me?'

Her head shot up, and she threw a burning glare his way, which seared his eyes. 'I trusted you once.'

He'd said the wrong thing.

Eloise called for guards. When three burly men dashed into the room, she gave her orders, 'Take this vile specimen of a human being to the cells. Keep him well away from Ms Novikov.'

She levelled a steady finger at John, who sneered at her. 'Don't be so bloody ridiculous, woman—'

His wife of so many years turned her back on him.

+++

Only after he'd shouted himself hoarse, demanding his release, did Ellie deign to visit him in his cell. Nonchalantly, she leaned against the wall near the exit, arms crossed, and watched him. Mixed malice and amusement contorted her features. What the hell did she have to feel happy about?

Revenge.

This was her taking her revenge. She didn't really think he'd killed the bitch Giles. Did she? Uncomfortable, not used to the shoe being on this foot, he sought refuge in righteous indignation. 'How dare you—'

'Oh, do shut up. It's about time you realised I'm not your little wifey anymore.'

John refused to give in. 'You can't keep me here with no proof.'

Ellie stood quietly, holding his gaze until he had to glance away. At this sign of weakness, she pounced. 'You do realise that I got exposed to the virus at the same time Ms. Novikov did?'

'So?'

'While she had access to a cure, I didn't.'

John didn't get it. 'Yet here you stand.' He stared into her eyes. 'You don't have the violet tint.'

She sauntered over to the narrow cot and perched on its end. Then she lowered her voice and spoke so quietly that John had to strain to hear her. 'The imprisoned infected at the rebel camp made for great guinea pigs. I managed to cure myself, using them.'

John sneered, 'So, little miss goody-two-shoes, why haven't you cured everyone yet?'

'I didn't have the means to replicate the small amount I'd made. Best to keep it under wraps, don't you think?'

Shocked, he could only stare. Her behaviour sounded so out of character. After a few seconds, he accused, 'They would have seen your eyes. When they rescued you. The rebels.'

Ellie chuckled. 'What with the severity of my injuries, and the healing drugs and nanos they gave me, that all lessened the effects of the virus. Nobody ever realised.'

'And you're telling me all this, why?'

Her voice dropped to a conspiratorial whisper, 'As part of my illness, I developed telepathy.'

Aghast, John gawped.

Ellie said, 'Because of all your lies and everyone's deceit, I quite liked that particular side-effect.'

His heart stalled, and his stomach dropped into his lap. How much could she see? His brain raced. 'And you stayed quiet about your en-hancement so you could use it against everyone around you. Without them being any the wiser.' Bitter, he shook his head. 'And I thought I had you fooled, but you simply gave me enough rope with which to hang myself.'

A grin stretched her lips and lifted her cheeks —even reached her eyes. 'And you fell for it. Silly little man.'

John snorted. 'You daft cow.'

Her mirth stuttered and stalled.

'If you wanted it kept on the down low, you shouldn't have confessed your abilities to me.'

Her confidence recovered. 'No one will take your word over mine. Not after everything you've done. You and Terrence. Not after what you did to Professor Stephenson. You messed up big time there.'

John crossed his arms and lifted his chin. 'No, but it will sow the seed of doubt. We both know that's enough.'

Ellie rose to her feet and strode to the door-way. There, she turned to face him. 'Enough for what, exactly? What crimes have I committed?

How can my ability possibly implicate me?'

John failed to come up with an adequate response. She had him there. Why *would* anyone care? As far as he knew, she hadn't used it for ill-gotten gains or nefarious purposes. Still, now he had one of her cards—but that was small fry to what else he could do if he could get out of here and to his computer terminal.

All of a sudden, Ellie stopped dead. Then she whirled on him, and disgust twisted her features into an animalistic snarl. 'Oh, you cruel bastard.'

His ex-wife stormed from the cell, leaving John wondering what she had just seen.

3

E121

Priya paced her small temporary apartment, wondering what she was still doing here. The rebels had invaded the capital and taken power. A good woman, Ellie, held the reins. So why did it all feel so wrong?

She had expected Ellie to hit the ground running and instigate vast and sweeping changes. Not so. Two full days now, and still everything remained the same.

No one had gone near the lab after finding Giles Stephenson's body. Which meant that no work on developing, let alone distributing, a cure had begun. Surely that was priority number one. Likewise, as far as Priya could tell, the army deployed around the planet on Terrence's orders to prevent the devastated populace from forming groups or communities remained active and on mission. Not a single one of them had been re-called.

Why?

The lack of change left Priya frustrated and concerned. What was Ellie's game? And why was Priya so bothered? That last question pulled her up short. Why *did* it upset her so much?

She'd done her job, hadn't she? Taken the vial safely to zone one and handed it over to people who could help. And therein lay her an-swer. She had thought she could hand over the bottle, and everything would get put right. Her life would be back on track, and she could get on with rebuilding her existence.

Now, however, she had her doubts. But what could she do? What should she do? Anything? Nothing? Leave it all alone. Let the people who knew what they were doing deal with it? Because the one thing that Priya knew within all this mess was that she didn't have the skillset. Nor the will. She wanted nothing to do with this.

And still, the doubts nagged at her. Gave her no peace. Refused to let her settle. After dinner— the best meal she'd eaten in a long while made from actual real spaghetti and meat and a tomato sauce, and they even had cheese—she went in search of the new leader.

As she walked down well-lit corridors, over polished and shining floors, she reflected upon other aspects that disturbed her. While her apartment was small, it was well appointed. The linen, freshly laundered and pressed, felt like too much luxury after her travails across Exxon 1. Everything in zone 1 smacked of luxury and privilege while the rest of the planet suffered deprivation and had to fight for its life.

What right did any of them have to sit here,

in the capital, enjoying every creature comfort, while the planet died a little more each day? And how could Ellie live with that? Why didn't she feel an urgent need to begin setting things right?

This dense cloud of doubt burdened Priya's every step forward. Eventually, she found Ellie in the president's offices. At the entrance, she set her jaw and straightened her spine, and then she knocked.

The camera above the door rotated and angled down to observe her. The portal didn't open immediately, indicating that the occupant didn't necessarily want to see her. When Priya discovered Ellie inside, instead of some minion, that hesitation unnerved her still more. Why wouldn't Ellie wish to see her?

More determined still, Priya strode into the office suite and up to the large desk, behind which her quarry sat. Uninvited, Priya dropped into one of the chairs opposite Ellie and studied the woman.

She appeared pale and drawn. Tired. Sudden guilt afflicted Priya. Of course all of this would feel overwhelming to a woman not prepared to handle it. Hadn't she just admitted that she herself didn't have the skills?

Priya changed tack. Quietly, she raised her first point, but less aggressively than she'd intended originally, 'The soldiers haven't come back in yet.'

Ellie watched her from across the desk, fingers steepled at her chin, and her expression inscrutable. The silence stretched.

Priya broke it, 'Since the virus hit, they've prevented any of us from forming protective groups or communities. Any gangs or clusters they find, they destroy.'

Again, she studied Ellie, who continued to watch her without speaking. This unexpected stubbornness helped Priya to get over her earlier flash of guilt. Once more, frustration took the lead. 'Why haven't you recalled them? Why aren't you stopping it?'

Ellie sat up straight and then dropped her head into her hands. With a pall of exhausted vulnerability, she spoke at last, 'And have every armed soldier back here? You expect they'll simply follow me? Any of us? We just killed hundreds of them, here in the capital.'

She pierced Priya with a hard stare. 'Did you know that Major Adams died yesterday?'

Oh. That changed things. Helped her understand Ellie's inaction. She shook her head and dropped her eyes. 'No.'

Ellie pressed the point, 'So, without a leader, they might have gone rogue.'

Priya mumbled, 'So that's why you've kept the portals closed too.'

Though she'd meant it as a statement rather than a question, Ellie nodded. Priya deflated. Then she tried for humour, 'I suppose the last thing you need right now is a helpful girl.'

Ellie raised her brows.

Priya grinned, abashed and embarrassed. 'I thought I was helping. But I don't have the skills or know-how for any of this.' She gazed at Ellie, once more a little in awe of the woman. 'I don't know how you do it.'

Ellie smiled and rose to her feet as if to say, *was that all?* Priya mirrored her and made ready to leave. Shamefaced, she said, 'Thanks for seeing me.'

Ellie nodded and walked with her to the inner door. Priya stepped into the outer office, and Ellie shut the door behind her. From within the inner sanctum, a phone rang. Priya paused, one foot raised an inch off the floor. Slowly, she lowered it to the plush carpet and listened.

Though muffled, she could hear Ellie's side of the conversation. 'Ah, Lady Morris. What a pleasant surprise.'

Indeed a surprise. Ruby Morris, the leader of Exxon 3, contacting Ellie. They must have heard of the coup. But how? Intrigued, Priya edged over to the secretary's desk and studied the phone. It appeared to be the exact same device she'd used in her days as an office worker.

For the first time since the catastrophe, her boring prior work allocation came in useful. Nervous, she watched the door to the inner office to ensure it remained shut fast. Then she pressed the party button on the phone, lifted the handset, and listened intently.

Morris seemed to be in mid-sentence, '… lot of good things about you.'

Ellie sounded cautious, 'Thank you.'

Morris probed, 'We were sorry to hear about yourself and Mr Martins. It's always difficult when a marriage fails.'

Ellie cleared her throat with a genteel cough. 'Quite.' After a short pause, she enquired, 'What can we do for you, Lady Morris?'

Give the other woman her due, she dove right in. 'We were relieved to hear of Mr Terrence's demise. As I said, your reputation precedes you. We'd hoped we could form an alliance. One that would help us all recover from this … unfortunate debacle.'

To Priya's utter horror, Ellie stated in a flat, hard voice, 'No. Thank you.' And then she hung up. Hurriedly, Priya pressed the disconnect button and fled the office in turmoil. What the hell had just happened? Why would Ellie refuse such a helpful union? Even if only temporary, it could assist every planet in the system in getting back on their feet.

Tears poured down her cheeks, stinging the few minor cuts she'd received in the initial flurry of fighting in the ambush. Shrapnel had ricocheted at her as she ran from the helipod, but her hands and arms had taken the brunt of it.

She and Eloise had fled the worst of it and made their way straight to the communications centre, where they'd worked at shutting down the radios so the soldiers couldn't talk to one another. Next, they'd sealed strategic areas of zone one, trapping many fighters to allow the rebels to reach them.

It had been a slaughter, but one that Priya had believed good and necessary. Not so now. What had she done? Most of all, she felt despair. She'd tried so hard, despite everything. Now, more than ever, she wished she'd died when Hank and his gang had raped her. What was the point? She was so useless and had nothing to offer. Why should she have to suffer like this? What had she ever done that was so bad?

A couple of hours later, Priya came back to herself, having traveled for miles around the zone, mourning her life. She found herself in a subterranean tunnel of some sort. Lost. Alone. Grieving. Without direction.

Listlessly, she trudged onward, with no goal in mind. A long straight stretch ended at a sharp turn. Priya walked around it. The landscape altered drastically. Instead of dim overhead utility lighting, bright fluorescents blazed. Either side, the drab concrete walls gave way to barred cells. The corridor stretched further than she could see. From a distance, she heard men laughing. Guards, perhaps?

Cautious now, she edged forward, glancing left and right into the rows of cells as she went. All of them proved empty. So why the men at the end of the line? Why would Ellie have stationed them down here?

As a child, curiosity had gotten her into endless trouble. As an adult, that spirit of enquiry hadn't lessened any. Nor had she learnt her lessons. She walked onward, drawn by she knew not what. About midway down the long hallway, she found an occupied cell. A black-clad army special lay curled in the foetal position on his narrow cot. His great mop of charcoal hair hung over his face, but she would have recognised him anywhere.

Kaleb.

Here in cells buried deeply beneath the capital. Her mind reeled. In a stage whisper, she hissed, 'Kaleb?' Her knuckles whitened when she gripped the bars hard enough to hurt.

At first, he didn't stir. She repeated her loud whisper. He shifted on the cot and raised his head to look at the bars. Evidently, he recognised her too, for he bolted upright and ran to her.

4

E122

Kaleb stared at the traitor. At her slender fingers curled around the cell bars. At the nine digits. Nine, not ten.

Flash.

A rat gnawing on a dead woman's hand.

Only she hadn't died, had she?

The missing little finger on her left hand filled him with a sense of dread. His brain shuttered. He blinked. Stared. Different thoughts— alien thoughts—came back online. Kaleb stared at the traitorous bi—no, at his *friend*. He stroked her fingers.

'Priya?'

Loud laughter reached them, and they both froze, listening. No footsteps or shouts followed. Kaleb struggled to see through the haze of his time with the major and what he had learnt. Another, more vivid, reality seemed to underlay that fog. The two stood at odds with one another. Each telling him vastly different things.

The more recent told him he should kill this woman before she could do any more harm. She'd led him astray. Had tricked him. Tried to steal the vial.

The older memories showed him a traumatised but brave young woman who had helped him see how the army had stolen not just his youth but his life. She'd enabled him, through her questioning of her own experience, to disentangle himself from some of that early brainwashing.

Once more, his brain shuttered. Stuttered. Some sort of reset happened.

Brainwashing … that was it. The major had brainwashed him. But was that true? Or was everything all lies? Angry and scared, he stepped back and glared at Priya.

'Who are you?' he demanded.

Shock paled her features and darkened her eyes. She, too, stepped away. In a whisper, she tried to clarify, 'What do you mean? You know me. You just said my name.'

In bitter tones, he said, 'Knowing your name has nothing to do with knowing you.' He took two aggressive steps to the bars and gripped them once more, staring at her intently. 'What are you?'

Confusion warred with fear. Her jaw worked soundlessly. After a few seconds, she found her voice, 'Kaleb. What happened to you?' Pity softened her words.

Still at a whisper, he managed to project a yelled order into his next words, 'Answer me!'

Priya swallowed audibly. Then she stepped to the bars and wrapped her trembling fingers around his. 'I'm the woman whose life you saved. Over and over again. You helped me.' She shook her head. 'We helped each other. Do you remember that Jenny died?'

A gory image of a woman covered in blood

and looking horrified burst into his consciousness. But it wasn't Jenny. It was Priya. 'You killed her?'

'No. Not me. Some men stormed the house. We got away.'

He hung his head, confused. Seconds later, he turned tortured eyes to her, 'But you had her blood all over you.'

Priya nodded. Smiled. 'You helped me change into a clean suit. Then we fled into the forest.' She gazed left and downward as if searching for a memory. 'You killed the raptor.'

That, he did remember. The way his chest had squeezed when he thought he'd shot Priya. Full recall had him stagger backward. His mouth filled with metallic-tasting saliva, and he spat on the concrete floor. Absently, he wiped the back of his hand across his lips.

He dropped to his knees. 'The major lied to me. Twisted it all up.'

Instead of agreeing like he'd expected, Priya told him, 'I don't know. I wasn't there.'

If she were as evil as he'd been told, she would have tried to ally herself with him. Would have agreed with everything he said. Would have attempted to make herself look good.

Priya went on, 'The rebels took me and that bastard, Martins. You were right about him. We never should have trusted him.'

Those words directly contradicted what his brain kept trying to tell him. He was supposed to trust Martins. But that conflicted with other things he knew, things buried at an instinctual level. He checked a memory with her, 'We came across him in a habitation pod. On our way to the rebel camp.'

'Yes. I persuaded you that we should let him come with us. I made a mistake.' Tears filled her eyes. 'I've made so many mistakes.'

Kaleb rose to his feet and returned to the bars. 'But you're here now. You came for me.'

For the second time in their brief exchange, Priya said, 'What happened to you?'

As though innocuous, scenes from the torture drifted lazily up to the surface of his mind—hiding their true brutality until they crashed and thundered on the shores of his pummelled brain. He clenched his fists. Priya backed away, looking nervous. Kaleb made a conscious effort to relax. 'The major had me brainwashed. He planned to set me up against you. Against everyone but him. He wants to force elections and run me as his puppet.'

Grim-faced, Priya told him, 'Not anymore. He's dead.'

Wordless, the two of them stared at one another, clueless as to where to go next. Movement from a neighbouring cell broke the trance. Priya glanced left, and her eyes widened. 'There are more of you.'

'What? Other specials?'

Priya nodded. Sudden hope lit her eyes. 'Let me help you. I'll get you out of here.'

'How?'

She checked the lock, and Kaleb followed her gaze. Electric, rather than mechanical. Good or bad? The controls would be at the guard station. Could they override it without going down there? These shared questions flew between them without words, needing only shared need to connect.

Priya leaned right in and dropped to her lowest whisper yet, 'Do you still have your pulse gun?'

Kaleb blinked. On automatic pilot, he'd opened his mouth, ready to answer in the negative. Instead, his hand drifted to his belt. Cold metal met his questing fingers. He glanced down. Another memory surfaced. The major had re-equipped him right before the fighting broke out, intending to release him. Before that happened, though, Adams got called away to deal with some emergency or other.

The rebel soldiers who had replaced the specials guarding the cells had neglected to open the bars to check the prisoners, assuming the army had taken care of that stuff already.

All at once, he knew where Priya's thoughts were headed. A grin blossomed on his face, stretching his lips and cheeks. After all this time, it felt strange. Nice. 'Here.' He held the weapon out to her.

Priya returned his grin, stepped back, aimed the gun, and fired a single discharge. The soft whump wouldn't travel to the guards. Neither would the soft sizzle of melting neostil or the click of the lock disengaging.

Heart hammering and palms sweating, Kaleb stepped from the cell and took the weapon back from Priya, still not too sure what to believe. For now, he would go with her. Anywhere had to be better than staying behind bars.

He dashed to the other occupied cell. A soldier he didn't recognise sat up and stared at him. Then pleased recognition smoothed his features. 'Hey, you're the one who said about the cure. Was it true?'

Priya stepped up. 'You bet your ass it is.'

The guy grinned at Kaleb. 'Let me out. I'm on your side, mate.'

Kaleb aimed and fired. This time, the door clunked loudly. Over-eager, the soldier had burst from his cell and shoved the barred door too far. Alarmed shouts to stay put had the three fugitives fleeing back the way Priya had come.

5

E123

For the next twenty-four hours, Priya kept

Kaleb close. She answered his many questions and mopped his sweaty brow when he awoke, screaming, from his nightmares. Though he seemed much improved, his resilience niggled at her. From what he'd divulged, the major had subjected him to a total brainwashing regimen. How had he not succumbed fully?

Violet still tinted his eyes, but not as prominently as previously, which warned her the virus had progressed. All of which left her nervous and jumpy. She would take care around him. Time and again he grew needy and clingy, only to swing wildly across the spectrum to cold fury, and then settling in the centre until something triggered him once more.

Over a cold breakfast of pastries and fruit muesli with fresh yoghurt, Kaleb ate contentedly, at his most settled since she'd found him. He appeared happy, jubilant. So when he looked at her with such warmth and smiled, she couldn't help but return the sentiment, even though she remained worried and vigilant—unsure what, precisely, she had liberated from the bowels of zone 1.

Kaleb grabbed Priya's hand. Unexpected and dramatic, the move startled her, and she tried to pull her hand back. He held onto it. A little too tightly—it hurt. 'Ouch, Kaleb.' She stared at him.

Fervour flushed his cheeks and brightened his eyes. In a rush, he declared, 'I love you.' He gripped her hand more firmly still. 'I've loved you since the first day I found you. It just took me a while to realise it.' His eyes implored on his behalf. 'Will you have me?'

Was that a proposal? Had Kaleb just proposed? No. Uh-uh. No way. Dismayed, Priya yanked at her hand again, this time with more force, and managed to extricate herself from his grip. The pressure left her with bright pink and shocking white patches on her skin.

'Kaleb …' She hung her head. What to say? At his profession of love, her stomach had dropped. Didn't that give her as good an indication of her feelings as any? Unbidden, another man's face loomed in her mind's eye. The last bloke she would have expected herself to fancy. Fortunately, she managed to stifle the laugh trying to burst out before her mirth made it past her throat.

The effort gave her hiccups. Across the table, Kaleb clenched his fists, and his face darkened. Ominous clouds gathered around his bunched eyebrows. Oh dear, and there she'd wanted to let him down gently. But then, she'd never had a good poker-face.

In a strained voice, she said, 'Kaleb, I care for you, deeply, but …'

He finished for her, 'But not like that.'

Priya shook her head and tried to take his hands, but he pulled them away and settled them on his lap, beneath the table. His refusal forced her to use her words. 'I'll be forever grateful for what you've done for me, but … I don't think I'm ready for any relationship. I'm sorry.'

Abruptly, he lurched to his feet and leant, straight-armed, over the table, glowering at her. Priya cringed back. The bridge of his nose, his cheeks, and his chin flushed a mottled shade of pink/purple.

'You *will* come to love me.'

Priya scooted her chair backward, scraping it across the highly polished floor. 'W-what do you mean?'

Kaleb straightened up and crossed his arms over his chest, staring down at her—a haughty expression pushed out some of his anger and indignation. 'You know I love you. And I believe, deep down, you feel the same for me. I know you can't commit because of what happened to you. Because of what people keep on doing around you.' He paused, took a couple of deep breaths, and declared, 'I can take care of you. Keep your enemies away. And you will come to accept your love for me.'

Priya shook her head. 'No. Kaleb—'

The finger at his tight lips shushed her. Everything about his stance, posture, and expression warned her that he was about to go supernova. She held her body and her breath, not daring to so much as flicker an eyelash.

She saw the very moment he committed to a definite course of action and wished, mightily, that she had a second sight to allow her to discern the nature of his intended transgressions. For transgressions she knew they must be. He wore his intent like a second skin.

Snake skin.

And, before her eyes, he shed his old self.

Alarmed, Priya eased to a standing position and edged away from him and toward the exit. Before she could reach it, however, he moved. At speed. Kaleb got to the door first. She gasped, expecting him to bar her way. Instead, he strode through the portal, stiff-backed and … what? … Angry? Determined?

Murderous.

Hurriedly, Priya squashed that thought. He wasn't capable, was he?

You know he is.

She couldn't squash that one quite so easily.

Distraught, she ran out of her room, intending to pursue Kaleb and try to talk him down. Left and right, she searched the corridor. She saw no sign of him. Just then, Leo walked around the far corner. Priya ran to him.

'Oh, thank goodness. You have to help me.'

Leo strode to her and cupped her elbows with his palms. 'What is it? Are you hurt?'

'No.' She shook her head and briefed him as succinctly as she knew how on what had just unfolded, as well as admitting her fears.

Leo checked, 'He was a special, wasn't he?'

'Yes. Why?'

'Come with me.' Leo took her hand and tugged her into following along.

He marched them both down corridor after corridor until they reached the door to the communications hub. Priya stared up at the rebel leader.

He took her glance for the question it was and told her, 'All the specials have extra implants.'

Priya hadn't known that. But then, she didn't know much of anything, did she?

Canmore continued, 'Those implants allow us to see and hear whatever they see and hear. We can tap in from here.' He grinned. 'Our friend, the major, kept that little gem quiet from Martins. Just as well, the way things have turned out.'

Leo accessed the nearest terminal, which one of the rebel troops vacated for him. Canmore spared the man a glance, 'Leave us.'

'Sir.' The guy saluted and left with haste.

Priya settled into the vacated chair, and Leo

sat by her side. Both watched intently as the screen opened. A camera jiggled.

'This is Kaleb?' Priya chewed her thumb.

Leo nodded. 'It's him.'

Tension thickened the air as they sat and watched Kaleb's progress in silence. The audio gave them harsh breathing and pounding footfalls. At the first intersection, he jogged left with no hesitation.

'He knows where he's going.' Priya's stomach dropped.

Leo nodded.

Kaleb took turn after turn, locked on target like a guided missile. But where to? For who? Which of her so-called enemies had he decided should die first?

Leo and Priya watched as Kaleb strode through a final door, marched across the room, and grabbed a man by the throat, pinning him to the wall. He'd found Major Adams.

Mute with shock, Priya watched. Ellie had lied to her. Adams lived. But why? What could the woman possibly achieve with her deceit? Then it dawned on Priya: it gave Ellie an out about not recalling the army. Eloise had blamed it on the troops being left leaderless. So, with Adams on her side, what was she really up to? At this point, Priya had no doubt whatsoever that Ellie knew not only that the major remained alive but also his precise location in the zone.

They watched and listened as Kaleb and Adams got into an altercation.

Kaleb accused, 'You lied to me.'

Adams held up his hands, 'No. Son, just listen—'

'I'm done listening. I know the truth now. All of it. I see what lying bastards you all are.'

Quickly, it turned a lot more violent. Still holding Adams forcibly against the wall, Kaleb pulled out his serrated belt knife and slit the major's throat. Appalled and horrified, Priya turned to Leo. 'Can we speak to him?' Her voice squeaked like a mouse's. Then she shook her head and cleared her throat. 'No, it doesn't matter. He used a two-way radio out in zone nine. So, of course, we can't.' Her voice cracked, and her eyes leaked.

Leo sat and thought about it. 'Who did he

communicate with?'

'I think it was Major Adams. But why wouldn't he use this hub to connect via the implants?'

'Might be that nine is too far out to reach by that method. Or …'

Priya nodded and frowned. 'Or it might be that he wanted those conversations to be held in private. On an untracked frequency. We've seen already how two-faced the man can be.'

Wordless, grim, Leo clicked on the two-way mic and nodded to Priya.

'Kaleb?'

The rogue special stopped dead on his way out of the major's office, having just cleaned his knife on the dead man's uniform. Then he stared up at the wall camera and grinned. 'I told you I'd take care of your enemies.'

Distraught, Priya begged him, 'Please, stop. I don't want you to do this.'

He laughed and shook his head. 'You love me, Priya. And once you trust me, you'll change your mind about us spending the rest of our lives together.'

Priya and Leo exchanged a glance. Priya hardened her heart and her voice, 'No. Killing people will never make me love you. How could I ever care for a man who murders people in cold blood?'

Kaleb's grin broadened. It made her feel sick. Still staring at the camera, he said, 'Next up is Martins, and then his little Russian whore.'

A sigh of relief escaped Priya. 'You won't get to them. They're in the cells. Too many guards stand between you and them.'

The camera showed Kaleb shaking his head, hands on hips. 'Then I'll go through them.' The deranged special set off at an easy lope.

Leo clicked off the two-way. Then he picked up the phone and called his chief of security. 'We have a fugitive on the loose. Army Special Moore. Identification number ZN669900. Sending you the tracking code now. Apprehend him immediately.' He spared a glance for Priya and then said, 'Use lethal force if necessary.'

A pensive expression settled on his face as he disconnected. He placed a hand over Priya's. 'I'm sorry.'

She hung her head and shook it slowly, from left to right to centre. 'He's left us little other choice.'

Leo pulled her into a hug. They parted and continued to watch Kaleb's progress on the feed.

He mowed down the first two rebel soldiers he came to. Without even breaking step or slowing his pace. Beside Priya, Leo flinched and pursed his lips. He turned to her, 'What happened to him?'

She shrugged. 'I don't know, not exactly. Adams brainwashed him. Seems he wanted to use Kaleb to take power for himself covertly. I think the virus Kaleb contracted got in the way of that. It didn't take properly.' Helpless, she flicked her hands up into the air and then let them drop to her lap. 'My turning him down was the last straw.' With her eyes, she pleaded with Leo to understand. 'He's a good man. Just, he's been through a lot.'

Leo nodded.

Together, they continued watching the feed.

At the main junction for the cells and detention centre, twenty troops amassed, armed to the teeth and waiting for Kaleb. Upon seeing them, he stopped, gauging the situation. After about three or four seconds, he spun around and ran back the way he'd come. Evidently, he'd assessed their numbers as too many and had disengaged.

Leo cursed. 'Why didn't they shoot him?'

Priya chewed her lip. 'More to the point, where's he going now?'

All too soon, they had their answer. Priya recognised the corridors he took as the most direct route from the detention complex to the presidential suite. Leo shot to his feet. Too late, though, as Kaleb blasted his way through the automated door and stormed into the outer office.

Which stood empty.

Enraged, he stomped across the plush carpet and pushed his way through the inner door. That sanctum, too, stood empty.

Both Priya and Leo let out loud sighs of relief. Then Priya voiced the question, 'But how did she know?'

Leo glanced at her, surprised, and then he nodded. 'She's always in her office at this time of the day.'

Priya had a suspicion, but not enough for her to risk giving voice to it just then. Old, painful memories hit her, flashing her back to the day she'd arrived, hungry, tired, and thirsty on the outskirts of zone nine.

On the screen, frustrated in his search, Kaleb stopped and stared up at the camera in the corridor, opposite the outer door. 'Leo.' He waited as if knowing they would need a second or two to react. 'I'm coming for you.'

CHAPTER TWELVE

1

E124

'It's all my fault.' Priya sobbed against Leo's shoulder, and he held her. 'I feel so guilty.'

Surprised, he pulled away and looked down at her.

'I caused all this.'

Leo pulled her in close again. 'No. What do you think you should've done? Slept with the guy just to keep him sweet?'

His words hurt. The trouble was, they also rang of truth. Hard to hear but true nonetheless.

She confessed, 'I still want to help him,

though.'

Leo's voice sounded soft and comforting when he spoke. 'Of course you do. He saved your life. That would mean a lot to anyone. You feel like you owe him a debt.'

Priya nodded, trying to sniffle away her distress. Grateful, she stared up at Leo.

His lips met hers.

She wanted his affection.

Needed the distraction.

They kissed.

A mere brush of the lips at first.

Then deeper, harder, more insistent. Demanding.

The last day had been a whirlwind, and she craved the contact. But also, just some simple human kindness—which Leo seemed more than willing to offer.

Though the episode lasted only briefly, rushed and desperate, it opened up something that Priya had buried, and she could no longer deny her feelings. She felt something for Leo. Not love—she couldn't call it that by a long way —but a deep and abiding friendship had formed over the last weeks. And, at last, at long, long last, she had a happy memory to paste over the horror. Leo had given her the means to recall a man's touch full of affection rather than of brutality. In her inner armoury, she now had something pleasant.

With their clothing put to rights once more, they surveyed the small office space. Leo stooped to retrieve a stack of spilled papers from the floor. Flushed, Priya watched him and grinned. Leo noticed, and soon, the two of them stood chuckling quietly. A knock on the door interrupted their gentle mirth.

Leo called, 'Enter.'

A young rebel trooper took a hesitant step through the door. 'Sir, we haven't located Moore as yet.'

Priya stilled, listening and forcing herself to keep breathing. Leo raised a brow. 'You haven't tracked him?'

The trooper blanched. Priya stepped in. 'Let's not kill the messenger.'

Leo spared her a glance and then pierced the troop with a hard stare. 'Well?'

'Sir. N-no. He … he appears to have disabled it.' The rebel cleared his throat. 'Well, to be precise, he removed his implants.'

Priya exclaimed, 'What? All of them?'

The young guy nodded. 'He left them down in chamber three.'

Leo's expression showed recognition. Priya asked, 'What's chamber three?'

The two men answered together, 'Torture.'

Her stomach plummeted. That's where they'd taken him to brainwash him.

The trooper left. Leo took Priya's hand. She felt torn. Should she have left Kaleb to rot in the cells, or was she right in trying to save him? Even at this cost?

She flashed back to Kaleb's words and actions the day before. Somehow, he had known of Priya's attraction to Leo even before she had. He'd recognised that she would turn to the reverend for help. Such a triangle of confused love, jealousy, and hurt could never end well.

Kaleb had set out on his murderous spree to try and win her affections. What a mess. Priya had to stop him. And she could trust only one man. Her thoughts must have shown on her face. Before she spoke a word, Leo told her, 'I'll help you.'

2

E126

With misgivings, Eloise appointed a new major for the army. Adams' death at the rogue special's hands came as a heavy blow. She didn't know the new man, Sergeant Straw, too well, but she'd heard he had the minds and hearts of the troops. Not that she'd trusted Adams, but he'd been a known entity with which she could make deals.

It would have been preferable to choose Leopold or another of the rebels, but that would have proven sheer folly. Ellie needed to try and win over the military as well as the populace.

Word had gotten out about the luxury in zone one, which contrasted sharply with the poverty and deprivation across the rest of Exxon 1 in the aftermath of the outbreak.

The people had revolted. Crowds protested around the perimeter of the presidential complex, calling for elections. No one wanted yet another ruler imposed upon them, despite it being that way since the first settlers had colonised the planet. While the other planets in the system had chosen to give democracy another chance, Exxon 1 had eschewed such foolishness, having learned the lessons well from a dead Earth.

Ellie cursed her current blind inner sight. Just lately, it had become intermittent, and she could no longer depend upon it to show her everything. Instead, she was thrown back to relying on the usual external indicators.

Straw had shown loyalty to her, which would have to do until she gained more strength and could take outright control of everything. Terrence had gone wrong in relying on too many people. She would rely on no one.

So far, the move seemed to have worked. Everyone around her believed that the appointment of Straw was the first step of many in setting things right and taking control of the chaos. Little did they know.

She couldn't enjoy her deception, though, as her conscience prickled uncomfortably, telling her she knew better than this. And she did. Perhaps when she'd taken care of Martins, she might return to her old self.

Her inner critic wouldn't stop its niggles, however. Even though she disliked what it showed her, Ellie had to give it credit. How good had she really been? She'd believed in her altruism and high moral standards. But then she'd allowed anger and hurt to take the upper hand and run things. Which had to beg the question of her actual moral worth.

A truly good person wouldn't have fallen so far nor so fast. Annoyed, Ellie tutted and shook her head, shooting to her feet and pacing. She couldn't deal with this useless inner searching right now. More critical issues demanded her full attention. And, at the very least, she was an improvement on Terror. Hell, anybody was an improvement on that man.

At her summons, Straw strode into the room, offered a smart salute, and sat stiffly in the chair she'd indicated. Sweat beaded his upper lip.

Amused, Ellie studied him. Once she gave her orders, there could be no going back. Her actions would out her as actively continuing the old regime rather than merely allowing it to roll on until she found her feet.

The longer they sat watching one another, the more nervous the man grew. Was she that intimidating? Or did circumstance have more to do with it? Resolved, Ellie leant forward. 'Major Straw ...' The man puffed up at his new title. 'Your first and most pressing task is to disperse the crowds from the perimeter.'

'Yes, ma'am.'

'While your second assignment will prove unpopular, I see the wisdom in the old president's actions. We'll continue suppressing the formation of groups or communities.'

At her words, Straw's eyes widened, just a fraction, and then he regained his composure.

Eloise pressed on, 'With the amount of anger people are expressing, we need to keep them from coming together—that won't help our recovery efforts at all. The last thing the planet needs is yet another regime change. All in its own time, yes?'

Straw nodded.

Ellie leaned back in her chair. She had him onside. 'Likewise, the portals will remain inoperative. All the better to prevent the other planets from interfering. Already, I've had Lady Morris from three trying to weasel her way in. That kind of political nonsense, we can do without.' She studied Straw and added, 'At least until we've sorted this mess.'

'Yes, ma'am.'

The man didn't recognise the prolonged silence as the dismissal it was. To emphasise the point, Eloise rose to her feet. Straw did likewise but, still, he just stood there.

She walked them to the door. 'That will be all.'

He gave another smart salute and marched from the room.

3

E127

Priya felt as though it had all come unravelled. Or had it not ravelled in the first place? Had she simply deluded herself?

Leo had disappeared, off searching for Kaleb in an effort to persuade him from his mission of needless slaughter. She worried about him and felt bad for both men.

On top of that, doubts about Ellie's fitness to replace the planet's leadership crowded in, threatening to suffocate her.

And then there was John Martins, whom Kaleb and she had helped bring back to the capital. Why had he attacked and killed the professor so viciously? What kind of man was he, really?

Utterly fed up with it all, Priya decided she wanted answers. Imprisoned in the cells, Martins was the easiest to get to just now. She took herself there, angry but not too sure what it was she actually wanted from him.

Indecisive, Priya hesitated at the bars. Her

quarry lay asleep on the narrow cot at the rear of the chamber. She had just made up her mind to turn away, telling herself that coming here was sheer folly, when he sat up and stared at her.

'Well, if it isn't the esteemed Ms Shaw. Finder of the vial. Saviour of the world.' He blinked up at her, a sardonic grin on his lips. 'To what do I owe the pleasure?'

Disgust flooded her mouth, coated her tongue with a metallic tang. Involuntarily, she took a small step backward. The man in the cell laughed. That got her ire up. She pushed herself forward and gripped the bars, glaring at him. Then she demanded, 'Why?'

The infuriating man just sat and stared at her.

Priya insisted, 'Why? After everything we did for you. We gave you a chance.'

At least he had the good grace to drop his gaze for a moment. 'That is regrettable. You seem like such a nice girl.'

'So, why?'

He shrugged and sighed. 'You were my ride back here.'

Priya rolled her eyes. As if such a reason

could suffice. 'But the professor. Why?'

Fury lit up his eyes then chilled into icy malice. 'That bitch did this to me. Her and her sidekick.' His hands fluttered around his aged face to help him make his point.

Priya stepped back once more, sure she would receive nothing of value from this fallen manipulator.

His next words stopped her in mid-turn. 'Ellie is keeping secrets too.'

Unwilling to face him fully and re-engage, Priya twisted her head over her shoulder and raised her brows. Despite a burning desire to learn more about his ex-wife, Priya didn't trust him. Wasn't at all sure she wanted to hear any more from his poison tongue.

John chuckled. 'As I said, a nice girl … but not particularly bright.'

Priya affected disinterest but didn't think she was too successful in her efforts. John leant back against the wall, watching her. 'Or am I the fool? Do you know about Ellie's telepathy already? Is there more to you than meets the eye?'

So much clicked into place.

How Eloise had known precisely when to attack zone one. Why she had imprisoned Martins without feeling the need to investigate further. Her anticipation of Priya's visit and her questions. The smooth way in which she had evaded Kaleb. And, the final piece of the puzzle, the speed with which she had replaced Adams. It had seemed as if the woman had known of his real death before any of them could have had a chance to tell her. That last pained Priya the most. How she would have loved to have seen Ellie's face when she confronted the woman with the truth.

Disoriented, sick to her stomach, Priya staggered. Her grip on the cold bars was the only thing holding her upright. Through the fog of her whirling thoughts, she accused John, 'You're just trying to sow more bad seeds. You hope it might yet give you another chance.'

To her shock, he smiled and nodded. 'But true, nonetheless.'

And Priya couldn't deny it. He had told her the truth. His motivations didn't change that fact. Unable to throw a parting shot, Priya walked away, deep in turmoil.

John's revelation had cast away the last of Priya's doubts and melded them into firm questions. Ellie was not fit for the role of president. Her hidden ability cast suspicion on her every action and—more importantly—her inactions. How many people had the woman manipulated with her second sight?

An unwelcome memory forced itself to the front of her mind. She tried and failed to shove it away, but it raped her again. Priya fell against the nearest wall and slid to the floor. The gang leader in zone nine, Hank, had developed the telepathy. No matter which way she spun it, Priya couldn't view anyone with the same enhancement through kind or trusting eyes. They all fell into the same filthy sack as Hank.

For ten minutes, she slumped there, victim to the flashbacks. When they relented, her breath came in short, desperate pants, and dizziness assailed her senses. Tears poured down her cheeks, and snot dripped in great gloopy gobs over her lips and chin.

Gradually, over the next five minutes or so,

Priya gathered herself. She brought her breathing under control and wiped her eyes. Then she pulled her sleeve cuff over her hand and bunched it in her fist, which she used to dry her cheeks and clear the gunk from her nose, mouth, and chin.

Until her recent interlude with Leo, Priya had begun to fantasise about getting away. Not just out of zone one but off the planet altogether. She'd heard good things about Exxon 3, which Lady Ruby Morris presided over. But then, at the end of last year, Priya would have sung the praises of Exxon 1 should anyone have sought her opinion. So how much could you trust what people thought? Their honesty and motivation didn't factor into it.

More and more dominoes tumbled. Ellie needed removing. Priya closed her eyes and chewed the end of her thumb. Who could replace her, though? Leo might do, but how well did she know him, really? How well did she know any of the people around her? How well had she known Kaleb?

For sure, she didn't want the job herself. She

wasn't built for it. Didn't have the equipment. All she'd wanted to do once she'd recovered from the assault was to go back to a quiet life. Then Kaleb had admitted to the vial's importance. Her job, then, had been getting the cure to the right people as soon as possible.

Look how that had turned out.

She hadn't signed up for any of this.

Priya eased to her feet and set off at a brisk walk. She had no destination in mind, only that she had to get away. Duty and desire warred with one another: Sort out this mess versus run as far and fast as she could.

4

E127

Distracted, Priya walked headlong into something solid yet yielding. Perturbed, she glanced up. And up again. Then up some more, craning her neck. The man loomed over her. She didn't think she'd ever seen anyone as tall or as broad as this behemoth.

A little afraid, and a lot annoyed, she mumbled 'sorry' and manoeuvred so she could edge around his massive frame. An out-swung arm blocked her passage. 'What the hell?' Priya glared up at him, putting as much fierceness into her expression as she knew how.

Some soldier had been her first impression. Now, though, his shoulder stripes warned her that she couldn't boss this guy around. He must be the new major. Straw, that was it. Heart thumping in cruel tandem with her headache, she forced a smile onto her lips and said, 'Major Straw.' Then out came the irony of all ironies, 'I didn't see you there.'

A frown crinkled his deep brown eyes, and then he blinked. 'I know you.'

Priya took a step back. She didn't know him.

'You travelled with Kaleb Moore. Priya Shaw.'

Uncertain, she nodded but kept her mouth shut.

His features softened. Then he cupped her elbow with the arm that had blocked her progress. 'We need to talk.'

Had Eloise put him up to this? Did she want the meddlesome girl out of the way? With her head feeling way too full and pressured, Priya walked with him down the corridor, continuing the direction in which she'd been headed but reversing his original path.

As they neared the presidential suite, her panic grew. But then he halted at the base of that corridor and took a left down the short T-wing. Priya understood, at last, that he intended to steer them toward his new office.

Rigid, she took the seat he indicated, opposite his across the imposing desk. She'd noticed that everything in zone one was about intimidation and excess. She felt grateful for her average family, her average upbringing in an average zone, and her average life. No wonder everyone in the capital was so arrogant and out of touch.

Silent, she watched and waited, letting the major make the first move.

He wrapped a meaty palm around his fisted left hand and leant his elbows on the table, dropping his chin to the cupped fist. 'Do you know where Kaleb went?'

Her shoulders drooped, and Priya shook her head. 'He disabled his tracker, the last I heard.'

Straw nodded. 'What are you doing about him?'

Without a clue of where this man's loyalties lay, she plumbed for the truth, 'Leo went after him.'

'To do what?'

Priya sighed. 'To stop him. Bring him back.'

Straw gave another nod. 'Moore always seemed like a sound guy. What happened?'

'Adams brainwashed him.'

The major's eyes went wide. Then he nodded again. 'I did wonder. When they brought him in. Did you know he told us—the troops—about the antidote?'

Priya shook her head. There was a lot she didn't know.

Straw flattened his palms on the desk and leant back in his chair. 'I support Kaleb. He's a good guy.'

Priya tensed. 'So, what are you telling me?'

'Mrs Martins gave me my first orders this morning.' Straw told her about the portals and the standing orders for the troops. Then he confirmed her suspicions that Ellie had no intention of distributing any cure.

He watched her and then seemed to come to a decision. 'She's no better than Terrence. In fact, she's worse. At least he was honest about his motives.'

Priya took the plunge, 'Do you know she has telepathic abilities?'

Straw rocked in shock.

'I just found out.' Priya chewed on the end of her thumb.

They stared at one another for a while, each gauging the other. Then Straw said, 'I have the minds and hearts of the troops. They'll back my decisions.'

'You're telling me this, why?'

'You can help.'

She shook her head and staggered to her feet.

Straw rose too and tried to placate her. 'Not on your own. We can help Kaleb. Get the other planets involved. God knows, we need all the assistance we can get. My sister lives on three. I like their system.'

He waited for a response, but Priya just stood there. After another couple of seconds, he said, 'Maybe it's time for a change.'

She snorted, both amused and appalled. 'For another change, you mean.'

Straw pressed, 'Are you with me?'

Priya edged to the closed door. 'I'm not against you.' Then she let herself out.

Straw didn't follow.

Dizzy and exhausted, she made her way back to her room. Priya felt sick to her stomach, and bile burned up her throat and flooded her mouth. Spent, she dropped onto her bed and lay flat on her back, staring up at the plain, low-hung ceiling.

It struck her that Eloise had allocated her these sparse quarters to keep her in her place. It was a non-verbal way of telling her precisely where she stood in the scheme of things. The lack of luxury rammed home just how unimportant Priya was to the new administration.

A single tear tracked down her cheek. Priya forced her breathing to follow a long and deep rhythm. She needed to think. To calm down. To gain some clarity.

The trouble was, she felt devastated. All her efforts had come to nothing. And, for sure, she was mightily fed up of the power plays. She'd done what had needed to be done. Had brought the vial to zone one. It wasn't her fault that the professor had died. It wasn't her fault that Eloise wasn't what everyone had believed. It wasn't her fault that nobody would be getting the cure. She might as well have left the stupid thing in the shit.

Despite her turmoil, exhaustion won, and Priya dozed off. When she awoke, the room had grown dim but not dark. Dusk, then. While she slept, she had reached a decision. As soon as she roused, determination flooded her system and drove her to action. She rose and got busy packing a bag.

These last months had taught Priya that she didn't need friends. Didn't need anyone. She was more than capable of going it alone. Needed to be able to go it alone. Couldn't trust or rely on anyone. Solitude would do her some good. Give her some much-needed space. Would help her to stand on her own two feet. It was high time she found her own way. Forged her own path in life.

At the door, a thought alarmed her, and she lifted her fingers to her neck, rubbing them over the old implant site that she'd had since toddlerhood. Even though it no longer worked, she worried that it held a tracker, much like the troops wore. Would it still be operable? Could somebody hack it?

Priya dropped her bag at the foot of the wall and strode to her small bathroom. From the cabinet, she retrieved a pair of nail scissors. They would have to do. Steeled against the expected pain, she clamped her mouth shut and screwed her lips together.

The useless things wouldn't open wide enough. She checked the rivet joining them. Loose. Quickly, she wiggled the scissors and forced them apart, loosening the joint further. A couple of minutes of manipulation had them fall apart. Now she had two sort-of-knives.

With the spare blade set aside on the sink edge, Priya reached behind her neck and located the small bump with her free hand. Then she pushed the tip of the half scissor against that hardened lump. The initial prick made her wince. But that would be nothing to the agony of digging deeper and gouging out the chip.

Nausea hit her in a flood of heat, and her hand shook. Priya paused to grab her toothbrush and jam it between her teeth so that she could bite down on it. Then she resumed her impromptu self-surgery.

Blood and tangled flesh dropped down her neck and below the collar of her suit. Goosebumps prickled every millimetre of skin. She gagged but carried on. And then she had the small device pinched between slippery thumb and forefinger.

Intrigued, she held it up and studied it. The thing seemed far too small to have done everything it had. A strange sensation started at her neck. Alarmed, she twisted and looked at the wound via the wall-mounted mirror.

Priya couldn't believe what she saw. Before her stunned gaze, her skin knitted together. Terrified now, she checked her eyes. The violet tint didn't come from the low lighting.

She was infected.

Kaleb.

Must have been.

It had come from him.

He'd given her the virus.

+++

Priya ran. Initially, she had no destination in mind. Blind panic propelled her headlong flight. She retained enough wits to grab her partially packed bag and leave the capital.

Perhaps her emptied mind saved her. Allowed her to get away unseen and unstopped. At every turn, she expected soldiers—whether rebel or army—to apprehend her. It never happened.

Some higher intelligence than blind panic must have driven her, however, because she made her way to the breach in the wall. It had taken a hit during the rebel invasion, and nobody had rebuilt it yet. Priya couldn't understand why Eloise would be so lax. There weren't even any soldiers guarding the yawning hole.

Furtively, glancing left and right in a continuous swivel, Priya dashed through the gap and picked her way through the rubble. The hairs on her neck rose, and she felt watched. She stopped and spun around, expecting to see rough hands grabbing for her, but she remained alone.

A thought had her shove out a breath and bite her lip. The wall wasn't guarded because Eloise wanted her to leave. Or was it Straw? Either way, she wanted to get away, and they were letting her. She'd take whatever she could get.

When she reached the edges of the zone, Priya halted and tried to order her thoughts. Memories of her finding Martins in his pod during her and Kaleb's travels gave her an idea. That was the one place she could pretty much count on to be empty and well stocked. It was all the way out on the far side of zone six, though.

Well, she'd made the journey once; she could make it again. And this time around, she had a lot more experience to work on. Priya tightened the straps on her bag, cinching it to her back, and set off at an easy trot, trying not to think about the many and varied predators she might encounter. Like the raptors edging ever closer to the cities, bold and fearless now that humans were in such disarray. Somehow, the creatures knew.

She kept going until dusk and then sought shelter for the night. A rising wind stung her cheeks as it flung dust at her. A storm was on its way. A small abandoned office building offered refuge. Hungry and thirsty, having neglected to pack any sustenance, Priya curled up beneath a desk at the rear of the one-storey, squat structure. It would have to do.

The small company hadn't provided a canteen area or any vending machines. Most probably, they'd expected their workers to visit one of the communal eateries around town on their breaks. If not for the storm and the descending dark, she would have pushed on and tried to find somewhere more suitable, but needs must.

Sleep eluded her, but she used the enforced downtime to at least attempt to rest. However, questions rattled around in her brain non-stop. How did she get the virus this late in the game? Surely, had it come from Kaleb, she would have contracted it well before now? And hadn't Canmore told her she was a natural immune? Was

Ellie releasing an enhanced version that geneti-
cally targeted her enemies as the professor and
the Novikov woman had? Did the new leader see
Priya as a threat? Or was someone else targeting
her and the others who had taken over Exxon 1?

Annoyed and jittery, Priya tried to clear her
head and rest, but every shuffle, rattle, and clang
made her jump. As did each floating shadow or
wafting breeze. And then, all at once, she wasn't
alone.

A deeper shadow moved within the night. It
came nearer. A man. Priya shot to her feet, grabbing for the knife she'd stuffed into her belt. If
only she could have planned better and gotten
hold of a gun. Anything that avoided close-quar-
ters fighting would have been preferable to this.

The guy halted, held up his hands. A flash-
light clicked on and dazzled her. Terror tried to
take over, but Priya fought it. She wouldn't let
anyone get the better of her ever again, not without giving her all.

The man shone the beam at his face.

Priya gasped.

'Leo. How did you find me?'

5

E128

Reluctant, but persuaded by Leo, Priya agreed to return to the capital on the proviso that he allow her to isolate herself to avoid the virus spreading to anyone else. At first, she'd begged him to leave her alone and to get out of there as fast as he could. She didn't want him infected too. Even though she still had her doubts that that would happen. Her thoughts on this being a targeted virus seemed the most likely despite the unanswered hows and whys.

While they walked, she asked the same question she'd blurted in her shock at seeing him, 'How *did* you find me?'

He took her hand, which felt warm and comforting as it wrapped her much smaller one. 'As soon as your tracker went offline, one of the crew alerted me.'

An ironic grin settled on Priya's lips. If she'd left the damn thing in, he wouldn't have come looking for her so soon. He would have carried on searching for Kaleb. 'Right, so you knew something had happened. But without the tracker …'

When Leo spoke, he sounded sheepish and a little unsure of himself, 'I asked the hub team to keep you on camera. When I saw that you intended to leave, I cleared the break in the perimeter.'

Priya stopped walking. 'Why?'

'I didn't want Ellie getting wind of it. There's something up with that woman.' He tugged at her hand and took a step. 'Come on. We'd best get back before we're missed.'

She fell into stride beside him once more, content with his answers so far. He cared for her, so he'd stalked her. Fair enough. It didn't feel sinister, not like it would if Ellie or her cronies had done the same thing.

A piteous mewling reached them. Priya freed her hand and followed the sounds. Leo cried 'wait' and then gave up and trailed her. She rounded a corner and gasped, sliding to a halt. A huge raptor lay in her path. Her heart thudded, and a sudden deluge of sweat soaked her jumpsuit.

The animal didn't move. More mewling came from behind it. Cautious, Priya grabbed a discarded metal rod and poked it. *Stupid,* she scolded herself. Still, the beast lay inert. Dead. With a sigh of relief, she edged around the vast corpse and toward the pitiful cries.

A baby raptor nuzzled into its dead mother's side. When it saw Priya, it gave her such a plaintive look it broke her heart. Then it mewled again. A tear—an actual tear—slid down one of its cheeks, and the tiny thing squirmed in an effort to get to her.

On impulse, driven by emotion rather than sense, Priya moved toward it and knelt in front of the cute orphan. It stretched its neck and pushed its snout toward her outstretched hand. Behind her, she could feel Leo tensed and ready to strike. In a whisper, she said, 'It's okay. It's safe. It won't hurt me.' Then she rubbed its nose in a gentle caress. The mewls changed from forlorn to content. 'There, there, you poor little thing. Come here.' It let her pick it up and cuddle it, nuzzling into the crook of her arm.

'What are you doing?'

She turned to glance at Leo, a warm glow in her chest. 'It's orphaned. We can't leave it here.'

Leo scowled. 'It's dangerous.'

His expression unnerved her.

He saw it. 'What?'

She snuggled in with the baby raptor. 'Now you remind me of that man who ordered his men to rape me. Behave yourself.'

Leo blanched. 'Sorry.'

Priya fixed him with a defiant gaze, 'I'm keeping it. The poor thing needs feeding and looking after.'

She paused, waiting for further protests, but Leo held his peace. Priya said, 'I've heard that if you get them young enough, you can tame them.'

Leo shook his head. 'You can't make a pet of a bloody raptor.'

It was one of the few times she'd heard him blaspheme. She set her jaw and walked away from him with the baby in her arms. 'I can, and I will.'

Because they travelled in the daylight, they had to stay alert for the infected and any gangs or groups or simple lone rogues. While nobody approached them, Priya did see plenty of movement from the periphery of her vision. The biggest threat came from the abundance of wildlife, which until recently, had avoided the cities and built-up areas. Now, however, they all seemed to have decided that the rich pickings on offer from vulnerable humans outweighed any risks.

Whether the juvenile bellows from the baby raptor kept most away, or she and Leo were just lucky, they made it back into the capital without incident. Even though Leo had left instructions with the troops, Priya had expected Eloise to show her face or make a move by now. That she hadn't, unnerved Priya.

All the way back, three things held her thoughts hostage: Who had given her the virus? She didn't want to infect Leo. And she worried about Kaleb and who he would kill next. As soon as Leo had escorted her and the raptor to the relative safety of her apartment, they shared a look. He, too, had kept the damaged special at the front of his mind. She took his arm. 'I'm sorry it has to be like this.'

Leo shook his head. 'It's not your fault.' He kissed her briefly. 'You need to stop taking responsibility for everyone.'

Priya swallowed around a hard lump that had risen to her throat. 'Keep me posted.'

'We'll have him back here in no time. I promise.'

She refrained from calling him out on making promises he couldn't ever guarantee. Instead, she nodded and watched him leave. Behind her, from the bed where she'd placed him, the raptor mewled for attention. With a soft smile, she picked him up. The little beast nipped her finger and drew blood.

6

E129

Tense, Kaleb stood his ground while some anonymous special walked toward him, hands held in the air and empty of any weapon. When the woman reached a few feet away, he bade her halt. She did as he asked. 'Well?' he demanded, wanting to know what she wanted and why she'd come.

She eased her hands to her sides and swallowed audibly. 'Straw sent me. He's the new major.'

Kaleb blinked. He hadn't expected them to replace Adams so soon. What did this mean? He nodded for her to continue.

'He wanted to speak to you, but you've ripped out your unit, so he sent me.'

Kaleb raised and readied his gun, aiming for her chest. 'What does he want with me?'

Pale and trembling, the woman pressed the intercom button at her chest so it would broadcast what she heard. A voice he recognised as the old sergeant's came through, 'Moore. Straw here. Do you copy?'

Kaleb lowered his weapon a fraction and aimed off to the left of the special. 'I copy.'

'I'm at the communications hub. From here, I can speak to every soldier via their implants.'

'And what do you plan to do with that, … sir?'

'I want you to come back, soldier. The troops

will rally around you.'

Kaleb laughed. 'On your command. Why would I trust you?'

The female special spoke before the major did, 'Not just on his command. What you said about the antidote got around. We'll follow you sooner than some privileged bigot from the capital.'

Over the comms, the major cleared his throat and chuckled. 'Well, I'm not too keen on hearing my orders have little weight, but I do second the sentiment.'

Kaleb opened his mouth to respond but held his words when the woman tensed and stared over his shoulder. Without turning or looking, he knew beyond a shadow of a doubt that somebody stood behind him. The hairs on his neck prickled, anticipating a deadly shot in the back.

'Drop your weapon.'

Kaleb would recognise that voice anywhere. It belonged to the man who had stolen his love from him. Rigid and waiting for an opportunity to attack, he lowered the gun to the ground and raised his hands in the air. Then, slowly, he turned to face the Reverend Leopold Canmore. Belligerent, he stared at him.

Leo waved the pulse gun and said, 'Both of you, stand side by side with your hands where I can see them.'

Preferring distance, Kaleb edged backward until he reached the woman special. 'Who sent you?'

Canmore held his ground and frowned. 'We both know the answer to that.'

Disgusted, Kaleb spat on the dirt. 'So, she did go running to you.' He shook his head. 'I should have known. The moment you accessed my comms, I should have sussed it out. I take it she made this worth your while?'

'It's not like that.'

'Bullshit.'

'We have genuine feelings for one another. I won't hurt her or use her.'

Although those words should have reassured —made him glad, even—Kaleb saw red. A burning rage torched any logic or sense he might have held onto until now. Priya was his. If he couldn't have her, then no one else would. He charged.

The special with him yelled 'no' and dove in front of him just as Leopold fired. Her cry died on her lips, and she thumped to the floor, limp and lifeless. Stupid woman. With his viral enhancement, the pulse would have just pinged off his skin, harmless. Probably, though, she hadn't known that. What a bloody waste.

Not giving the man a chance to reset his aim, Kaleb grabbed him around the neck. How the reverend had learnt to fight, he had no idea. He showed enough skill to make it unlikely he had done so only after the outbreak. In a fluid motion, one well practised, he shoved his hands between Kaleb's arms and broke them apart.

Canmore stepped backward, reversed his weapon, and jabbed the heavy stock at Kaleb's chin. The blow stunned him momentarily, and he dropped to one knee. He hadn't expected such a move from a man who professed to be of the cloth. Kaleb had underestimated him. He wouldn't make the same mistake twice.

Blood dripped from his lower lip, and he wiped it away while rising to his feet. Pity his lips weren't as hardy as the rest of him. What

was that all about? He'd never tried to understand nanotech or biology and wished he'd made
more effort. The two men stood staring at one
another. Why hadn't Leopold finished him off
while he had the upper hand? Why had the fool
let him recover?

But he hadn't. Not really. He had used the
pause to put a little distance between them and
put Kaleb in the crosshairs once more. Pity he
didn't know about the viral enhancement. Otherwise, his move showed the action of a professional. What was his story?

Kaleb's pulse raced, and his heart thumped
hard enough to pound in his neck and temples.
He wanted this man dead in the worst of ways.
Right now, though, things weren't leaning in his
favour. Too quickly, he'd lost the upper hand
he'd gained for brief seconds. Now, he didn't
even have the lower hand—he had no hand at all.
At any moment, Leo would shoot him dead and
then go crawling back to Priya, claiming it had
been self-defence.

At least, events played out that way in
Kaleb's mind because he still didn't entirely trust

his new abilities. But then two things happened almost simultaneously. Canmore pulled rigid wrist cuffs from his utility belt and said, 'She wants you home.'

On the heels of that proclamation, booted feet pounded the ground all around them, the noise echoing off the neostil walls. Both men tensed, ready for trouble.

A second later, special after special rounded each corner until the two adversaries stood surrounded. The army had arrived. At first, Kaleb couldn't grasp what had just happened. Then he remembered the open comms on the fallen soldier. Of course. Straw had heard and seen it all. True to his word, he'd sent help.

Without needing to be told, the reverend dropped his gun to the ground and raised his hands, then he lowered himself to his knees and awaited his fate.

Though still furious, Canmore's final statement rang through Kaleb's mind, *She wants you home.* In spite of everything, Leopold had come for him with the intention of returning him to Priya and, presumably, help. However, he doubted that little old Ellie would have allowed it. So, what was their game?

All of that processed in a mere second or two. Canmore's final words ended up saving his life. The reverend's little speech had given Kaleb an idea. It would work in his favour to return Leo to Priya unharmed. He needed her onside.

Kaleb's travels outside zone one had shown him that, somehow, the population had known of he and Priya and their mission. Had the rebels spread that tale to aid their takeover? One of the first things they'd fixed was the newsnet, albeit with just the one channel, which they promptly got broadcasting via the large communal screens in the centre of each zone. It seemed that the two of them, along with Eloise and Leo, had become heroes of some sort. Then Ellie had let herself down. And because Canmore had supported her, the people also doubted him. But if the rebels had control of the newsnet, then who was spreading the latest propaganda, and to what end?

He shook his head. Those questions would have to wait. Still, if he played his cards right, he and Priya could run the planet together. Although he had the army behind him, he would have a much easier time if he also had the civilians onside too. And to accomplish that, he had to have Priya.

7

E131

Stiff-backed, clench-jawed, and tight-lipped, Priya stood on the far side of the enormous presidential desk, ignoring Kaleb's entreaties to sit. This extravagant slab of mahogany had seen so many different masters come and go recently. If it could talk, what tales would it have to tell?

Leo had found the errant special, all right, but hadn't brought him back. No, that had happened the other way around. And now Leo languished in the cells. Where was Eloise when you needed her? Why hadn't she intervened? Surely she must be seeing this? Or had she foreseen it and fled? Maybe Kaleb and Straw had apprehended her already and just wanted to get Priya publicly onside.

Kaleb sat before her, relaxed and leant back in his plush chair. To her rear, blocking the doorway, the gargantuan Major Straw stood watch.

Both men had just made it clear to her that the army ranks stood behind Kaleb. Which, of course, changed the power balance yet again.

Kaleb straightened and held her gaze. 'Another rebellion is coming—as I'm sure you've heard.'

Mute with fury and apprehension, she settled for a nod.

'I don't know who's running the newsnet, but I do know that the people love you. I suppose folks always love a pretty, plucky heroine. To take advantage of that, we have to move quickly.'

'And if I say no?' Her voice sounded thin and tight.

'Then more people die.' He grinned. 'Perhaps people you care about.'

The thinly-veiled threat to Leo hit her like a punch on the nose. She blinked. Tried not to react. Then Kaleb's boyish side took the upper seat, and his grin softened to a warm smile. 'We're good together. You know that.'

Priya folded her arms. 'Why not leave me out of it altogether?'

A frown erased his brief warmth. 'The people are angry at the army and the regime we represent. For years, we've done the president's bidding.'

Priya snorted. 'And nothing's changed yet, has it? No matter who's in charge, you just jump.'

Kaleb gazed down at the desk, fingers steepled. 'That's about to change.'

'No.' She glared at him. 'The army still supports the regime. Only this time, it will be your regime. In the end, nothing ever changes.'

The man she now ceased to think of as a friend, rose to his feet and returned her glare. 'The populace will route for you more than for me. You will stand by my side—'

'Or you'll kill Leo.'

'Amongst others, yes.'

The violet tint in his eyes glowed brighter. His skin appeared a pale, chalky-white in the artificial lighting. How much had the virus advanced? Subjected to its ever-increasing ravages, how did he stay so strong? Priya trembled at the thought of what her infection might do to her.

She couldn't see that he had left her with an awful lot of choice. She cared deeply about Leo. Feared Kaleb. And taking joint control had to be better than leaving this madman free to do as he pleased, didn't it? A bitter laugh bubbled up and out; let him think of it what he would. Of course it wouldn't be better: Kaleb had no intentions of sharing anything with her. She was the public face … a leader in name only.

Nevertheless, to help Leo, she said, 'I'll do it.'

If nothing else, it might buy her time.

CHAPTER THIRTEEN

1

E127

Ellie's telepathy kept trying to show her something, but she couldn't quite see what. It nagged at her to do something. If only she could see that bit further. Frustrated, she paced her office suite, thankful for the thick carpet which deadened her footfalls and prevented anyone from hearing her struggle.

A little later, slumped in her chair and half-way through a now-tepid cup of coffee, clarity hit her. Sasha Novikov. Whatever this was, it had something—everything—to do with her. Drink forgotten, Ellie rose and strode to the door. At her inner-sight's prompting, she headed straight for the cells.

The girl sat deep in apparent meditation, staring at nothing Eloise could see. Impatient, she uttered a curt, 'Novikov.'

The petite woman stirred and turned her gaze on Eloise. A small smile played with the corners of her lips but got no further. 'We meet again.' Her voice sounded saccharine. 'I wondered when you'd come.'

Ellie turned to Major Straw, 'Open it.'

He did as she bid and unlocked the cell door. Inside, Eloise stood by the cot and glared down at the impertinent little slut. What her husband had ever seen in the girl … but, no, she hadn't come here for that. Swallow by bitter swallow, she gained control of her rage and addressed the point at hand.

'You did something. I need to know.' God, but her inability to see this left her shaking with mixed anger and fear. 'Tell me.'

Despite Ellie's threatening posture, Sasha chuckled. 'You haven't even opened it yet, have you?'

Eloise stood stock still. She managed to whisper, 'The vial?' Then she took a step closer and leant down, 'Tell me what you did.'

With a demure shrug, Sasha stared up—fearless—into Eloise's eyes. 'The vial holds nothing but water, you stupid cow. ... It's useless.'

Shocked and appalled, Ellie slapped Novikov across the face. She rocked to the side, then sat holding her cheek and staring at her. 'You ignorant bitch. How could you?'

Sasha laughed. Big mistake.

Eloise pulled her weapon, intending to shoot the whore who'd ruined everything. She locked her arm, cocked the gun, and tightened her fingers around the trigger. Just one tiny squeeze. And it would be done.

Major Straw stepped up to Eloise and placed a placating hand on her upper arm, using gentle pressure to ease the barrel away from Ms Novikov. 'She may well come in useful later, ma'am.'

The black-out curtain lifted, and Ellie saw the sense in the man's words. But how dare he touch her? He would pay for that. She grabbed viciously at the little bitch's arm and yanked her to her feet. Then she spun on her heels and dragged the girl from the cell, along the corridor, and to the stairs leading to the lower basements.

At the top of the flight, she shook Sasha to punctuate her words. 'I'll incarcerate you down there, in the lowest cells. Nobody will realise you're there. You're mine now.' Then she threw her down the stairs. The woman tumbled head over feet all the way to the bottom, bouncing off every second or third concrete step. At each impact, a cry of pain and fear escaped her.

Once the girl had settled at the bottom, Eloise took her time descending, and then she stood looking over her. Did she realise what she had done? The vial was useless. Stephenson was dead. And Ms Novikov hid something from Ellie yet. Unfortunately, her enhancement chose this moment to play up again, and she couldn't quite see what else the slut hid from her. Ellie's lack of sight worried her.

The red veil of rage descended again, and Ellie drew back her leg and hefted a nasty kick to

Sasha's kidneys. On the floor, the girl writhed and screeched, which only fuelled the attack. She would pay. Eloise would make sure she felt the consequences of her selfishness.

Vaguely, somewhere to her side, some man demanded that she desist. Eloise chose not to hear. Not to yield. This had gone too far. The girl had done too much. It wasn't right. First her husband, then the virus, and now this ... this scheming tramp had ... had ...

A sharp prick stung her neck. Eloise whirled to face her attacker. Major Straw leapt backward, a syringe in his hand. An empty plunger held a drop of liquid suspended from the tip of the needle.

'What did you just do to me?'

But she knew. The traitor had drugged her. When he spoke, his words sounded distant and fogged. 'You're not yourself, ma'am. Just a little sedation, to help you calm.'

Even as she succumbed, she desperately wanted to go at Novikov again. Find out where the rest of the cure was. Although she hadn't used it yet, she did have plans for it. And she couldn't work her telepathy. They were all against her. Every last one of them.

Eloise stumbled. Major Straw caught her by the elbows. She blinked, fighting the drug and trying to stay awake. Against her will, she went all floppy and slumped into his arms. This couldn't be happening. She wouldn't allow it.

2

E128

Ellie awoke in her room, alone. Sprawled on the bed, she did a quick body check. Dressed, not dishevelled. No aches or pains other than the thumping headache from the drug. Good. Nobody had messed with her while she was out. She shuddered. A little out of fear at how vulnerable she had been, still was, but more from fury at the man's audacity. Obviously, she couldn't trust Major Straw.

Cautious, she eased to a sitting position, with her feet off the side of the bed and planted on the floor. The room spun for a couple of seconds and then settled to its standard orientation. Ellie rubbed at her temples, which continued to throb and pulse with a dull ache. Her tongue felt like cotton wool, and she couldn't work up any spit.

Tired and out of sorts, she rose to her feet and staggered to the kitchen, where she ordered cold water from the auto-dispenser. When it came, she grabbed the glass and gulped greedily. Already, her mind ran through the ramifications and what her next steps should be.

The biggest mistake those around her had made was to believe her to be an altruistic person. Just because she had previously always taken the moral stand and never said much, it didn't mean that she presented what she was. Human, just like everyone else, she fell victim to anger and hurt and made mistakes. Just as she had discovered since that fateful helipod crash. Nobody was perfect, and it was sheer stupidity to believe otherwise.

People's erroneous perceptions also put her in this difficult position now. She simply couldn't give them what they expected. Not yet. And she couldn't trust anyone enough to tell them why.

Not until she found *him*. He might have fooled the others, but she had seen.

Once she'd put herself back to rights and felt about as good as she was going to, Ellie strode into the presidential office and ordered Major Straw to attend with haste. After only a couple of minutes, the man knocked tentatively. When she called 'enter', he did so, but he looked edgy. As well he might.

Ellie didn't waste breath or time. 'You're fired.'

He hung his head. Didn't try to protest or explain.

Unbidden, her sight flashed to brief life. She saw it all. His dismissal would set him up for allowing Exxon 3—where his sister lived—to invade. By that time, it wouldn't matter. Not for her. Straw would see, very soon, that he had made a mistake in putting himself behind … Kaleb … ah, so that was what was afoot. She hid her tired, ironic smile. The man didn't yet realise that Priya and Leo were infected too. That would change things. There and then, Ellie decided she would wait a while until she revoked his comms access. Let him do what he would. It might even work in her favour. Or, at the least, in the planet's favour.

Meanwhile, she had to find the remaining stocks of the cure. The ones that Professor Stephenson had worked on under Terrence's rule. She glared hard at Straw. 'You're dismissed.'

He gave her a sharp salute and marched from the office. The newly-built outer door closed so quietly that she couldn't hear it. To make sure he had left, she got up and opened the inner door. The outer chamber stood empty of anything alive. When she tried to turn her vision to discovering Leopold's location, it stuttered and died. Just like that, she'd gone blind again. Sod it.

Something was wrong. The certain knowledge that she was missing something plagued her. With a shrug, Ellie got to work organising search teams to tear the zone and the labs apart if needs be. She had to find that cure.

And there, that day in zone one, Ellie realised something. That no such thing as free will existed. How could it, when nobody lived in isolation? Other people acted, the laws of the universe worked and interacted. Within that, you could make choices, but not necessarily on anything you wanted. Sometimes, your only options were terrible options. And still, the fundamental human right to have freedom of choice retained utmost importance within those damned universal laws. Ellie would have her way yet.

The final search-team head came to tell her the same news that all the rest had delivered already. They could find no stocks of the cure. This guy had led the search of the main labs, and he had more to say. 'We found fridge upon fridge of empty shelves. The incinerators show signs of recent use. And we found this.' The man held out a hand.

On his palm sat a piece of orange neoplast, singed around the edges. Stickiness coated the curve of its inner surface. Water wasn't sticky. Nano proteins and their carrier were. Eloise clenched her fist. Through gritted teeth, she said, 'Thank you. That will be all.'

Not wanting to be the messenger that got shot, he turned and dashed from the office. Furious, Eloise marched from the room and headed for the lower cells. She would get the rest out of the selfish little whore, one way or the other.

As before, Novikov sat staring into space, appearing far too serene for Ellie's liking. Swollen flesh and purpled bruises marred her pretty little face and throat. When she spoke, her voice came out as a hoarse croak. 'You again.'

Without wasting time, Eloise had the guard open up the cell and strode in, where she grabbed Sasha by her already traumatised neck. 'Tell me. Everything.'

Within the choke-hold, Novikov gurgled a laugh and pointed to the fingers pressing her windpipe. Ellie let go. Sasha said, 'I destroyed it all.'

Shock rocked Ellie on her feet, and she staggered back. 'Why would you do such a thing?'

The girl had the humility to hang her head. But Ellie soon realised it wasn't out of shame or remorse, more like sadness from betrayal. From things gone wrong. Staring at the floor, Novikov admitted, 'They used me. Betrayed me. All of them.' She glanced up at Ellie and shrugged then returned her gaze to the grimy floor. 'Before I left zone ten, I'd vaccinated myself, and by the time I saw how it was here in the capital, I just didn't care anymore.'

Betrayal, Eloise could relate to. She eased herself down onto the end of the cot and listened, waiting for more.

Sasha wiped an eye and sniffed. 'Giles did the most damage. I loved her, and she used that in the worst way. I've had enough. So why don't you just kill me now?' She stared at Eloise. 'All my life, it's been like this.'

Silent, unable to put her warring emotions into words, Ellie stood and walked from the cell. She bid the guard to lock it again. Right now, she wanted to kill the girl. But on the other hand, she could understand her pain and suffering. Understand her anger. Could Understand why she'd done what she'd done in a fit of pique. What gave Ellie the most pain and difficulty to swallow was the knowledge that both of them had responded in similar ways to hurt and betrayal. To anger.

That didn't sit well. And to add insult to injury, it seemed that nobody had any cure to combat the awful devastation of the nano-virus that raged throughout the Exxon system. The fallback could have been Priya Shaw's natural immunity, but she had succumbed to the virus too—or some mutation of it. Which amounted to the same thing. If it could mutate, nobody was safe. Was this the end of humanity?

3

E131

Right now, Priya hated herself. She'd locked her squealing, protesting baby raptor—which she'd named Toothy—in her room and snuck her way through the zone to the upper cell block where Kaleb and his crew hid. Although she didn't want to back him, she felt she had little choice—or, at any rate, no good ones.

Once she met up with him, Kaleb wasted no time. They marched for the presidential suite, shooting any rebel troop who tried to stop them. Priya felt duty-bound to warn Kaleb of Eloise's telepathic ability, but he shrugged off her caution.

They broke down the door, and Kaleb stormed into the room, with Priya at his heels. Like a dog. Which fitted her situation quite nicely, she thought. A defiant dog brought to heel. At least he hadn't stuck more than a metaphorical a muzzle on her. Not yet.

Ellie stood ready for them, as Priya had known she would. Instead of trying to persuade them from their planned course, she raised her pistol, aimed it at Priya, and fired.

Kaleb leapt in front of Priya.

Took the bullet for her.

Priya screamed.

When he dropped to the floor, everyone stood frozen.

A couple of seconds dripped out, and Priya stood waiting for copious pools of blood to form. They didn't. After another second, Kaleb groaned and pushed himself to a sitting position. Then he laughed. Still chuckling, he shoved to his feet.

Kaleb had taken the bullet meant to end her life. This, more than anything else, highlighted what a mixed bag of good/evil he had become. And, evidently, he did care for her, in his own twisted way.

Nonchalant, he told her, 'I'm impervious to bullets.'

So, he hadn't risked anything for her, after all.

Shaken, Priya followed his gaze. Where she'd expected to find a stricken Eloise, she found only empty space. In the initial confusion and shock, the woman had managed to slip away. But how? She hadn't left by the door.

On edge, propelled by curiosity, Priya eased around the far side of the enormous desk just in time to see a trap door slide shut on silent hinges. In the beam of sunlight from one of the vast windows, the dust motes danced and slowly settled. Once the portal closed fully, it left no traces. Had she rounded the furniture just a second or two later, she would have missed this completely.

Kaleb came and stood slightly behind her. A soft curse left his lips. Then he ordered one of the soldiers present, 'Find her.'

Everyone except Priya and Kaleb scrambled to action, and soon—too soon—the two of them stood alone. As far as she was concerned, this alliance couldn't be any unhappier, but he seemed delighted. As if his overpowering Leo and forcing Priya's hand had made it all right again.

Though their mini-coup had removed the corrupt element, Kaleb confused the picture. He was no longer a good person. Nor was he entirely bad. The brainwashing and the virus had damaged him. But, at times, the old Kaleb shone through. It left Priya so confused.

Even though he'd already dismissed any input she offered, Priya tried one more suggestion. 'I don't think you need to worry overly much about Ellie. You have Leo. You have me. And that means you have the rebels. Let him out of the cells, and he'll cooperate.'

Kaleb shook his head and sneered. 'You're clueless. Leave the politics and tactics to me.' With that, he strode from the room.

Alone, at last, Priya stood with pursed lips, deep in thought. This tension between them couldn't endure. Again and again, Kaleb put down any ideas or requests that Priya offered. Fed up, she wondered if she'd done the right thing. Was there any way she could extricate herself from this useless arrangement? She cursed Leo and all he stood for. He never should have talked her into coming back.

The telephone rang.

Priya leapt in fright.

Sudden guilt washed through her, and she glanced around. In that tiniest fraction of a second, Priya knew she intended to answer the call even though Kaleb had said she shouldn't involve herself in anything. Her furtive glance told her she remained alone. Nervous, but also morbidly curious, she reached out trembling fingers to pick up the handset. 'Hello?'

An educated, formal-sounding female voice greeted her. By name. 'Miss Shaw. Lady Ruby Morris here, from Exxon 3. May I call you Priya?'

Again, Priya glanced around the presidential inner office. The room was, supposedly, impregnable. But someone had bugged it. They must have, or how else would Lady Morris have known that here Priya stood, alone? She cleared her throat. 'Yes.' Priya paused to sort her thoughts. 'What can I do for you, Ruby?'

Her use of the minister's first name hit the mark, and it took Lady Morris a second too long to reply. 'If one can put aside petty differences, one can achieve much. The rest of the Exxon system has come together. Were you aware we have developed a cure?'

Priya gasped.

Lady Morris said, 'I thought not. We wanted to liaise with Exxon 1, but thus far, its leaders have proven unwilling.' Another pause ensued. Then Ruby spoke again, 'I wonder will you be any different?'

The question, it seemed, was a rhetorical one, for the minister went on without waiting for a response from Priya. 'We have administered the cure to our people. We have assisted our populations in reforming society and repairing. Your planet needs us. Your people need us. You need us.'

Stunned, still processing how much the five planets had achieved by banding together, Priya slumped down into the nearest chair—the president's seat. Lady Morris and her cohorts had gained the upper hand. They had something to hold over Exxon 1 and whoever took charge. And no matter who held the reins, the planet's people desperately needed that something.

Alongside all those thoughts, Priya's brain managed yet more calculations. A light-bulb lit up in her head. 'You have control of our newsnet. You're the ones who've been spreading all that propaganda. But, why promote Kaleb? Me?'

'You are a bright girl. Neither Terrence nor Martins—the Mr or the Mrs—would cooperate with us. So, naturally, we turned our attentions to yourself and Special Moore.'

Priya nodded, deep in thought. 'I can see why you no longer want Kaleb in power, which is why you waited until he'd vacated the room, but I don't understand why you want me. Why would you put the people behind me? I'm no good to you. Especially not with this virus.'

'We have the cure, my sweet child. Let us help you. Together, we can achieve much.'

It didn't take her long. Only waiting long enough to suck air into her tired lungs, Priya said, 'Yes. I'll work with you. But I don't know what to do about Kaleb. And someone is still spreading the virus. They have to be, or I wouldn't have contracted it this late. I had to have been immune to the original. Or do I sound crazy?'

Lady Morris chuckled. 'Not at all. I would have to agree with you.' She hummed while she worked out her words. 'We have identified another player. One we shall help you take care of.'

'Who?' Priya held the handset in a white-knuckled grip.

'That I cannot tell you just now.'

Priya nodded. Then, resolved and newly determined, she jumped into the deep end, 'Tell me what you need me to do.'

4

E141

The 24-hour deadline that Lady Ruby Morris had set yesterday had just expired. Worried, Priya chewed her thumbnail. Ten days on from their telephone conversation, the prime minister of Exxon 3 had grown impatient of Priya's protestations that Kaleb simply wouldn't listen to her.

Eloise Martins remained at large, and Priya didn't believe that Major Straw—whom Kaleb had reinstated—was trying particularly hard to find her. She didn't trust the man. He was up to something.

Leo still languished in the upper cells, along with his fellow rebels, so she had no one to help her. She was on her own. Damn it. Damn everyone. Damn everything.

In a bad mood, which he always seemed to be in these days, Kaleb stormed into the presidential suite and beckoned Priya to follow him into the inner office. Once again, desperate now, Priya tried to talk to him about their next steps.

'What's the point? If we don't accept the cure that the other planets are offering and give it out, why did we take over? We might as well have just left Eloise in place.'

'The bloody point is—' Kaleb stopped and dragged a hand through his overlong and wild-looking hair. It was as if his brain had stuttered to a sudden stop. That happened a lot lately. Priya believed it was partly because of the brainwashing, but more so because of the virus. He didn't have long left to live.

She held out a hand and touched his elbow lightly. 'Kaleb, please.'

He jerked away as if scalded. 'Shut up!'

The door burst open.

Unknown troops dashed into the room.

Quickly, efficiently, they subdued and secured Priya and Kaleb. A suited man walked in and studied them. He settled a smile on Priya, which replaced the consternated frown he'd just levelled at Kaleb. 'Miss Shaw. A pleasure. Lady Morris has told me so much about you.'

Kaleb shot her daggers from narrowed eyes.

The suited man held out a hand, which she took and shook.

'Johnson Bartholomew at your service.'

'You're from Exxon 2?' She didn't have much knowledge of the world away from Exxon 1.

He nodded. 'I represent all five planets.' Then he smiled and shook his head. 'My mistake. As of now, I represent all six.'

Rather uselessly, in Priya's opinion, Kaleb

burst out, 'The alarms didn't activate. We didn't hear any fighting.'

Bartholomew's smile held a tinge of sadness. 'I'm afraid we had help.'

Priya named the traitor, 'Major Straw.'

'Lady Morris was correct. You *are* a bright girl. Yes, with his assistance, we hacked the presidential portal to bring in our troops undetected and—thus—unchallenged. That same hack disabled your alarms. We decided that enough blood had been shed on one and that stealth was the better part of valour.'

Priya said, 'Not just the presidential portal. You had to have hacked and used the army portals in the zone too.'

Bartholomew smiled broadly. 'Just so.' Almost immediately, a frown settled onto his lined face. 'We had so hoped you would cooperate as promised.'

Priya swallowed. 'I'm sorry. I tried.' She flicked a glance at Kaleb.

Bartholomew pursed his lips. At that moment, soldiers dragged in Ellie and John Martins. Priya's jaw dropped. She shut it with a snap.

'How did …?'

Both of them appeared bedraggled and un-kempt.

The minister of Exxon 2 shook his head and looked pained. 'We discovered Mrs Martins attempting to sneak her husband from his cell.' He pierced Priya with a hard stare. 'Now, it's time we got to the bottom of events here in Exxon 1's capital, I think. Just what the dickens has been going on over here?'

'Betrayal upon betrayal.' Eloise showed her teeth in a smile full of malice.

Priya protested, 'From you and your bloody husband.'

John laughed. 'So that's it? You're trying to drop my wife and I in it to save your own skins? Nice.'

Bartholomew watched and listened.

Shock and outrage made Priya's voice sound all breathy and weak, 'You're twisting it.'

Eloise caught the minister's attention. 'I tried to do some good. I really did. But at every turn, I had to fight the young Miss Shaw and the army she had behind her. She even turned the Reverend Canmore against me.'

Priya gasped. 'That's not true.'

Bartholomew held up a hand, palm outward. 'That's enough.' He sighed and dropped his head for a few seconds, and then he raised it and stiffened his spine. 'Quite obviously, I shan't get to the bottom of this anytime soon. Right now, I don't know who to believe. Mr Moore, you're staying quiet ...'

They all turned to stare at Kaleb.

He lay on the floor, unconscious. He'd passed out.

The minister grimaced and then glanced from one to the other. 'In the event that I cannot get to the truth of the matter, you leave me with no choice. The time has arrived for a clean sweep. Executions are set for seven days hence.' He nodded to the guards, who had assembled at the entrance to the outer office. 'Take them away. Separate cells, well away from one another.' He stared at Priya, 'I believe you might benefit from a little company down in the cells.'

Despite having just heard her death sentence pronounced by this invader, her heart leapt. Did he mean Leo? Appalled and hopeful both at once, she didn't protest when two armed soldiers, wearing uniforms she didn't recognise, took her arms and led her from the suite.

Within minutes, though, her hopes shattered. She never saw Leo. They took her to the lowest level of the cell block, where dampness and mould thrived on the despair of the prisoners. Once in the depths, with only stale air to greet her, they dragged her—reluctant now—to the furthest end of the dim corridor.

Completely ignoring her protests and pleas, they opened a barred door and shoved her into a tiny cell. The door clanged shut with a bong of finality. Saddened and deflated, Priya turned toward the one bunk in the room. A pretty—if unwashed—blonde girl occupied it, staring at Priya.

With a glare, she said, 'Who the hell are you?'

CHAPTER FOURTEEN

1

E141

Scared, unprepared, Priya backed up until the bars dug into her spine. Over these last months, she'd lost far too much weight. Her bones poked through where once she'd boasted soft curves. The cell's occupant watched her, both women wary.

Then the woman stood and adopted a menacing stance. 'I won't ask you again. Who the hell are you?'

Priya squared up too. 'Hey. Knock it off. We're both in the same ship here.'

'Right. Of course we are. You don't have a death sentence hanging over your head.'

Priya perched on the very end of the small cot. 'I wouldn't be too sure of that.' Then she relented and held out a hand. 'I'm Priya Shaw.'

After a short hesitation, the blonde shook Priya's hand. 'Sasha Novikov.'

She, too, dropped onto the further end of the cot. They sat in wary silence for a while—the small gap between them looming like a vast canyon.

Priya grew antsy. She'd never felt comfortable with prolonged silences—not when in company. Her own company, she liked just fine. Eventually, her discomfort joined forces with her natural curiosity: she'd heard a lot about the Russian-descended young woman. None of it good.

'Did you do what they say you did?'

Sasha watched her for a few seconds, wary and working out her words. In the end, she settled for a shrug, which fell a long way short of satisfying Priya. 'You released the virus.'

A nod.

'Deliberately.'

Another shrug.

Priya shot to her feet and crossed her arms, towering over the other woman. 'Oh, come on. You killed all those innocent people, and now you won't own it?' Disgusted, she turned her back on Novikov.

From behind her, Sasha said, 'It wasn't just me.'

Priya spun back to face her. 'That's your excuse?'

Sasha started to shrug again, then stalled. Instead, she let out a long, heavy sigh.

Priya pressed, 'You killed Terrence. Aged Martins. And—craziest of all—you destroyed all stocks of the cure. Why?' She bent over Sasha, who cowered back against the wall. 'Just tell me that much.'

At the sight of the cowed woman, all her energy dissipated in a rush, and Priya slumped down onto her end of the single cot. Why had they put her in this cell with this woman? Obviously, it was only meant to hold one person. What did they hope to achieve? Two blondes stuck together in a tiny room, opposites in everything but hair colour. So, why put them together?

In the smallest of voices, Sasha opened up. 'I just wanted to be safe.'

Despite the strong urge to berate the woman for her stupidity and selfishness, Priya forced herself to remain silent. To listen.

'My whole life, that's all I wanted.'

Priya's restraint broke. 'What, and sod everyone else?'

Sasha recoiled.

Priya sighed. 'Sorry. Go on.' She jammed a thumb into her mouth and chewed it.

'In this world, people take whatever they want. Whenever they want. However they want.' She stared up at Priya, all at once defiant. 'So, tell me, why should I care?'

Her words made Priya pause for thought. She removed her thumb from her lips and wiped the saliva off on her jumpsuit bottoms. 'I got hurt too. Do you see me breaking the planet?'

Sasha hung her head. 'I'm sorry.'

'Can you not tell me why?'

'I didn't realise it would turn out like this.

Terrence and Martins lied to me. Manipulated me. And then Ellie … she … I guess I broke her too.'

Priya nodded. 'I thought she was a good woman. Someone who could help get us all back on our feet. How wrong was I?'

Sasha squeezed her hands between her knees. 'We both got it wrong. That's my fault. Look how much I hurt her by trying to protect myself. Oh God, I've done so much damage.'

Priya shook her head. 'No. I keep getting it wrong. I keep trusting people and expecting them to do the right thing. I swear, I'm begging to get hurt again and again.'

Sasha stared at her. 'So, what's the right answer?'

Priya shrugged. 'Fucked if I know.'

In spite of the tension and brevity—perhaps even because of it—the two cellmates burst out laughing. Their mirth held an edge of hysteria, however, and after a few seconds, tears mingled with the uncontrollable snorts and guffaws. A few seconds more elapsed. The pair quieted. Sniffled. Coughed. Couldn't meet one another's gaze.

Slowly, rational thought reasserted itself. Now Priya did look at Sasha. She'd just realised something. 'Maybe you can help.'

Surprised, Sasha jerked. 'What? No. You've got the wrong girl. I'm not good for anything. Anyone. You have to realise that.'

'You don't have any choice.'

A sarcastic laugh escaped Sasha. 'Oh, sweetie, we all have choices. Not always good ones, but we do get to choose, all the same.'

Once more, Priya rose to her feet—weary this time, rather than angry. 'And you choose this?'

'Right now, death's about the best thing that could happen to me.'

2

E141

For the next hour, Priya left the girl alone. Instead of pressing her, she worked hard to make small talk and put her at her ease. After a couple of halting starts, she even opened up about the rape and assault. Then, on an impulse, she finished by telling Sasha, 'You made that happen. You let the virus out. What did I ever do to hurt you? Why would you not help me now? In my direst need?'

Tears streamed down Sasha's cheeks as she sat and sobbed silently, sucking in great lungfuls of air and expelling it in sharp bursts of pain. Breath and words hitching, she tried again to deny Priya's request. 'I—c-can't. They—they'll k-kill me. I'll be s-signing my—my death warrant.'

'You're dead anyway. Won't you see that?'

'I don't know what to do.' On the last word, Sasha's voice broke down into a long, drawn-out wail, and she turned imploring eyes up to Priya.

Relentless, hating herself for being so cruel, Priya pushed harder. 'You can at least die for a reason. If they're going to kill you anyway, why won't you help us? Surely you want to put right whatever you can?'

Priya dropped to her knees and gripped the woman's hands. 'Please. You have to at least try.'

Sasha cried harder, and then she dropped her

head into her hands, rocking back and forth on the cot and sobbing. Priya let her be, for now. If she pushed her into a nervous breakdown, the woman wouldn't be good for anything.

Another five minutes passed. Sasha calmed and did her best to wipe her face with her hands. She looked a mess. Chagrined, Priya offered, 'I'm sorry. I am. But you're our last hope.'

Sasha nodded and gave one final sniffle and hand swipe under her runny nose. 'I'll do it. I'll tell them everything they want to know. You're right. It won't make any difference to me. I'm dead anyway.'

Relieved, Priya threw her arms around the Russian and hugged her tight. Sasha tensed and then wriggled out of the embrace. Her expression showed horror and distaste. Instead of feeling repelled and rejected, Priya found herself pitying the woman. What had happened in her life that was so bad? What did it take to make an innocent child grow into such a ruthless, evil adult who could take comfort from nowhere?

But was she so bad? Could Priya honestly say that anyone was either all good or all bad? Or were they simply human—prey to the vagaries of life, love, and hurt? Could she say of herself that she was a good person through and through? She thought of the man she'd knifed to death so viciously. Yes, he'd been infected. Yes, he'd attacked them. And, yes, she'd fought for her life, and for Kaleb's. But, at the end of this week, when she faced her maker, would that excuse prove enough? No. She didn't have to be so brutal. Didn't have to respond so violently to her fear and pain. She could have stopped sooner. A lot sooner.

Sasha broke into her thoughts, 'So, what do we do now?'

Priya cleared her throat and got to her feet. 'We talk to Bartholomew.' To that end, she crossed to the bars and called for the guards.

A sultry young man ambled down the corridor and to their cage. There, he slouched against the wall and undressed her with his eyes. Then he gave Sasha the same treatment. Priya bit her tongue until she drew blood. If she could get him alone … and there she went again. How could she, in all conscience, call herself a nice person?

No, just like everyone else, she was a mixed bag. Capable of much. Scary thought. But then, thinking a thing wasn't the same as doing a thing.

'We want to talk to Mr Bartholomew.'

He sneered and shook his head. Sasha joined Priya at the bars and gripped them with both hands. 'I have something to tell him.'

Priya added, 'It's important.'

Sasha said, 'Believe us. He wants to hear this.'

Still adopting a lazy demeanour, the guard turned away and ambled back the way he'd come. Would he pass on their message or not? With a sigh, Priya resigned herself to waiting. So much for always having a choice.

Sasha's earlier words had rattled her more than she cared to think. Was she trying to say that even in her worst extremity, being taken against her will by Hank and his men, that she'd had some sort of choice? To say that she found that hard to swallow would have to be the understatement of the millennium. *I mean, for crying out loud.*

About twenty minutes later, the same lazy

footsteps approached from down the dimly lit corridor. Unspoken, both Priya and Sasha held their positions, not deigning to show him the respect of rising to their feet. They made him stand and clear his throat before they even acknowledged his presence.

'He'll see you.'

Priya nodded and shoved to her feet. Sasha stood too. In silence, both watched him unlock and open the door. Priya stepped forward, showing bravery she didn't feel. Her heart thumped at her rib cage, and her throat felt tight. She didn't have to do this. Go with Sasha. But then again, of course she did. Didn't she?

An escort of four armed guards waited for them at the station at the end of the corridor. Priya felt thankful that they'd left Mr Sultry behind them, for the time being. The guards remained silent and alert but behaved well enough. No inappropriate touching, nor prodding, nor jabbing. And no innuendo either. In these reduced circumstances, she'd take what she could get.

Their escort led them to the presidential suite. Once again, Priya wondered what the monstrosity of a mahogany desk would say could it speak. What stories it might tell. Would any sound stranger than what Sasha was about to say?

Johnson Bartholomew sat in the president's chair and studied them when they came in. With a wave of his hand, he dismissed the guards. Uninvited to sit, the two women remained standing. The minister steepled his fingers on his chest, reclined in the sumptuous chair. 'You had something to say?'

He arched a brow at Priya. 'Not me, sir.'

Sasha stepped forward. 'I do. I know things you should hear.'

Impatient, he flicked a hand at her to get on with it. Priya's heart sank. Even before Sasha told her tale about Terrence, Mr Martins, Ellie, and herself, he had decided to disbelieve them. To label them all liars. And Sasha, in her own words, had just labelled herself a manipulator of the highest order. Priya should have seen it coming. But she had harboured some small hope that he had imprisoned her with Sasha for a purpose. Why else would he have stabled them together? Why else would he have thought that Priya would benefit from 'a little company', as he put it?

To give him his due, he did sit and listen without interruption until she'd finished speaking. He even sat quietly, contemplating, for a few minutes.

'Such an abundance of secrets and lies. Such an abundance of fools.' Curtly, he dismissed them, 'Go.'

The guards must have waited, listening, somewhere nearby, for they strode in and marched Priya and Sasha back to their cell without her seeing Bartholomew summon or signal them in any way.

Deflated, dejected, neither woman struggled or tried to resist their fates. Priya consoled herself with the knowledge that she had tried. Had done her best. What else could anyone ask of her?

3

E142

The day of the execution drew one day closer.

What was happening with the others? Ellie and John, she didn't much care about. But Leo and Kaleb? And what about herself and Sasha? How would they die? A swift all-but-painless death, or long and drawn out—sadistic?

If they died now, the world wouldn't ever discover the truth. Their names would live on in ignominy. While little miss Novikov had striven for power her whole life, all Priya had ever wanted was peace and quiet, anonymity. Everything regular and ordered and known. Except that it hadn't been known, had it? That had been a mere illusion. Or should she call it a delusion? As far as she could see, it amounted to the same thing.

The night had passed uncomfortably, with the two women taking it in turns to share the narrow cot. At first, they had tried sleeping sitting leant against the wall, but neither one had managed to drop off. And then Priya had slumped in a half-doze of exhaustion and fallen onto the hard, damp, cold, and unforgiving floor. After that, they had agreed to take it in turns lying down.

They spelled one another in two-hour shifts. For the majority of the morning, they followed the same routine, each restless and giving out copious sighs. Eventually, Priya had had enough. She couldn't stand to stay still any longer. In desperate need of a distraction, of solace of any kind, she rose from her crouched, uncomfortable position on the floor, and paced the tiny cell. Three steps to the rear, three to the bars, and back again. Until Sasha snapped at her to stop.

Priya turned her frustration on her. 'What the hell else do you want me to do? For God's sake. None of this would have happened if not for you and your sick ambition.'

Sasha recoiled as if slapped.

Guilt and shame flooded through Priya's body. She felt that she ought to apologise but choked on the words. Her tongue glued itself to the roof of her mouth. Mute, furious, ashamed, she continued her useless pacing. The small confines soon made her dizzy.

Sasha stood. 'I'll make this right.'

Priya's guilt made her one word sound angrier than ever, 'How?' She scowled and crossed her arms.

The young blonde shuffled over to the bars

and peered out. 'I'll use my body.'

'What?' Then Priya's brain sprinted across the half-mile chasm she'd lagged behind. 'No. You can't.'

Novikov gripped the bars. 'We have no other choice.' She stared at Priya, looking sad and wrung out. 'We'll die, and no one will ever discover the truth of what happened here. Worse still, that bitch and her husband might yet end up back in control.'

Priya blanched. 'That can't happen.' She shook her head and returned Sasha's gaze. 'They wouldn't, would they?'

Sasha shrugged. 'Would you have predicted any of this?'

Slumped back on the cot, dismayed, Priya shook her head in the negative. 'Of course not.'

The young Russian seemed to find some resolve, and her spine straightened. 'Well, then, there's nothing else for it.' She renewed her grip on the bars and yelled, 'Guard! Guard!'

Both women held their breath and waited. Who would come? Would anyone? Urgently, Sasha whispered, 'While I occupy him, you steal his keys.' A moment's hesitation had her change her mind. 'No. You'll have to kill him. Do you know how to break a man's neck?'

Appalled, Priya held up her hands, palms blocking in a defensive gesture. 'We can't murder him. He's just doing his job. That's barbaric. I'll steal his keys, yes, but not that. No way.'

Steel glinted in the blonde's narrowed eyes. 'You have to. He'll raise the alarm if you don't. Stop being so soft.'

Priya retreated all three steps to the far side of the cell. 'I won't do it.'

Footsteps drew close, halting their hushed argument. One final glance lingered between them, and then it fled. The same young guard from yesterday appeared at the exit. His expression held even more disdain and boredom than the day prior. Instead of speaking, asking what they wanted, he just stood and glared at them.

While Priya shrank into the shadows, Sasha shoved her shoulders back, which pushed out her chest. She undid the zipper enough to show a teasing glimpse of tight cleavage and licked her lips. Head bent close to the bars, she murmured,

'A girl gets lonely down here, you know.'

The greedy glint in his eyes showed Priya that he did know. It showed her how lonely the guards down here got too. What had they gotten themselves into? Could they do this? Could she kill him?

No.

Definite.

Simple.

She couldn't do it. But he was here now. Already undoing his zipper and juggling the keys at the lock in a clumsy frenzy to get at the girl. Shit. She *had* to do it. Priya couldn't let Sasha sleep with him for nothing. They were counting on each other.

Priya watched which key he selected. Burned it into her memory. And then tried to go away somewhere in her head.

Disgusted, terrified, and torn, she melted as far into the shadows as she could, trying not to watch but not having much success. She waited until his grunts and pants grew frantic, and then she eased up to the side of the copulating pair.

The guard grew alarmed at her approach, and

Priya had to force a smile and caress his naked buttocks. 'Me, too,' she whispered.

He bought it and returned his focus to Sasha's skilful ministrations. Swallowing her bile, Priya inched the keys from the lock, where the guard had left them in his horny zeal. The bunch jangled. Priya froze. Sasha covered with a loud moan and writhed beneath the young man, feigning the edge of orgasm.

Somehow, despite her shaking, Priya managed to ease the keys into her pocket. Suspicious again, the guard glanced at her. Revolted but committed, she returned to caressing him until he stopped thrusting into Sasha and bucked, groaning.

Bile rose up her throat, and she worked hard to swallow it back down. After all, Sasha had taken one for the team, not her. Acutely aware of the need to distract the young man long enough that he forgot about the keys he'd left in the door, she leant against the open entrance and smiled at him.

Flushed and satiated, he grinned at her. 'I'll come back for you later.'

'Be sure you do.'

A moment of terror snatched her breath when he slammed the door shut, but the lock auto-engaged and he sauntered away down the corridor, humming a soft tune. For the time being, unaware of his loss.

4

E142

Not wasting any time, Priya fumbled the keys from her pocket and dropped them. With a curse, she bent and grabbed them. Shaking more than ever, she shuffled through them until she held the big key in her grasp. Then she reached through the bars and bent her wrist as far as it would go, trying to angle for the lock on the outside of the bars. On the first go, she missed, and then she had it. The large, heavy key slid in and turned the bolts with a satisfying clunk. Behind her, Sasha put herself to rights. Thank God these lower levels didn't have electronic doors like the main cell blocks.

As soon as they stepped foot into the corridor, the alarms blared. Both women froze. Then they ran. Down the hallway away from the guard station. Priya hoped Sasha knew where she was going. If not, this was no better than the blind leading the blind.

With each footfall, she scolded herself for her squeamishness. She should have done as Sasha wanted and killed the guard. He must have discovered the missing keys almost immediately. Of course he had. She should have known better.

While the alarms blared, Sasha led Priya to the central lab. What was she doing? That would be one of the first places they'd look, wouldn't it? But then she took them into some sort of storage closet. Did she think this would hide them from their pursuers? They mustn't get caught. This was their one chance. She'd heard they'd discovered the professor's body in some sort of hidden lab, and now wondered if—perhaps—this was where Sasha intended to lead them. A panel at the rear of the room slid back and silenced Priya's doubts and questions. A secret place. That would work. They could wait it out until the pursuit died down. Most likely, the invading Bartholomew had no clue about this space. Brilliant.

Sasha led them through the dark. Priya stumbled at stairs and had to grab a banister to keep her balance. Sasha hissed at her to be careful. The change in sounds and echoes, as well as the air, alerted Priya to the fact they'd entered a larger chamber. When she reached her arms out to each side, they no longer found walls. She sucked in a sharp breath.

The lights came on. They stood in an underground lab. Sasha spared her a brief grin and then dashed to the far side of the room, where she levered herself up onto one of the counters. Priya envied the girl's agility and poise. If she'd tried a move like that, she would've ended up flat on her back and looking a right fool.

The Russian removed a ceiling panel and reached up into the dark above, where she rummaged around for a few seconds. Then her face lit up in triumph, and she lowered her arm. In her hand, she gripped a tightly wrapped package.

Impressed with the woman's reserves and

ingenuity, Priya stood and watched, astounded, as she slid on nimble feet to the floor and undid the fastenings. A small flash-drive glinted in the bright overheads. Sheets of paper followed from the envelope. Intrigued but cautious, Priya eased over to Sasha's side.

'What is this?'

'Redemption.'

Wide-eyed, Priya asked, 'It will save us?'

Sasha settled the papers on the gleaming countertop and held the drive aloft. 'If this doesn't, nothing can.'

For the first time in a while, hope returned. True hope which believed that Priya—together with Sasha—could actually make a difference. She straightened her spine. 'What do you need me to do?'

'I got this from John Martins' apartments before I tried to run. I had to keep Stephenson from finding them. This—' She twirled the drive in her hand '—will show us how to develop a truth serum.'

'What, to make people tell the truth? Get Eloise and Martins to have to confess?'

'Not quite. If I get it right, it will force anyone injected with it to see everything at one single touch. Nobody will be able to hide from whoever has this serum in their blood.'

Priya squinted then frowned. 'I was supposed to be immune to the virus. Would this work on me?' She shrugged, helpless. 'And look at me now—infected. How does that even work?'

Sasha rested a hand on Priya's shoulder and gave it a gentle squeeze. 'If you really were immune to the original virus, then someone must have engineered a strain targeted at you.' Fear clouded her features. 'As to who or why, I couldn't begin to guess. But, anyway, this serum should work on anyone. It's different from the nano-tech in the virus.'

'I'll have to take your word on that. This is all beyond me.' For the time being, Priya tried and failed to ignore the rest of what Sasha had just said. Who could have targeted her deliberately? Who would have? Not Leo. Ellie? Someone else? Kaleb? She doubted it. That wouldn't fit with what he'd said he wanted from her. One of his allies, then? Major Straw? But why?

Perturbed, she forced herself to return her attention to the young scientist. 'How do you know all this stuff?'

Sasha shrugged, humble. 'I grew up with it. This is what I've always wanted to do.'

'Okay. So, how can I help?'

'Keep a lookout. Make sure nobody comes through that panel from the box room. If they do, shout. It might give me time to hide.'

Surprised, Priya swung her gaze around the pristine room. 'Where?'

Sasha shook her head. 'Best if you don't know.'

Priya nodded. 'Then I can't give you away.'

Just then, her stomach rumbled. The women shared a chuckle. Sasha said, 'I can't feed you, but we do have water on tap. Grab a drink and then go and stand as lookout.'

Priya did as Sasha suggested and then settled herself to watch and wait on the far side of the door, which led into the hidden corridor and stairs. The seconds stretched into minutes, which stretched into hours, which stretched into seeming days. More than a few times, she had to shake herself from a doze. Again and again, sleep tried to sneak up on her, demanding payback for the unsettled night she'd had the night before.

A distant yell brought her to sudden wakefulness. Alarmed, Priya leapt to her feet, spun around, and … stopped. How the hell could she get back into the hidden lab? Stupid girl that she was; she'd neglected to ask Sasha how she'd activated the sliding panel. From behind, she hadn't seen how she'd gained access upon their hurried arrival.

Frustrated, she stood and studied the flat expanse of wall. Her heart thumped hard. What had Sasha's yell been about? Did it portend more trouble yet? God damn it, where the hell was the switch?

The wall slid aside. A beaming Sasha Novikov stood on the threshold. She held a gleaming vial aloft. 'I think I've done it.'

Priya's heart pounded harder, now from joy rather than apprehension. She returned the Russian's triumphant grin. 'Now what?'

Sasha beckoned Priya to join her in the lab. 'We try it out.'

Behind Priya, the door slid shut soundlessly. She felt trapped. Without the young scientist saying a word, Priya understood that it made sense for them to use the layman as the guinea pig. The thought of those helpless little test animals reminded Priya of her pet raptor. What had happened to it? Was it still in her rooms? Did it have enough to eat? To drink? More than ever, she needed to get out of here. She rolled up her sleeve and extended her bared arm. 'Inject me.'

Sasha paused, assessing her, and then she nodded. It took her a couple of minutes to get the serum into a syringe and to ready the sterile field. Then she swabbed Priya's arm, put on a tourniquet, and tapped over her veins. A plump green vessel rose to the surface. With practiced efficiency, she lined up the needle and pushed it at an angle beneath Priya's skin, seeking the prominent vein. Deftly, she depressed the plunger.

Both women watched the slightly brown liquid slide into her arm. Sasha released the tourniquet and slid the needle free. Next, she pressed a cotton swab over the entry point and bade Priya apply pressure for a minute. Once she'd applied a dressing patch, both women waited to see what would happen.

They didn't have to wonder for long. Sasha squeezed Priya's hand in a gesture of reassurance. Neither of them had expected such a quick response, but Priya got hit with everything. In that one touch, Sasha's whole life laid itself bare for Priya to see.

A cute, young girl. Carefree and full of vitality and energy.

Abused and used her whole life.

A big man doing unmentionable things to this sweet child. A man Priya feels she should recognise but can't quite place.

A girl growing old before her time.

Growing cold. Calculating.

A young woman, trying to keep herself safe.

Her every decision about being the one on top.

Priya yanked her hand free of Sasha's and recoiled. It was all too much. Devastated, horrified, she broke down sobbing. Over and over, she could only tell Sasha, 'I'm sorry. So very, very sorry.'

A few minutes elapsed unremarked. Eventually, Priya found her equilibrium and the courage to look Sasha in the eyes. She opened her mouth to speak, but the other woman beat her to it.

'Leave it.'

'But—'

'Not now.'

Sasha's hardened features ensured Priya's silence more than her few words. Appalled at what the serum had revealed of Sasha's life, she waited for her to make the next move.

Novikov's voice came out clipped, 'It worked. Now we take it to Bartholomew.'

5

E143

The heralds of dawn nudged at the windows of the main lab, harrying and hurrying Priya and Sasha. With the truth enhancement, they crept from the lab, each terrified of the cameras as well as the patrols. They'd come this far. They couldn't fail now. It couldn't all be for nothing.

The truth needed to get out.

Worms of hunger and nerves crawled in Priya's belly. Gnawed at her gut. A reminder of both the urgency and the direness of this situation. As she and Sasha edged down the too long, too bright corridor, Priya tried to recall when she had eaten her last meal. They hadn't had breakfast before Sasha had seduced the young guard, so that meant she'd not eaten since the evening of the day before. Over forty-five hours. No wonder she felt ravenous.

She hoped their plan would work, paltry and simple as it was. What else could they do but go to the presidential suite, to Bartholomew, and inject him with the serum? Surely, once he saw what was what, he would free the two of them, as well as Leo. Most probably not Kaleb. He was too dangerous. Too far gone with the virus. Too unstable after his brainwashing. Her lips tightened and thinned. She could only accomplish so much.

All at once, they stood frozen in place. Surrounded. No alarms had sounded. Priya had heard no footfalls of approaching troops, but here they were, guns at the ready. She and Sasha traded dismayed glances. It was over. They'd lost. Their last play had failed.

Two of the soldiers secured wrist ties on the women and spun them to face the other way. Johnson Bartholomew stood watching them, his expression inscrutable.

Sasha demanded, 'How did you find us so soon?'

He crossed his arms and narrowed his eyes. 'We've watched you this whole time.'

Sasha shook her head. 'No. Not underground —'

'Yes, my dear. We knew about that secret little facility too.'

Priya spoke up, 'Why didn't you just come for us straight away? Why wait?'

Bartholomew smiled. 'We had some curiosity as to what you would do.'

A soldier delved into Sasha's pocket, rummaged, and produced the box containing one syringe of the serum. They'd left extra stocks in a fridge in the underground lab. Not that those other vials would make any difference at all. Not now that the invaders knew all about the underground complex.

It was all over. Priya's shoulders slumped. The execution day was four days hence. She'd done her best, but her efforts hadn't been good enough. She would rot in her cell for another few days, and then they would kill her. They would execute them all. Some deserved it. Others didn't. No matter. They would all die, all the same. Sadness weighted her bones, making her feel leaden and sluggish.

Without protest, she allowed the guards to return her to the damp, dank cell in the bowels of zone one. Sasha also came along quietly. All the rebellion had leached from both of them. Back in their tiny prison, any slim hope of making another play crashed to the ground and committed suicide—evidently, Bartholomew had ordered a triple guard on them.

The naive youngster they'd tricked was nowhere to be seen. Absently, Priya wondered what they'd done with him—fired, killed, reassigned? Even if he'd been watching them alone, he wouldn't have allowed them to fool him twice.

6

E144

Three days to go. Just ninety hours or so until her death. Priya suspected that it would come as a relief for the long-suffering Sasha, but not for the rest of them. And was killing them all really the answer? What did that make the invading planetary leaders? Surely they were no better than Terrence, not when it came right down to it. That man wouldn't have blinked at executing anyone who might—*might*—go against him either. It seemed that nobody in power bothered too much about waiting for guilt to be proven over innocence.

For hours after their return to the cell, Priya had paced relentlessly, ignoring Sasha's repeated tuts and sighs. Only now, exhausted, did she stop and slump to the floor with her knees bent up to her chin. She dropped her head onto those bony joints and gripped her shins with sweaty palms.

On the bed, Sasha sighed yet again.

Her dry tongue stuck to the roof of her equally sapless mouth. With an effort, she unglued it and tried to moisten her parched and cracked lips. But all that achieved was to make the splits smart more. Since leaving the lab yesterday, she'd not eaten or drank. Their captors appeared utterly unconcerned with their prisoners' wellbeing. Once or twice, Priya had gazed longingly at the damp oozing down the rear wall of the cell, but common sense had thwarted desperate longing. If she wanted to die publicly vomiting and soiling her pants, then licking that mouldy mess was the way to go.

Faint and dejected, she closed her eyes and buried her forehead atop her knees, seeking oblivion from it all. Despite her urgent need for the world to grind to a sudden and abrupt halt, for it all to just go away, the hours ticked on by.

These lowest levels contained no windows, being so deep beneath ground. Still, Priya imagined it must have reached somewhere around evening time by now. Ages ago, Sasha had—inexplicably—fallen into a deep slumber. Now, her snores filled the cell and fled through the bars to rattle down the corridor. Fed up and frustrated, Priya tapped the back of her skull against the wall in time to the annoying and steady drip-drip-drip from a leak or some water sauce in the top left corner of their cage. Again, she licked a useless tongue over dry and split lips. Again, she winced at the sting. Again, she gave up and leant back with closed eyes. This had to stop soon. She couldn't go on like this for another two days. It would kill her.

And then Priya laughed aloud. Come what may, by the end of two days, something would kill her. Maybe boredom, but most probably, she wouldn't get that lucky. She suspected a shooting or a hanging. Hoped for a death that came quickly and relatively painlessly. Reckoned on them wanting to make an example of the rogues from Exxon 1. So, no, they wouldn't make it painless or easy.

Soft, rhythmic clicking pulled her from her dark imaginings. Priya opened her eyes, lifted her head, and listened. The click-click, click-click, drew nearer, became louder, but never varied its pace. A long, slim shadow preceded the maker of the noise. A woman. But what made the clicking noise?

Soon, she had her answer, but it had her stare in consternation. She'd never seen footwear like it. Dainty shoes wrapped tiny feet, but the heel wasn't anything Priya could identify. A long, thin, pink column ran up from the floor to a heel that blended into the rest of the pink shoe. From there, Priya's gaze travelled up slim, shapely calves which disappeared beneath a neat hem at the knee.

The skirt suit the woman wore matched her footwear, and her whole appearance screamed neatness and order. When she spoke, Priya identified her. Mrs Ruby Morris of Exxon 3. Come to gloat, no doubt.

The minister smiled down at her. 'The shoes are called stilettos, my child. I'm sure, never having left Exxon 1, that you've never set eyes on the like until now.'

Priya held herself still and kept her silence.

Lady Morris surveyed the minute chamber, and a frown marred her perfectly made-up features. Then the odour of unwashed bodies and a lack of toilet facilities must have reached her, for she wrinkled her nose and took a dainty step away. A smile pulled at Priya's lips, which hurt, and she killed her mirth with haste.

'I had no idea they were keeping you like this.' She turned to the nearest guard, who wore a uniform that Priya assumed signified he came from Exxon 3. 'Open this door at once and bring water.' Once more, she studied the two prisoners. 'And fresh clothing.' At his hesitation, she clapped her hands sharply. 'Chop, chop.'

The guard scurried away.

Lady Morris stepped into the cell. Two steps. Click-click. From her pocket, she withdrew a box. One that looked familiar. Priya struggled to her feet. From the bunk, Sasha did likewise, rubbing the sleep from her eyes.

A different guard hurried up to the open cell, holding two glasses of water, deliciously condensed on the outside. Priya's stomach rumbled. Lady Morris gave a pained smile. Sasha snatched the tumblers from the man and held one out to Priya, who took it and finished it off in one long gulp. Then she belched.

The moisture got her tongue working. 'You brought the truth serum.'

'I did, indeed.'

Sasha stood at Priya's side, a solid presence. 'Why?'

A different frown from the one minutes before settled onto the minister's face. Her arms twitched, as though she wanted to cross them but refrained. Priya and Sasha watched and waited.

'While some may be content to make a clean sweep, others of us would like to learn the truth.'

She held out the box, which now contained five syringes filled with truth serum. Priya took it from her. Sasha remained quiet and unmoving. She looked stunned. Just how Priya felt.

Lady Ruby Morris said, 'I want you to inject me.'

CHAPTER FIFTEEN

1

E145

Sasha blinked. Something had just happened in the back of her skull, but she couldn't pinpoint quite what. It almost seemed as if someone had joined her to watch the proceedings. But that was craziness. With a shake of her head, she repressed the feeling and tried to focus.

So much had changed in so short a time. Priya had injected Lady Morris with one of the syringes of truth serum. The minister of Exxon 3 had then grabbed hold of Priya's arm and held on for at least half an hour. Throughout that period, her facial expressions had morphed through many changes, which included horror, dismay, amusement, pity, anger, and—finally—understanding.

After a few minutes of silence, while she absorbed what she'd seen, the woman had then taken hold of Sasha. While the flux of expressions followed a similar pattern, they were not the same. And at the end of the ordeal, she had flushed with fury then paled. With her jaw set, she had given Sasha a brief hug and then walked away, her shoes click-clicking firmly down the corridor until they faded into silence.

A while later, guards had come and taken Sasha and Priya to an empty office, where clean clothes awaited them. Now, Sasha's skin itched. She felt desperate for a shower or a wash of any kind. But while Lady Morris had given them water and clothing, getting them clean didn't seem to be on the immediate agenda. Not after what she'd just witnessed via the serum.

Sasha cast her gaze around the room and its occupants. John and Eloise Martins stood alone in a far corner, watching everyone else—much as

Sasha was doing, only she had Priya with her instead. Leo sat huddled with Kaleb against a wall. Kaleb didn't look in great shape. Not at all. It surprised her to see the two men supporting one another. From the look on Priya's face, this turn of events had caught her unawares too.

Interestingly, Major Straw was nowhere to be seen. What did that say? A second glance at Ellie brought Sasha up short—the woman looked haggard and unwell.

Along the whole of one wall stood a buffet table, heavily laden with sandwiches and finger food of all sorts. Sasha's stomach rumbled, and saliva flooded her mouth. She couldn't ignore the feast any longer. Not caring what anyone may think or say, she strode to the table, grabbed a plate, and got busy heaping it high with a bit of everything.

After a beat, Priya joined her and heaped her plate even higher. The woman then scurried away again, hugging her food to her torso. A snide chuckle sounded from the corner of the room, and Sasha glared at Ellie. The tension thickened. If not for that bitch's lies, none of this would have happened. Before the tenuous thread of civility could snap, however, John stepped between the two of them and oozed up to Sasha. What the hell did he want?

He took her by the elbow and guided her to an empty corner of the conference room that Lady Morris had housed them in. Sasha shrugged away from his touch and shoved a whole sandwich triangle into her mouth. Hmm. Flavours overwhelmed her. Tuna and sweetcorn and mayonnaise. Real from the taste of it. How had they gotten hold of *real* tuna?

John bent low so that he could murmur into her ear. 'You owe me. Remember?'

Sasha leaned away from him, cringing. 'You're joking, right?'

He shook his head and smiled—a sad, twisted effort. 'You promised. When I helped you with Denis.'

Her eyes went wide, and the food on her tongue turned sour and unwelcome. She struggled to swallow the soggy mess. 'After everything that's happened? You seriously think—'

He put a finger to her lips.

She wanted to bite it right off.

Instead, she shrugged him away. 'Get your filthy hands off me.'

John tutted. 'Now, now, my little Shura. I own you. That was the deal.'

Sweat broke out on her chilled skin and dripped down her spine. She wanted to walk away from him but didn't quite dare. Not yet. Not until she knew what Lady Morris and the others had in store for them.

John took advantage of her hesitation and pulled her by the elbow until he could murmur into her ear again. His words made her feel nauseous. He couldn't expect her to do that, could he? Was the man insane? More than likely. She willed her body to move away from him, but it wouldn't obey. She tried harder. But something had gone wrong with the controls. What the hell?

John gripped her arm more tightly. 'Do this one last thing for me, will you? You'll find what you need on the documents and drive you stole.' Then he let her go.

Just then, Priya approached them. 'Everything okay here?' She turned concerned eyes on

Sasha.

John chuckled and sauntered away, ignoring the food laid out on the long table. All at once, Sasha's powers of movement returned. Mute, and shocked and angry and torn, Sasha nodded and let Priya lead her back to their patch of wall. What had just happened? Had it been fright that had pinned her in place? No. She didn't believe so. Not for one single second. Someone else had been in control.

The double doors opened. Lady Morris entered first, followed by Johnson Bartholomew. Then three other men that Sasha didn't recognise. Major Straw brought up the rear. Which seemed to answer Sasha's earlier question—the man was colluding with the invaders. Most likely, he had helped them right from the get-go.

From his huddled position on the floor, Kaleb spoke up, 'You won't catch me, you know.' Amusement laced the words, and the damaged soldier held his gaze on Lady Morris.

Priya grabbed Sasha's arm. She wished people would stop doing that. Annoyed, she faced the other woman but held her peace when she saw how pale and scared she looked. 'What? What is it?'

Priya turned desperate eyes on Sasha. 'That wasn't Kaleb. It wasn't his voice.'

The two women stared at one another, each trying—and failing—to process.

Lady Morris, however, seemed unperturbed. She simply smiled and continued whatever conversation she had been engaged in upon her entrance. Sasha watched the other ministers, and none of them appeared in the least upset either. Something was afoot, and she didn't like it. Not one bit.

2

E145

When John returned to her side, Ellie distanced herself from him in every way possible: mentally, emotionally, and physically. She wanted nothing to do with the man she had once called husband. What had he said to the young Ms Novikov? She cursed her sight for playing up as much as it was. Cursed the fact that it seemed to have grown worse. She felt terrible, and her whole body hurt.

With forced poise and equanimity, she strolled over to the generous buffet—were they trying to make a point?—and helped herself to a couple of sandwiches, a sausage roll, and a piece of quiche, even though she felt not in the slightest peckish, despite her days of starvation. She needed her wits about her, and a satiated stomach would only put her to sleep. She couldn't allow that. Not yet. The food also gave her a reason to move away from John without raising any alarms.

Then Kaleb spoke and changed everything.

John's eyes went wide, and his face blanched. He dropped his plate and dashed back to Ellie's side. What the hell did he think she could do?

Ellie, meanwhile, stood stock still, in the grip of another sight. Her vision had kicked in again. She saw Lady Morris re-imprison everyone except for Priya, Sasha, and Leo. The woman had made a decision, and the other leaders would follow her. As for she and John and Kaleb …

they would all die, one way or another.

All at once, her vision cut out. It didn't matter, though; she'd seen what was coming. Quickly, quietly, she took John's hand and eased them toward the door, using Kaleb's handy distraction to slip out unseen. It proved more challenging to navigate the heavily patrolled corridors, however, and only Ellie's intermittent inner vision got them away.

Time and again, her neck prickled a warning, and she dragged them out of sight—once into a cleaning cupboard, another time into a storage space, and finally, into a foul-smelling waste chute, which shot them into a basement area. This proved useful, if distasteful, as it took them away from any of the invaders' patrols.

Disgusted, Ellie did her best to brush off her suit, but it was ruined. Faintness hit, and dizziness rocked her on her feet. John caught her in his arms and wrapped them around her. 'What's wrong? Are you all right?' He sounded concerned.

Her strength returned—or, at least, some of it. She straightened up and pulled away from John.

To ease the rejection, Ellie rested a hand on his elbow. 'Thank you. I would have fallen.'

John nodded. 'What now?'

Ellie crossed her arms and set her jaw. Steel determination glinted in her eyes. 'We do what needs to be done. For certain, things cannot remain as they are.'

John grinned. If only he knew. For the most part, Ellie enjoyed her second sight, but sometimes—like now—she cursed her ability and the added responsibility it brought with it. Once she'd seen something, it couldn't be unseen. And this one was a whopper. It left her no choice: she had to do something about it. First of all, though, they had to get out of this dump.

Without bothering to get her husband's attention, trusting he would follow her, Ellie found the door and gripped the begrimed handle, thankful for the meagre lighting in here. They must have installed it to aid the waste workers in their distasteful tasks.

The basement corridor stood empty, and she broke into a jog. As expected, John stayed close on her heels. In many ways, he was like a puppy, only a little more housetrained. Ellie bit down on her smile when pain lanced throughout her torso, and she stumbled. The wall on her left bounced her back to her feet, and she continued to dash down the damp and dusty access tunnel.

Behind her, John pushed for information, panting as he spoke, 'We'll work together? Get rid of anyone who stands in our way?'

Ellie checked the overhead signs and darted right. The floor sloped upward. Impatient, in pain, and needing all her energy to keep going, she snapped, 'I just said we'll do whatever we need to.'

At last, at long, long last, they reached an abandoned housing wing. Recently, the lower-level workers had been reassigned to newer accommodation closer to their job allocations. The power and water continued to supply the building, and the pantry held canned and dried food. They could exist here for a good while if they needed to.

Ellie waited until John had closed the door, then she fished her master-code list from her pocket and scanned it for the one which would lock them in. She found it and activated the panel on the wall to the side of the exit. Sloppiness had left it unlocked in the first place. If she didn't have more important things to think about, that would be another one for her long list of to-dos.

And a big, important thing occupied her thoughts continually. Sasha, and what else the girl had kept hidden. If not for her enhancement crumbling, Ellie would have seen it already. She cursed inwardly. It might prove vital. And she couldn't see it. In that area, she found herself blind.

Not eliminating the virus fully at the start, when she first contracted it, lay at the heart of these hiccups. Ellie had to admit that now. Accept that she had made a mistake in believing herself cured when, in actual fact, she had merely delayed it.

Ellie didn't want to die. She had someone she had yet to stop. In complete disregard of her needs and desires, though, the virus had gained in strength, and she was forced to concede that it had now begun to affect her brain. Shortly, it would warp and change her, and she could no longer deny the trouble she was in. Her decline threatened everything. She hadn't anticipated this. Would she have time?

3

E145

John smarted at Ellie's continued rejection of him, not to mention this unconscionable delay. Why hadn't she acted yet to take back control? Why wasn't she talking to him? If the daft cow thought she could exclude him, she had another think coming.

He watched her dozing on the narrow bed and grinned. The way things were looking, all he had to do was bide his time and let those gorgeous nanos do the hard work for him.

On the thin mattress, Ellie snored—a short but powerful honk—and woke herself. She sat up and glanced around, looking disoriented for a few seconds. Then her gaze settled on John, and her expression hardened.

Annoyed, he crossed his arms and scowled.

'You might show a little gratitude.'

Ellie blinked and stared. Then she recovered her wits. 'You think? Who just saved who? You do realise we were dead meat in there, yes? Morris intended to carry out Bartholomew's original plan of executing all of us.'

John rolled his eyes. 'Not all of us, surely.'

Ellie tutted. 'You know what I mean. Stop splitting hairs.'

He dropped onto the end of a facing cot. 'What else did you see?'

Her shoulders slumped. 'Not a lot.' Ellie rubbed her forehead and sighed.

John dropped his bombshell, 'Denis once told me about a second vial.'

Ellie jerked her head up and gaped. 'And you kept that to yourself?'

'Amongst other things. Anyway, what's it matter? The other planets have their own cure to offer.'

Ellie shook her head. 'It changes everything, you imbecile. How can you not see that? If Exxon 1 has its own antidote, it's free of Lady Morris and her cronies.'

John's smug smirk faltered. 'You can't talk to me that way.'

'I can and just did. You're a baby, John. You need to grow up before it's too late.'

Furious, he shot to his feet and towered over her. 'And you need to stop your stupid bloody temper tantrum.'

His words shut them both up, and a tenuous silence fell, punctuated only by Ellie's heavy breathing and John's frustrated sighs.

After about thirty seconds, Ellie spoke in soothing tones, 'You have to let go of your arrogance and ambitions and see your true position in the scheme of things. You never had a chance at being in control or taking power for yourself.'

Though her voice came out soft and measured, her words felt like a punch to the gut as well as a slap in the face. No, forget that; she'd just done the equivalent of kicking him in the balls. His ire rose further, and he clenched angry fists.

Ellie held up her arms, palms facing him. 'Let me show you what I saw.'

John stared at her, wary and struggling to

suppress the rage that wanted to strangle the life out of the little bitch. 'Show me how?'

'I know about the backdoor access. You're not the only one who's used it.'

His mouth worked like a fish. It took him three goes to get his words out. 'How long have you known?'

Now it was Ellie's turn to roll her eyes. 'Always with the useless questions. It doesn't matter how long. What matters is what we do now.'

Defeat sucked all the juice out of him, and he slumped forward, bracing his hands on his knees. He turned pained eyes to Ellie. Thankfully, she didn't look triumphant or gloating, not like he would have were their situations reversed. She just looked sad. He forced himself to ask the question, 'What do you have in mind?'

Her next words shocked him to the core.

'Let me access your chip. I won't be the first.'

Even before she acknowledged his guess, he knew it to be true. 'Terrence?'

'As he did to countless others.' Ellie hung her head and took in a deep breath. 'Myself included.'

Nausea crippled John, and he fell to his knees on the cold, pitted, concrete floor. Hot vomit spewed from him in one long, violent rush as his stomach ejected the fresh food he'd not long since ingested. When it was over, he knelt in place, panting and gagging. Ellie got up and put a hand on his shoulder. 'We can stop him.'

John flinched. 'He's dead, Ellie.'

She shook her head. 'No. That's what he programmed into you, but you know the truth. Look within, and you'll see.'

He tried. He really did. But his anger and self-recrimination got in the way.

Again, Ellie said, 'Let me show you.'

Utterly defeated, realising that the president had been running things all along, John croaked out a single word, 'Okay.'

Not wasting breath or energy on more words, Ellie took him by the hand and led him to the locked door, where she reversed the code and pulled him into the corridor. John didn't need to ask—she was taking them to the military mainframe hub.

Shock robbed John of thought, other than 'you bastard' on repeat loop, and had him walk on numb feet. It was just as well Ellie stayed sharp, or he would have had them apprehended within minutes of leaving their refuge. At every turn, she avoided troops and general workers and got them to the hub. New respect for his wife fuelled his self-pity and self-recrimination. What an idiot he'd been. How much they could have achieved together. Was it too late?

Mercifully, they found the hub empty. Evidently, the invaders hadn't populated it yet. Ellie sighed and patted her pocket. For the first time, he realised she carried a gun. How in hell had she gotten hold of that? Or had she managed to keep it when Bartholomew sent her to the cells? He shook his head. Too many questions. Too many unknowns. Too much to get his head around. Had he felt useless and helpless after Sasha had infected him? That paled into insignificance next to this.

Listless by now, overwhelmed with it all, John plodded to a chair and sat down. Then he bent his head forward to expose his neck—it would be easier for Ellie to gain access via the old-fashioned hard-wired route. It would take too long to walk her through an ether hook-up.

She surprised him again. At the console, Ellie tapped a few keys and brought up the back-access login screen. How had she done that so easily? The program was well hidden. Without hesitation, she keyed in the code for his chip. John felt an itch at the back of his skull. Then she was in.

After a momentary sensation of weirdness, he was aware of nothing amiss. How many times had he dismissed that initial not flush and itch? How many times had Terrence taken him over and used him? His eyes found Ellie's, and they stared at one another. He gave her a small nod of permission.

Ellie closed her eyes, typed in a few more commands, and a series of video-type reels played in his mind. Entranced and repelled at the same time, John watched himself running into the presidential suite's inner office, expecting to find a dead president. The alarms continued to blare, which matched his recall, but there was no body. John blinked. His brain stuttered. Simultaneously, he saw both what he thought had happened and what had actually unfolded. Two visuals overlaid one another … a dead Terrence, surrounded by blood and vomit, and a bare carpet—unstained and unblemished.

Distantly, more keyboard taps reached his ears and penetrated in a vague fashion. The feed changed. Now he watched Terrence at the controls, accessing one chip after another in quick succession. With his wild hair, deranged manner, and shining eyes, the man looked crazed.

Tears streamed down John's cheeks. 'Stop. Please, make it stop.'

Ellie did.

John sobbed.

His wife pulled him into a hug. Then, inexplicably, she apologised. He twisted so that he could look at her. She grimaced. 'All along, I thought you had betrayed me of your own free will. Now I see it wasn't so.'

John shook his head and wiped the tears from his eyes and cheeks. 'It was a bit of both, I suppose.'

Ellie waited for more.

John sniffed. 'Terrence didn't have me under his control the whole time. That would be impossible. He accessed so many others too.'

Ellie nodded. 'And you can only access one chip at a time.'

'Right. So, even though he used me, I did have free will too.'

Ellie rubbed his shoulder. 'Never for very long, though, sweetheart.'

Her endearment brought his tears to fresh life, and a sob escaped him. Shamed, he hung his head and looked away from the woman he had betrayed.

She pulled him in for a hug and murmured soothing words in his ear. After a while, Ellie eased back and took John by both shoulders so that she could look him in the eyes. 'We have to stop him, John. We have to end this bloodshed once and for all.'

Martins stared at her, torn and in turmoil.

'Will you help me?'

4

E145

Ellie watched John and waited, studying the varying emotions that flitted across his features in quick succession. She saw his decision before he nodded. Relieved, she embraced him for a couple of seconds and then let him go.

Though she suffered and was weakening fast now, she felt elated. If nothing else, she had knocked John from his course. That had to count for something. And she had to give her husband credit where credit was due—though still in shock from his new knowledge, he had agreed to help. Even knowing he could never have any hope of having any power for himself.

'How will we stop Terrence?'

Ellie took one of his hands in both of hers and squeezed it. 'We have to out him. If we can get into the newsnet, I can transmit the memories from your chip. We can show the world that he isn't dead. That he orchestrated this whole thing.'

'Why would he even do something like this? Why release the virus and then pretend to be dead?'

'Snakes in the grass.'

He looked at her, eyes questioning.

'Think about it. What better way to flush the snakes hidden in the grass. To out all those against him or harbouring secret ambitions.' She grinned. 'I bet he never counted on Priya, though.'

John shared her chuckle. 'Talk about a wild card.'

Ellie pulled a flash drive from the computer terminal and stood. 'Let's get this done before we get caught.'

He nodded and joined her by the door, which she eased open, and they peered into the corridor beyond. Though she heard voices, she saw nobody. With a building sense of urgency, she pulled him into the passageway.

John came with her willingly enough. 'The bastard has to be crazy to pull a stunt like that, though.'

Short of breath, Ellie settled for a nod. She

couldn't hide her cough, though.

Concerned, John gripped her arm.

She shrugged him off and carried on walking at a brisk pace. Twice, she had to lead them down an alternative route to avoid patrols. The third time proved unlucky. Thank goodness she'd pre-empted this and had her weapon in her hand.

The lone soldier held up his hands. His Adam's apple bobbed when he gulped. Though she hated herself for it, she pulled the trigger. She could see no other way. If she left him alive, even injured, he would raise the alarm too soon. The gun discharged with a soft thwump. Grateful for the technology that muffled the shots indefinitely, Ellie grabbed John and ran onward.

By a circuitous route, they finally made it to the newsnet broadcasting station. Ellie shot the two guards at the door and pushed her way inside. A lone technician leapt to his feet, hands in the air. She waved the weapon at him. 'Sit down. Do as I tell you, and you won't be harmed.'

He did as he was told.

Ellie and John pulled up chairs either side of

the terrified man. Then she told him what she wanted of him. As he listened, his eyes grew round and big. At the end, he nodded and got to work, his fingers moving feverishly over the keyboard.

At last, he had them hooked up to the one broadcasting channel. 'All yours,' he told them.

'Thank you.' Ellie gestured toward the door. 'You can go now.'

The man wasted no time and dashed from the room. Ellie inserted the flash drive into the player and hit send. The newsnet broadcast all of what John had just seen when Ellie had back-accessed his chip. Now the whole planet would see it too. They would see how Terrence had tricked them all. Hopefully, this exposure would force him into the open. Sharp pain lanced through her skull, and she had to fight to hide her wince. She didn't have long left now. This had to work. And because she wouldn't be around to end it, she could only hope that one of the others would be able to finish the job.

The reel stopped, and Ellie stared at John. Then she pressed the intercom button. 'President

Terrence experimented with nano enhancements and alterations, which eventually drove him crazy. That and his insatiable greed messed with his brain. His madness started this catastrophe we've all had to live through. He believed he was all powerful and had found a way to make everyone weak and subservient forevermore. He also thought he had found life eternal. But while he still lives, there are those that can and will stop him.'

She paused and stared hard into the camera lens, piercing anyone who watched the live feed. 'Terrence, if you're seeing this, you have to come out and face the consequences. If not, you'll be flushed from hiding like the rat you are.'

Ellie lifted her finger from the intercom, and the room plunged into silence. Then she pressed a button, and the monitors went dark.

John sat by her side with an awed look on his slack face. 'What do we do now?'

Ellie gave him a sad smile—all she could manage right then. 'Now we atone for our sins.'

He stood and backed away. 'Ellie, no. It doesn't have to end like this.'

'It does. And you know it. They'll execute us regardless. And I'm dead already, or near enough. I want to go before I do any more damage. I can't trust myself anymore.'

'But, darling—'

She fired the gun. Blood and brains erupted from the back of his skull and splattered the desk, equipment, and wall around him.

A lone tear slid down Ellie's cheek. She put the weapon to her temple. Her finger twitched. With gritted teeth, she closed her eyes and held her breath. She pulled the trigger.

CHAPTER SIXTEEN

1

E145

Still reeling from Kaleb's speech in an altered voice, Priya blinked back to the present and glanced around. The room seemed emptier. She looked again. Eloise and John Martins had disappeared. Kaleb slumped against the wall, done in. Priya went to kneel by his side. Over Kaleb's head, Leo tried to smile for her, but it came out muted and more of a grimace.

Across the room, Lady Morris cursed. 'Did anyone see them?' She turned her accusing stare on the remaining people present. A few shook their heads in the negative, while most simply stared back at her.

Sasha turned her pent up anger on the woman, 'Why the fuck do you think any of us—' she indicated herself, Priya, Leo, and Kaleb —'would help *them*? I mean, seriously? And you run a bloody planet.' In disgust, she turned her back and stormed from the room.

Nobody tried to stop her.

Priya watched the door ease shut and waited to see what would happen next. Who needed drama when you had real life?

Ruby Morris got busy giving orders, which she seemed good at. Priya hid a sardonic grin. Now wasn't the time. When she'd done, she turned her attention to Priya, who wished she hadn't. She'd quite liked sitting there in relative anonymity. As ever, the good times hadn't lasted.

'Priya, dear. We need to secure Special Moore.'

Priya struggled to regain her feet. 'What? No. He's sick.'

Lady Morris approached her and rested a manicured hand on Priya's elbow. 'This zone has a secure hospital complex, yes?'

At a loss, Priya sought Leo's gaze. He nodded. Lady Morris withdrew her hand and folded her arms across her ample chest. 'That's settled, then. We'll incarcerate him there.'

Priya started to protest again, but the minister held up a preventative hand. 'No. It's the safest way for us all, your friend included.'

The woman studied the remaining three of them. 'Priya, you and Leo and Ms Novikov are free to do as you wish. We have no further need to detain you.' With that, she turned and left the room. Her entourage followed on her heels.

Over an unconscious Kaleb's head, Priya stared at Leo. 'So, that's it? Just like that, we're free? We can go home?'

Leo eased Kaleb onto his side and settled him in the recovery position. Then he got to his feet and came over to Priya, where he pulled her into an embrace. Into her hair, he said, 'I don't think it's as simple as that, my love.'

Seeking comfort and reassurance, Priya pulled back and looked at Leo. His loving eyes held an ominous violet tint. He had the virus too.

She yanked back, horrified. At his frown, she said, 'Leo. Your eyes.'

The conference room held no mirrors or reflective surfaces. He grabbed one of the knives, but it didn't hold enough of a sheen to show him. Perturbed, he said, 'I'll be back,' and left her alone with Kaleb.

Not for long, though, as a couple of medics came and stretchered the damaged soldier away. Now it was just herself on her own. And she had some serious thinking to do. Leo contracting the virus changed so much.

Kaleb was beyond help, even if they administered an antidote straight away. Priya didn't believe for even an instant that he had any sort of a chance. Leo and herself, however; now, that was a whole other matter.

Priya came to an unhappy decision and went in search of Lady Morris. A hunch took her to the infamous presidential suite, and that's precisely where she found the minister. The woman didn't appear at all surprised to see Priya.

She rose from her chair and extended a welcoming arm. 'Please, take a seat.'

Priya sat in the over-large upholstered chair, facing the leader of Exxon 3, who seemed to have taken nominal charge on behalf of the other planets. Mr Bartholomew, it appeared, only played second fiddle and didn't have any actual weight when it came to interplanetary relations.

Instead of looking Mrs Morris in the eyes, Priya stared at her fingers and fidgeted. She mumbled, 'I've come to a decision. A way forward.'

Lady Morris watched her, and though her lips remained straight, her eyes lit up. 'Go on.'

'I'll take your deal.'

The minister leant forward. 'Which is, in your understanding …?'

'I'll lead Exxon 1 to recovery, under the guidance of yourself and Bartholomew and the others, in return for bulk supply of your cure.'

Lady Morris stood and extended a hand. 'And yourself and the Reverend Canmore will receive the antidote within the hour.'

Priya mimicked the minister, and they shook on it. 'You noticed Leo, then?'

Ruby Morris smiled. 'It's my job to notice

such things, my dear.' She walked them to the door. 'If you head for the hospital wing, I'll ensure the Reverend meets you there. We have a limited supply of the vaccine with us.'

Duly dismissed, Priya did as she was bid. What she hadn't told the mighty Morris was that she fully intended to hand the power to someone else just as soon as she could.

2

E145

In the worst turmoil of her life so far, Sasha took herself off to the underground lab alone, so that she could think. On the way through the main lab, she made herself a cup of coffee, remembering the first time that Giles had offered her a brew and the banter they had shared. If only she'd heeded the warnings of her inner voice. So much of this mess could have been averted.

In the underground lab, it surprised her to see that the flash drive and paperwork remained out in the open, laid out on one of the workbenches.

The last time she'd seen these, she'd been in too much of a hurry to make the truth serum to take much notice. Not so now.

After sipping her drink, she settled the cup on a counter and meandered over to the documents. The paperwork outlined the contents of the flash drive and from where the information had originated. Apparently, the nano-code was derived from soldiers with different enhancement effects of the virus. Terrence had experimented on his troops, aiming to make super soldiers. The ability to see the past from the eyes of anyone you touched was one of those enhancements. While Sasha and Priya had developed and administered that aspect, the files showed many more. Some of them highly dangerous.

The rest of the paperwork concentrated on various high flyers and government ministers, as well as Eloise Martins and even Sasha herself. John had accumulated enough blackmail material to finish everyone had he so chosen. Thank God she'd found and hidden this before Giles had caught her. She shuddered to think of the damage John or Giles could have done otherwise.

That train of thought took her straight back to the promise he'd demanded of her. She felt torn at his request. She owed him, but …

She shook her head. Could she do that? Poison the water and kill everyone in the zone? If she did, it wouldn't be for that man. If she did anything from here on in, she had to do it for herself.

It might offer a way out for her. A way to undo all the harm she'd caused. She could drink the water too. Make a quick end of it. That way, she would leave a clean slate for whoever came after. The planet could start clean and fresh. As could the others. For Sasha realised that, were she to do this, she would have to ensure she got the leaders of the other five planets too. And what better time than now? When next would they all come together like this?

Still torn, she shook her head. Could she do that? And then she found a resolution. It came quickly and decisively and filled her with sudden calm. Just then, Priya burst into the room.

'Quick, turn on the holo-screen. You have to watch the newsnet.'

.

Impatient, not waiting for Sasha to catch up, she snatched the remote from its perch on the wall by the entrance and switched it on. Sasha watched, fascinated, as Ellie's face filled the screen.

'Hang on,' Priya said and hit buttons.

The reel reset and ran from the beginning. As she watched, Sasha grew increasingly horrified. What John's chip revealed of Terrence's actions was bad enough, but then—on screen for all to see—Ellie shot John and then herself.

Sasha slapped a hand to her open mouth. 'Oh, my good God.'

Priya held her hand. 'I don't think we were supposed to see that last bit.'

Sasha stared at her.

Priya rewound to the end of Ellie's speech. Sasha gasped. 'No. I can't watch that again.'

'You don't have to. Look, see the monitors? See the button Ellie presses?'

Sasha studied the screen, which Priya had—mercifully—paused. She nodded. Ellie had switched off the monitors.

Priya said, 'I think she meant to turn off the

camera feed, not just the monitors. She wouldn't have wanted Terrence to see that last part.'

3

E146

Priya desperately needed to occupy two places at once. If only technology had evolved that far … but then again, given all that had happened recently, perhaps such limitations were for the best. She wanted to stay with Sasha and comfort her, for the young woman was obviously in a bad way, but she also needed to go and see Kaleb. He didn't have long left.

Upset, she slipped into his private hospital room and sat on a chair by the side of his bed. He lay with his eyes closed and breathing laboured. By now, everyone knew her face, and the guard at the door had given her no trouble. In fact, everyone she encountered treated her with a deference and respect that she just wasn't—and could not get—used to. Maybe in time.

At one glance, she could see that Kaleb's

virus had come to end stage. He couldn't fight it anymore and was beyond Priya's or anyone's help now.

Absently, she patted Toothy's head. The young raptor wouldn't leave her side. Their recent separation had affected the little creature deeply. Probably because it came so soon after its mother had died. They gave each other mutual comfort.

Her hand paused in mid-stroke, and Priya laughed aloud. Her pet might be responsible for the new deference that people showed her. Yes, that was more than probable. The notion struck her as amusing, and she laughed again. Toothy left her lap and climbed beneath the bed—he loved to hide under things, so long as Priya stayed near. On the bed, Kaleb stirred. Then he opened his eyes.

In his gaze, Priya saw hate and murderous intent. Immediately, she knew that the brainwashing had now taken full effect in the final throes of his illness. His damaged mind had succumbed. He sat upright and lashed out at her, catching her back-handed across the face.

'You bitch. It's all your fault. You did all this. Everything that's wrong is because of you.'

Priya swayed but managed to keep her seat. She touched a tentative palm to her smarting cheek and gaped at him. In pain and reeling from the shock of his sudden transition, she wasn't ready for his assault.

He leant over to her side of the bed and wrapped both of his meaty hands around her delicate throat. His grip locked and choked off her airway.

Panicked and frantic, already short of oxygen —having being caught after an out-breath—Priya thrashed and writhed. Her attempt to scream proved vain. She needed to breathe to yell. Beneath his hold, something in her neck twanged and twinged. Pain lanced up into her skull and down into her left shoulder. Tears poured down her cheeks.

It couldn't end like this. Not after everything. And Kaleb didn't know what he was doing. He wasn't in control of his faculties. It was too sad. Too bloody stupid.

From beneath the bed, a low growl rumbled

up and over her. Then Toothy leapt. He fastened his jaw around one of Kaleb's wrists and bit down hard. Then he wrenched his mouth from side to side until he forced Kaleb to let go.

Priya fell to the floor, gasping and rubbing her throat. Swollen and inflamed, it made catching her breath difficult and painful. For a few seconds, she lay there sobbing and wheezing. Then she remembered Kaleb. She couldn't let Toothy kill him. He couldn't die like that.

'It's okay. Come here.' She eased the young raptor away from Kaleb, and it released his arm with reluctance. Priya crooned at it in a broken voice, 'Good boy. You did real good. Thank you. It's okay now.'

The raptor snuggled in under her chin. Priya grunted. The thing had grown heavy. Before too much longer, she wouldn't be able to hold it like this.

On the bed, Kaleb lay limp and twisted on his side, and blood poured from the bite wound on his wrist and hand. Sweat glistened on his pale skin, and his breathing sounded worse than did Priya's. His eyes had rolled up so that only the whites showed.

After one last stroke of Toothy's head, she eased him to the floor, and he slipped back beneath the bed. With her hands now free, she gripped Kaleb's wounded hand in her two. She sat that way for three minutes, and then he breathed his last, but not before she'd seen the truth about him hunting down Hank and his gang. Kaleb thought he'd gotten them all, but he hadn't.

4

E146

Sasha paced the underground lab, which she had been unable to bring herself to leave. The shock of what the newsnet had shown had brought her to her senses. All of this had to stop. Terror had to stop. She had to stop.

Part of her wanted—needed—to forgive herself. But another part held her back, unable to accept all she had done. Even John couldn't make the change at the end, when it counted.

Ellie had done it for him.

The only way forward that Sasha could see right then was a complete reset. That would be best. Yes, she would kill herself and take them all with her, thus paving the way for a fresh start. Let a whole new creature rise from the ashes.

Would she commit one final act of vengeance? … For she saw, now, that her whole life had been about nothing but vengeance, disguised under other names, but vengeance nonetheless.

Priya, though. She couldn't murder her. That girl had done nothing but try and help, in spite of everything she had suffered and seen. Unlike Sasha and Ellie, she hadn't turned her anger or pain into hate or ambition. She'd stayed true to herself.

Then the thing of most import struck Sasha—Terrence was still running the show. He had accessed Kaleb's chip, just like Ellie and John had shown. It had to be Terrence who had spoken through Kaleb in the conference room yesterday morning. … Was it only yesterday morning? It felt like a lifetime ago. Which meant it was also

Terrence who had back-accessed her and prevented her from leaving John's side. Surely that
wasn't the first time. The realisation left her even
more traumatised.

What had Terrence made her do? And how
much had she done of her own free will? Was she
actually responsible for most of this, then? Or
had he just made her think so?

Her mild relief at not being in control was
short lived. Because, of course, he hadn't used
her chip continuously. Terror had also accessed
many other chips, and he could only manipulate
one at a time—or so she believed. So what did
that mean to her? For her?

Sasha slumped to the floor. Because, by God,
she'd exercised free will the rest of the time.
While Terror's actions offered her partial exoner-
ation, it wasn't enough. Not nearly so.

5

E146

Priya stayed by Kaleb while nurses washed

and prepared his body. Only after the morgue technicians had removed him, did she leave the hospital complex.

All the while, Sasha had stayed on her mind, nagging at her. There was more to do there. Priya tried the lab first. The woman seemed to live down there, given the chance.

Sure enough, she walked through the final entrance below ground to find Ms Novikov seated at a bench, studying something complicated-looking on a monitor. A flash drive poked out of a port below the screen. For some reason, a chill ran down Priya's spine.

To announce her presence, Priya cleared her throat. Sasha startled. Quickly, she flicked off the monitor and turned to face Priya, a fake smile pasted on her features. Priya didn't buy it.

'Everything okay?'

Sasha beamed. 'Yes. Fine. You?'

Priya gripped the back of a stool and pulled it toward her, then she eased up onto the high seat. 'I'd feel better if I knew you were all right.'

Sasha blanched and flinched. 'I'm fine. Really.'

Priya shook her head. 'No, you're not. I don't believe your smile for a moment.'

Before her eyes, the other woman wilted— just like a flower left in a hot room with no water for too long. 'Tell me.' She held out a hand, and Sasha scooted over to take it. 'I won't judge.'

Tears leaked slowly from Sasha's eyes, and she looked at the floor. 'That's part of the problem. You're so good.' She sniffled. 'Not like me.'

Priya squeezed Sasha's hand gently. 'We're all the same, really.'

Sasha jerked her hand free and stared at Priya. 'How can you say that? We're nothing like one another. And Terrence and … and the others ..'

'We all make choices. We all love and hate and hurt.'

'But we don't make the same choices.'

'Not all the time, no. But I don't believe that any single person is all good or all bad. Not at heart.'

Sasha shook her head. 'That's just naiveté.'

Priya chuckled without mirth. 'That's why I need help.'

'You?' Sasha raised her eyes and studied her.

Priya smiled. 'I'm not worldly-wise enough to lead a zoo, let alone a nation.'

Sasha wiped her cheeks dry. 'And yet here you are, trying to make me feel better.'

Priya shrugged. 'Not without an ulterior motive, I'm afraid.'

'You think I can help you. ... Why would you trust me? Of all people, why should you want me around? What about lover-boy Leo?'

Priya flushed a pretty pink colour. 'I take it everyone knows about that, then?'

Sasha grinned. 'It's kind of obvious.'

Priya scrutinised Sasha. 'So, will you do it? Will you help?'

She shook her head. 'I can't. I'm no good. Not for you. Not for anyone.'

'You only need to be good for yourself.'

Confusion creased Sasha's features.

Priya retook her hand. 'I want you to lead.'

'No.' Again, Sasha jerked her hand free.

'You get to have a do-over. You get to put it all right. I'll help you. As your second in command. I just can't do it all myself. I'm no leader.

You've just said how naive I am. I don't have the first clue.'

Sasha stood and backed away. 'I won't do it.'

Priya stood too. 'Then what will you do?'

Her words brought Sasha up short. Made her stop and contemplate. All of a sudden, her murderous, suicidal thoughts seemed preposterous. This wasn't the end. It was the beginning.

If she could forgive herself.

But that would take work. And a lot of time. Perhaps, for now, Priya's acceptance might be good enough. Just for a little while. After a few seconds, Sasha lifted her head.

'I'm the last person who should take all the power. We've seen where that can lead. But I'll assist you.'

And if that didn't work, she could still end it, one way or another.

CHAPTER SEVENTEEN

1

E150

It will happen today—Priya Shaw, the little bitch, will officially accept the leadership of Exxon 1. All the planets and people stand behind her. ... But Denis Terrence isn't dead.

Mr and Mrs Martins go that right. Damn them. They had made him vulnerable. Since that broadcast, he'd had to hide more deeply. And he hadn't been able to risk accessing any terminal anywhere. They were watching.

Oh well, things had gone about as far as they could without him anyway. He'd achieved his objective and brought the traitors out into the open. Just that he would have preferred a little more time, and to come out on his own terms.

He would show them all. First, though, he had to stop Ms Shaw. Once someone else completed an official swearing-in, it would all be over for him. He would no longer have any claim or right to the presidency. With her out of the way, however, he could retake charge. Not that he'd ever really given up his power, but this time it would all be in the public view.

Ms Shaw was his biggest surprise. A player he hadn't counted on. He hadn't even known who she was. Just some unlucky girl that came into his sights by accident. He'd been playing around in Jimmy's head when she showed up out of nowhere. And what fun he'd had watching Hank and the rest have their way with her. When it was all done, he'd left the gang behind, thinking they'd killed the woman, and put that happy episode to bed.

How could he have known how wrong he was about that? She was an unknown. A nobody. Not part of the elite few he'd had his eyes and focus upon. Today, he would put that oversight to rights.

Once the population saw the miracles he had achieved, the enhancements he had created and adopted, they would rally around him. And with Ms Shaw and that whore Novikov out of the way, as well as that meddlesome Morris, he would become the people's last hope for a cure. And he would give it out to all who offered their allegiance. He didn't anticipate that many would refuse.

Terrence knew the secret passages around zone one and the presidential complex better than anyone—he'd made it his business to know. Now, he used that knowledge to gain access to the presidential inner office. He entered via the same trapdoor that Eloise Martins had used to make her escape when Special Moore had initiated his coup. With all that had unfolded, folks seemed to have forgotten about it.

As expected, Denis found Priya in the main office, preparing for the big ceremony. Wordless, soundless, he lifted himself from the floor hatch and approached her from behind. Until he grabbed her arm, she didn't even know he was there. An erection strained at his pants.

At his touch, the girl stiffened and jerked. He held her fast, expecting her to scream or call for help. She did neither. Instead, she seemed enthralled. Then he saw what she saw. He grinned. So, his truth serum worked. And it didn't matter what she knew now because he would kill her before she could do anything about it.

The flashes of vision and insight reached the present, skimmed through a presentiment of what would come, and then stopped. The woman's eyes cleared, and she glared at him. She drew a breath in, probably ready to scream now. He didn't give her a chance.

Terrence attacked.

Faint bruises ringed her throat and neck, and he aimed for that obvious vulnerable spot. In vain, she tried to pry his hands away. He towered over her and grinned. Just a couple of minutes more, and it would change everything.

All at once, a snarling beast threw itself at him and latched onto his throat, ripping and tearing. He dropped the girl to the floor and grappled with the animal.

The raptor proved too strong for him. Blood streamed down his neck and onto his chest, ruining his good shirt. Terrence dug his nails into the creature's thick hide. The animal went crazy. Then it locked on to his jugular vein.

CHAPTER EIGHTEEN

1

E150

Priya staggered backward and fell into a chair. Terrence lay on the floor, bleeding out. Other than herself, Priya's final obstacle was now gone. In the fight for her life, she realised that she could do the job. Wanted to, in fact. In her old existence, she'd reached the level of office manager. And she'd enjoyed the challenge. If she could lead a team successfully, it meant she could lead people, which meant she could lead the planet, didn't it? After all, Exxon 1 was kind of like a large team. She just had to take it one step at a time like she always used to. And she knew the art of delegation.

The door separating inner office from outer burst open, and Sasha came running in. 'I heard a commotion.' She saw the body and stumbled to a stop. Priya could understand her shock. Terrence was the last person she'd expected to have to face right before her inauguration ceremony.

And then he'd grabbed her. And in the grabbing, had inadvertently shown her the truth of her rape and beating. It was a strange one, for in some ways, seeing why it had happened to her changed how she felt about it, and about her attackers—they had been Terrence's victims as much as she had.—But in other ways, in the real world, in her physical experience, it changed nothing.

Then there was the what else that she'd seen. When Sasha's story had unfolded before her after receiving the truth serum, Priya had felt she should recognise the man who'd subjected Sasha to the worst of the abuse. Well, now she did. Terrence had inserted himself into the girl's life right from the beginning, and her parents had colluded willingly. Priya made a split-second decision. She grabbed Sasha's hand and got more than she had bargained for.

All at once, Priya saw Sasha's indecision. Understood her wavering. Knew what havoc the woman might yet wreak. The information simply reaffirmed her decision, and she pulled the woman to the corpse on the floor and pressed Sasha's hot hand to Terrence's cold one.

This would either kill or cure. But Priya had to know one way or the other. She stood back and watched the horror settle onto Sasha's face. Waited while the horror morphed to pain morphed to anger morphed to hate. The way of the world. A choice we all had to make: whether or not to go with it or let it go. In the end, our free will amounted to the same choice: choose the good path or choose the confused path. And, no matter what we chose, it didn't always come out clean. This life offered no guarantees. So, which way would Sasha go?

Eventually, the woman stilled and rose to her feet. She stood and faced Priya with a resolute expression on her face. 'There's something you need to know.'

Priya nodded. Waited.

'I kept a second vial. Not water, this time. It contains a universal antidote. One that attacks nanobots in their entirety. You should have it.'

Priya rocked on her feet. 'So that's what I saw after you gave me the serum. I didn't recognise its importance or what it was.' This changed the balance of power. Exxon 1 no longer had to live at the mercy of, or in debt to, any of the other planets. With their own cure, they were free to rebuild themselves and run themselves.

Priya rubbed her arms. 'Where is it?'

Sasha patted her pocket. Then she held out a hand. 'You should see the rest.'

Priya took the outstretched palm. Saw that Sasha had turned the corner. Had made her choice. No more nonsense about poisoning the water or killing herself. Priya's gamble had paid off, and the truth had, indeed, set the woman free. Together, the two of them could lead the planet back to greatness.

CHAPTER NINETEEN

Epilogue

E1602 (Or, New Era, Year Three)
  Zone 9

Priya stood and surveyed the vast fields, ready for harvesting. In the distance, farmers and labourers bantered as they worked. A fresh breeze riffled through her long hair, cut into the latest style. By her side, Sasha smiled. 'We did it.'

Priya nodded. Just then, the lunch siren sounded. 'Let's go and meet the men.'

'And women.'

The two of them chuckled and climbed into

the waiting jeep, and the driver bounced them across the edge of the field to the gathered workers. Priya jumped from the cab before the driver could disembark and assist. Jubilant and at peace, she approached the group.

She recognised the man right away. Jimmy. The guy who'd led her into the trap. She'd believed Kaleb had killed the whole gang, but when he'd tried to strangle her in the hospital, she'd seen that he'd missed about half of Hank's cronies. She could recall each and every face. In the three years since, she'd vowed to find Jimmy and try to discover what sort of person he really was.

Would the man know her? Did he even remember? She got her answer when he bolted to his feet and backed away. He looked terrified of her.

A couple of burly farmers manoeuvred into position to prevent him from fleeing if that's what he chose to do. They'd picked up on the undertones. Priya spoke quietly while the others looked on, intrigued.

'It wasn't your fault.'

The farmers either side of him relaxed. Jimmy didn't.

Priya took a step forward. He held his ground. 'Denis Terrence—' a few workers spat on the ground at the name— 'controlled you that day and, I'm sure, on many other days. It wasn't your fault.'

Jimmy gave a curt nod. Priya stepped forward again. 'I'm sorry.'

He looked surprised. As did many of the others. Priya walked to within a couple of feet of him. 'I'm sorry that happened to you. I'm sorry you have to live with the memory of that. I'm sorry I was naive enough to go with you. If anyone made bad decisions that day, it was me.'

He shook his head. 'I should've known.'

'None of us knew. The important thing is what we do now that we have our freedom.' Priya turned away and took a step. 'Walk with me?'

He joined her, and she led them away from the group. Her security detail kept a steady distance behind. She took Jimmy's hand. He let her. After putting it to a public vote, the population had opted unanimously for everyone to be given a sanitised version of the truth serum at age fifteen.

No more secrets or lies.

Having seen what she needed to, she stopped and released Jimmy's hand. 'You'd make an excellent inter-planetary minister. Come and work with us.'

He shook his head. 'I'm not educated like you. Not ever done nothing good my whole life.'

Priya stopped walking and faced the man. 'Lacking good schooling has nothing to do with lacking intelligence. And if you're willing, we can implant everything you'd need to know. You're a good person, Jimmy Archer.'

'No, miss, I'm not.'

'Then, tell me. How have you suffered such torment and regret these last three years if not for being a good soul at heart?'

His shoulders slumped, and relief showed in his eyes.

Priya held out a hand. 'Come and work with us.'

Jimmy smiled and wiped away a stray tear. 'I'd like that, President Shaw.'

THE END

Made in the USA
Columbia, SC
12 April 2021